NEXUS CONFESSIONS:
VOLUME ONE

NEXUS CONFESSIONS: VOLUME ONE

*Edited and compiled by
Lindsay Gordon*

In real life, make sure you practise safe, sane and consensual sex.

First published in 2007 by
Nexus
Thames Wharf Studios
Rainville Road
London W6 9HA

Copyright © Virgin Books Ltd 2007

www.nexus-books.co.uk

Typeset by TW Typesetting, Plymouth, Devon

Printed and bound by Clays Ltd, St Ives PLC

ISBN 978 0 352 34093 1

Contents

Introduction

Who can forget the first time they read a reader's letter in an adult magazine? It could make your legs shake. You could almost feel your imagination stretching to comprehend exactly what some woman had done with a neighbour, the baby-sitter, her best friend, her son's friend, a couple of complete strangers, whatever . . . Do real women actually do these things? Did this guy really get that lucky? We asked ourselves these questions, and the not knowing, and the wanting to believe, or wanting to disbelieve because we felt we were missing out, were all part of the reading experience, the fun, the involvement in the confessions of others, as if we were reading some shameful diary. And when Nancy Friday's collections of sexual fantasies became available, didn't we all shake our heads and say, no way, some depraved writer made all of this up. No woman could possibly want to do that. Or this guy must be crazy. But I bet there are reader's letters and confessed fantasies that we read years, even decades ago, that we can still remember clearly. Stories that haunt us: did it, might it, could it have really happened? And stories that still thrill us when the lights go out because they have informed our own dreams. But as we get older and become more experienced, maybe we have learnt that we would be foolish to underestimate anyone sexually, especially ourselves.

The scope of human fantasy and sexual experience seems infinite now. And our sexual urges and imaginations never cease to eroticise any new situation or trend or cultural flux about us. To browse online and to see how many erotic sub-cultures have arisen and made themselves known, is to be in awe. Same deal with magazines and adult films – the variety, the diversity, the complexity and level of obsessive detail involved. But I still believe there are few pictures or visuals that can offer the insights into motivation and desire, or reveal the inner world of a fetish, or detail the pure visceral thrill of sexual arousal, or the anticipation and suspense of a sexual experience in the same way that a story can. When it comes to the erotic you can't beat a narrative, and when it comes to an erotic narrative you can't beat a confession. An actual experience or longing confided to you, the reader, in a private dialogue that declares: *yes, if I am honest, I even shock myself at what I have done and what I want to do.* There is something comforting about it. And unlike a novel, with an anthology there is the additional perk of dipping in and out and of not having to follow continuity; the chance to find something fresh and intensely arousing every few pages written by a different hand. Start at the back if you want. Anthologies are perfect for erotica, and they thrive when the short story has tragically gone the way of poetry in other genres.

So sit back and enjoy the Nexus Confessions series. It offers the old school thrills of reading about the sexual shenanigans of others, but Nexus-style. And the fantasies and confessions that came flooding in – when the call went out on our website – are probably only suitable for Nexus. Because like the rest of our canon, they detail fetishes, curious tastes and perverse longings. The thrills of shame and humiliation, the swapping of genders, and the ecstasy of submission or domination. There are no visiting milk-men, or busty neighbours hanging out the washing and winking over the hedge here. Oh, no. Our readers and fantasists are far more likely to have been spanked, or caned, feminised into women, have given themselves to strangers, to have dominated other men or women, gone dogging, done the unthinkable, behaved inappropriately and broken the rules.

Lindsay Gordon, Autumn 2006

viii

Mandy's Evening

My unforgettable evening began, quite unremar-
kably, at home. I was feeling like a loose end,
struggling to find anything that engaged me or
seemed worthwhile, and the television offered little to
distract me. The noise of a party down the street only
served as a taunting reminder of the emptiness of my
diary that week.

My usual answer at times of such self-pity is to dig
my large knobbly black dildo out of the bottom of
my bedside cupboard and indulge in a little self-love.
I don't know who designed it, but they got it just
right: at full setting the end of it plays and vibrates on
my clitoris perfectly, and it's just the right thickness
for me, stretching me beautifully and plying its many
knobbles against my beauty spot. It's not too long
either, which can be a problem with many such toys.

I have often mused that a lot of men are overly
concerned about the length of their members, with
little regard for the important attribute: thickness.
Long and thin is no good to me – give me short and
thick any day. So many teenage boys waste time
measuring themselves with their school rulers, time
that would be better spent, I think, comparing
themselves with the holes in their mums' spaghetti
measurers.

But somehow the idea of my toy just didn't seem enough that evening. Sometimes it can seem a little clinical, cold and lifeless, and I really felt I needed something more real, something more pink, more fleshy, more hot, more likely to shoot warm and soothing semen into me. My boyfriend was being a right bore that evening, sitting across town in his flat watching some vital, unmissable football match – a match at least as vital and unmissable as the last must-see important match the previous week, he assured me – his beer can taking my place at his side.

At that moment, with my pussy gnawing my leg off, I became intensely jealous of football. Why, after all, should football lay claim to my boyfriend's cock when I had so much more need for it? It wasn't as though he really needed it to watch football, was it? From that moment football became the enemy and I resolved to liberate that cock from its armchair prison and ride it to heaven and back. David would just have to wait until the next must-see important match, which wouldn't be until at least next week, most likely.

Formulating a plan was rather easy. The two main ingredients, a horny female body and a penis, were not exactly difficult to bring together. I just had to make the former look as alluring and available as possible and the latter would be compelled to act. The requirement then was to don the most irresistible costume in my arsenal and deliver it to my penis's doorstep unexpectedly, giving its owner little time to think about the football it might miss before I was upon it and it was inside me scratching my itch.

The air gushed around me as I threw the double wardrobe doors open to look for a suitable dress. I needed something short and tight, to display the curves of my hips, abdomen and thighs. The whole effect would also require a matching pair of high heels, of course.

I took a moment to imagine the sweep of my leg muscles and the way that the dress would cling to my skin and ride up my leg as I posed for David at his front door.

I threw half a dozen dresses and skirts on to the bed and spread them out so that I could see them all in array. Dresses of red, black, blue, lime-green and white were laid out before me like some erotic rainbow, and picking out just the right number was proving difficult. I peeled off my day-clothes as I considered which to wear, and eventually found myself standing there naked, my hand wandering absent-mindedly to rub my pussy lips, still trying to cogitate on the matter. Inspiration was slow in coming to me so, to give myself some thinking time, I decided to put on my underwear.

I pulled out the drawers of my dresser and, after a quick rummage, plumped for my black lacy knickers, which had a matching bra set. I grabbed a similar suspender belt. It was from another set, but went well enough with them. I suppose I had decided without realising it that I was going in stockings.

I squeezed my warm, soft, cherry-nippled handfuls into the push-up bra and thrust my chest out at the mirror on the dresser. They looked magnificent, and I blew myself a kiss in congratulation. I wrapped the belt around my waist and sat on the bed, admiring myself gratuitously as I rolled some smooth black nylon stockings up my long legs, pointing my toes as I did so. It looked and felt so sexy, and I felt a quiver of excitement in my tummy as I stood to straighten the seams. The feel of the nylon was divine, so cool and light against my slender, shapely legs, and I exhaled deeply to calm my excited body. My hands were excited too as they attached the clasps to the black bands of my stocking-tops halfway up my well-defined thighs. I rubbed my clitty, not too much, just quickly to wish it a farewell for the time being, as I pulled the knickers up to my waist. Now, even more excited than before, I returned to my bed to choose a dress.

Still nothing seemed to inspire me, so I distracted myself again by choosing a pair of shoes from the bottom of the wardrobe. The heel had to be high – to tense my buttocks, to bring out my calf muscles, to present that turn of the ankle and display the smoothness of the instep – all of which are known to catch the male eye. There is a vein that faintly contours my instep and I have it on testosterone-driven authority that it is mouth-wateringly sexy.

I picked out the shiny black high-heeled courts or pumps, which felt so right with the hosiery I was wearing, and slipped them on. Again I admired myself in the mirror, posing like a whore in just my lingerie and hose, a hand on one hip, one leg out before me, the other to the side. Yes, I would fuck me, I thought, if I were a cock-controlled football fan.

As I posed, my eye caught sight of my long black coat, hanging on the back of my bedroom door. I looked at it. I looked at myself in the mirror. I looked at the dresses fanned out on the bed.

An idea so delicious and naughty entered my head that I felt butterflies in my pussy at the very thought. I could go out without the dress and just the long coat, couldn't I? I reached for the long cloak-like garment and put it on my back.

Yes. It covered me up completely, and yet underneath I felt so exposed and vulnerable. I put my arms into the sleeves and swirled the coat around me as I swayed my legs and hips from side to side, admiring my sexy attire and shapely body in the mirror. I could not wait to go out like this and surprise David at his door. I buttoned up the coat.

Before I left, however, there was one more thing to do. I reached up under the hem of the thick black coat, pulled down my knickers, let them slide down my nylon-covered legs and stepped out of them. I picked them up and flung them on to the bed, then clicked the light out behind me.

I sat in the back of a taxi and gave the driver the directions. He was a scruffy-looking chap, a few years older than me and perhaps a little overweight, judging from the way he filled his lumberjack shirt. I sat across from him where he was able to see me over his left shoulder. It was not a conscious act, but I know that in my excited mood I would never have sat directly behind out of view, for deep down within me I craved attention.

My body felt alive. I could feel the smooth, cool sensation on my buttocks and upper thighs where my tingling skin pressed against the silky purple lining of my long coat. I rubbed my legs together sensuously to feel all the sensations available to me, of my fresh skin, the sleek coat lining, the slightly coarser stockings and the projected surface of the stocking tops. My pussy started to seep.

How surprised would my chauffeur have been to know that beneath the single layer of my coat I wore such provocative attire, and that I sported my exposed pussy and arse? Very surprised indeed, I would imagine, as well as rather aroused. I began to fantasise about flashing for him as I got out, holding the flaps of my coat apart and standing before him, watching him drinking in the image of my body and my bushy minge. I imagined watching the sap rise in him as he admired me, and how it would turn me on even further. My pussy wept tears of lust.

Even naughtier thoughts came into my head: I imagined flashing my eyes at him and telling him he could have me any way he wanted me, and I imagined his rough hands all over me as he ravished me and took me over the bonnet of his cab, compliantly making myself putty in his hands.

I reached under my coat and rubbed at my clitoris with my middle finger, borrowing moisture from my pussy to lubricate it the way I like it. I had not expected to become so very worked up, and I began to pity my poor boyfriend for what he was in for.

We entered the neighbourhood where David lived and I found myself wishing that the journey could last just a little longer. The sensations my clothing was giving me and the naughtiness of what I was doing behind that poor man's back were so good, I did not want to stop.

'Actually, driver, could you take me somewhere else first?' I said without thinking.

'Whereabouts, Miss?' he asked, glancing into his mirror. He still had no idea that I was semi-naked and frigging myself in his licensed taxi.

I had to think of something quickly. 'Erm, The Attic on Shawlands Road,' I said, thinking of a pub at a reasonable distance.

'OK,' he said into the rear-view mirror.

To be honest the journey still was not long enough, but I could hardly make him drive me back again like some dotty bimbo, so I climbed out of the cab and paid him his fare. The chugging of the diesel engine faded away into the night and I was alone, standing outside the pub, feeling the cool night air around my legs and clutching my coat around me, the only preserve of my modesty.

I was still as horny as a mare, and revelling in the danger of what I was doing. In fact, I craved even more thrills and, without any real thought for why, I pursued the feeling and stepped inside the big red doors.

I supposed that the only thing to do was approach the bar and buy myself a drink. Eyes turned to regard me, as they tend to when an attractive girl enters a bar-room. I should be used to it, but on this occasion I was intensely aware of them burrowing into me, as though they could see through my coat, greedily appraising my wares and judging me for a whore. I tried my best to rein in my imagination, telling myself that no one could know, but the rationalisation didn't seem to make my cunt any drier.

I ordered a glass of wine and slid my curvy behind on to a stool, sitting side-saddle to the bar with my legs crossed, one heel hooked on to the footrest, the other shoe dangling on my foot. My coat cut the view of my legs at mid-thigh, only just hiding the stocking-tops and clasps. I sipped my wine and watched for stolen admiring glances.

I saw many a head turn here and there and it became obvious to me that, at least in an illicit sense, I was the centre of attention. The males of the pub suddenly became curiously generous or thirsty and my part of the bar became quite busy with men buying rounds and surreptitiously stealing glances at my flexing legs as I dangled my shoe for their entertainment. The closeness of the men as they came by, brushing past me, pushing the smooth lining of my coat against my thigh, giving me a cool sensation on the naked part of my leg, reminded me how vulnerable, how close, I was to every one of them.

I was very much on autopilot now, acting before thinking, and I found myself flashing my eyes at a

7

fit-looking fellow in dark blue jeans and a white shirt. He was surprised to catch my eye, and I must admit I was surprised I had made the move, but, as I say, I was acting without thinking. I had left my wisdom behind with my knickers, it would seem.

I gave him a kind of half-discouraging, half-friendly smile as he approached, hoping he would pick up that I kind of regretted my actions and would really rather he did not speak to me. It seemed to work at first as all he did was take up the perch on the bar right next to me and lean on it with his elbows, making himself visible to the busy bar staff. Not a word was said.

I breathed an inward sigh of relief and gazed again around the bar as I practised the ancient art of shoe-dangling for the audience. The same heads were turning to steal glances without giving themselves away and I became quite excited again. Perhaps too excited. I tensed my leg just a bit too much and accidentally – I think it was accidental, anyway – clipped the back of the fit-looking chap's leg. He turned around.

'Careful,' he said with a smile.

'Sorry,' I said, flashing my eyes again – I don't know why, I just could not help it.

'Nice shoes,' he said, genuinely admiring them.

I was impressed. I like a fellow who can appreciate the finest things in life.

'Thank you, I'm glad you like them.'

I tried to make out the contours of his pectorals through the shirt and liked what I saw. I crossed my legs, almost daring myself to flash him a stocking-top, and I noticed his eye flick to steal a glance at my inner thigh.

'You in alone?' he asked.

'Yes, I'm on my way somewhere but I couldn't resist coming in for a drink first,' I told him. It was largely the truth, I suppose. My pussy seeped some more as I thought about my skimpy outfit and how exciting it was to be talking to someone, casual as anything, while wearing practically nothing.

'I'm out with my pal,' he said, pointing to a slimmer chap sitting at a nearby table, swirling the dregs of a beer.

'Going somewhere later?' I asked.

'We don't really know yet.' He shrugged. 'You must be off somewhere posh then.'

Of course, to him I must have looked quite dressy: a long plush coat, expensive high heels and seamed stockings. No doubt he thought the coat hid an elegant dress.

'Oh, not really,' I said.

'Do you normally dress like that, then?'

I laughed.

'I'm not dressed how you think,' I said.

It was only after I had said it that my heart skipped a beat – I realised that I had inadvertently moved the conversation towards dangerous territory.

'Oh no? How are you dressed?' he asked, leaning in towards me as befitted the intimacy of the question.

I pressed my slender, long-nailed hand softly to his chest to compel him to lean back again.

'Shouldn't you be buying a drink for your friend?' I suggested to deflect his attention away from my attire.

'Its OK, he's not thirsty,' the handsome fellow said with a smirk, now clearly intent on taking our conversation to the next level.

On the one hand my situation was making me feel horny and susceptible. The imprudence I had shown in getting into this ridiculous predicament would have made a whore blush, yes, but the naughtiness of it all was feeding my libido and titillating me greatly. I decided to continue – there was no harm in teasing him and flirting with him if I was getting so much pleasure from it, was there?

'So, what are you wearing? Show me,' he insisted, bringing the subject back to meatier matters.

'Well,' I said, closing my eyes for a moment and leaning in towards him, so he could just feel my breath brushing his ear, 'I can't show you, but I could describe it.'

He smiled. 'Go on then.'

'I've got a nice pair of high-heeled black courts on,' I told him, lifting my leg and pointing my toe to show him the lines of my foot and ankle and how they formed a perfect curve into my shoe, as if the heel was merely an extension of myself.

'So I see.'

'And I chose a pair of sheer black seamed stockings to go with them,' I said, running my hand softly up my shin.

'Very nice,' he responded, as though he was observing them for the first time.

'Of course, they're not hold-ups, so I needed a black lacy suspender belt to keep them from slipping down.' I smirked.

He rolled his tongue around his mouth and flared his nostrils. The very mention of these evocative garments was clearly causing the sap to rise.

'I've got a pretty good bra that matches it quite well, so I put that on too.' I stuck my chest out, and pushed my shoulders back, as though it made my bra visible through the thick black wool of my long coat, and leant back again, crossing my legs slowly and sensuously. I saw his slim friend at the small round table start to take notice of us – he and a few other men had been attracted by my leggy display.

'Go on, what else?' pressed my suitor, eager to be teased further.

I gave him a silence accompanied by a discreet smile and an arched eyebrow.

'What else? Tell me more.' He was near to begging now, I was pleased to note.

I gave him the same look.

'Don't stop now,' he said, turning his head to the side, as though looking away would help to deflate the bulging in his jeans.

Should I say anything else? Should I invent a dress or pair of knickers and describe them to him before leaving? What was my exit strategy? I should not dare to take this further, or I might have to fight him off me. I gave him another helping of silent subtlety. Perhaps that was the best way – retain the mystery and let him come to his own conclusions. I smiled and turned demurely on my stool to face the other way.

I noticed a pair of very jealous-looking men had been glowering at us during our discourse. They turned away in a vain attempt to hide their curiosity.

'Would you like a drink?' my new friend asked. I had not expected him to continue the conversation, which he clearly did not feel had reached a natural conclusion.

I nodded over my shoulder and showed him my current drink as a hint for what he should order. To his credit he did not need to ask and ordered perfectly just from sight of it. I supposed that it was only decent to turn back again and give the generous fellow a few more minutes of my society.

'Thank you,' I said.

'You're welcome,' he replied, with deference. 'Now how about describing for me the rest of your outfit?'

He picked up his two pints and shaped to head towards his table, pausing lest I reply to his request.

More danger lay in that direction, I knew, but I also knew more excitement and titillation would be the trade-off, if I were to tell him about my state of undress. I took a deep breath and rubbed my legs together.

'There's not much else to tell,' I ventured. A thrill of excitement ran up my pussy and into my stomach as I spoke.

'What do you mean?'

'I mean,' I said, gasping for composure, 'that I'm not wearing anything else.'

He laughed again, taking my revelation in good humour, but when his laughter had died away and he saw that I was still staring at him with the same arched eyebrow and the same half-smile as before, the truth dawned on him.

'You're not joking.' His mouth gaped in amazement.

'No. I'm not.'

By now I was experiencing the sort of dread excitement that one feels at the top of a rollercoaster. Fear and pleasure really are the most potent of cocktails.

'I don't believe you,' he said through narrowed eyes.

'OK, I'll prove it,' I answered, and I folded back the bottom of my coat, as though I were folding the corner of a napkin, to reveal the black band of my stocking top, the clasp of the suspender belt and the quivering white flesh of my inner thigh.

His attitude completely changed. I remember it as vividly as though it were happening now, because it is without doubt the most erotic moment of my life. He looked me up from the tip of my shoes, along my legs, over my crotch, past my breasts and into my eyes.

'You little tart,' he said. There was no smiling or flirting any more; he was looking at me now as an object, an object of desire, yes, but nonetheless an object. And it thrilled me.

Suddenly I was acutely aware that my pussy had no cock in it. It's something a little hard to describe if you have never experienced the feeling before. Our stomachs spend most of the time empty, but we only become aware of their emptiness when our bodies crave food and tell us that we are hungry. It is much the same thing with my pussy: it spends most of its time empty, and for the most part I give it no thought, except for these moments when it feels like the most empty space in the world, a vacuum in need of filling.

Suddenly my game of flirtation changed into a need to have this man inside me; it was like flicking a switch.

I did not even look back at him. I just looked down at my own legs and said: 'Would you like to see more?'

He abandoned his drinks on the bar top and clasped my arm with a strong hand. I took to my feet and looked up at him. I blush now to say it, but I needed to fuck this complete stranger, or rather, I needed him to fuck me.

Oh, that I could recapture the feelings that coursed through me as he led me, firmly but not roughly, to his table to tell his friend we were leaving. My genitals buzzed, my toes tingled, my tongue seemed to bathe in saliva, I was sensuously aware of the contact of every part of my body against the clothing I wore: the glassy nylon sheen on my legs, the lace belt around my waist, the lining of my coat against my bare buttocks, my bra tight against my nipples. I knew I could back out at any moment and do the right thing, but that would mean breaking this trance-like nirvana and I could not leave it.

As we approached the friend I did not know what to do with my eyes. I could barely face meeting the burrowing eyes of that man at the table, who was unaware that I was just about to shag his friend; my face would have burned crimson. So I looked down at my feet.

'I just met this lovely-looking girl at the bar,' my new friend told his patient pal. I smiled at his flattery.

'She's out in her underwear. Do you want to come and fuck the little tart?' he added. I felt my knees buckle.

My stomach filled with adrenalin, and my face did indeed burn at the suggestion; I was mortified that he would act so arrogantly. I had been debating with myself whether what I was doing was right, but now I knew I was being very naughty indeed. I knew I should stop, but if I walked away it meant calling an end to my incredible state of arousal and wasting the delicious juice that now filled my soft pink entrance. I could not refuse, I needed a cock in me as soon as possible, and if accepting the cock on offer meant taking another too, then so be it.

I heard the slim guy's chair scrape back on the floor as he stood. He followed behind us as my guiding escort led me out of the door. I kept my head down, watching my shoes as we left, unable to meet the gaze of anyone who might be watching us. My legs were like jelly and I felt goose-pimples running from the top of my head down my back.

We crept around the back, into the deserted beer garden, past the picnic tables, and followed a series of six small paving slabs set into the damp lawn to act as stepping stones to a table that sat behind a large evergreen hedge. We set off the spotlight as we passed, but no one from inside appeared to notice as we slipped behind the hedge. Its light bathed the sides of our faces in a lemon-orange glow.

I stood before them, hardly able to breathe with the excitement.

'Show us then,' said the fellow from the bar, looking down at me with crossed arms.

Diffidently, I unbuttoned my coat from the bottom to the top and, in the very same pose that I had planned to adopt on the doorstep of my boyfriend's flat, I peeled it open and revealed my provocative costume. I rubbed my right knee against my left leg. I could tell they were impressed though I felt too shamefaced to meet their eyes directly.

I stood there for what seemed like an age, swaying slightly for their entertainment and arousal as they devoured every curve and line of my body. My bush glistened in the half light and I felt the cold night air on my wet lips. Despite the coat and the underwear I felt emphatically naked.

Finally, they could wait no longer and stepped toward me, the stockier chap pressing downward on my shoulder to encourage me to crouch. I heard a zip being undone near my right ear and I reached forward to open the other fly, which I found in front of me.

My handsome seducer's penis sprang forth between the two rows of zipper teeth and eased itself to erection. Eagerly, I licked the head with a flicking tongue and began to suck it, tasting all that I could of it. I heard myself humming with pleasure. Soon I caught sight of the second penis in the corner of my eye, winching itself to a vertical position. I grabbed it too, and began to alternate between the two as I crouched there behind the hedge, my legs wide open, exposing my pussy to the world. I felt wondrously wanton and devoid of responsibility.

I was not out here for the undeniable pleasure of sucking two cocks, however. I had been driven to this by one need and one need only and I felt it was time I fulfilled that need. I stood up and, turning my back to the boys, I bent over in front of them to touch my toes, lifting the flaps at the back of my long coat apart to allow my blushing buttocks and my wet pussy to peep through. I gasped as I felt the coat lifted roughly and thrown over my head, exposing me completely and shrouding my head in the long dark garment.

They stood admiring the elongated heart shape that my arse and legs, crossed over at the ankles, now formed. My sleek legs, encased in black, tapered outwards to my stocking-tops where the contrast of my creamy thighs, bisected by the harsh black line of the suspender strap, guided the eye to the bountiful mounds of my buttocks. And in the centre of it all, my red pussy and tight anus beckoned all comers. What man has not dreamed of such a vision?

The two men discussed me like I was not even there.

'I can't wait to get it up this little tart,' said the first.

'You go first and we'll tag team her,' suggested the second.

From my position I could see nothing but their legs and I watched like a deer in the headlights as their jeans fell to the floor. Listening to them was an eerily detached experience, in my enclosed space inside the coat. I felt almost as though I was eavesdropping on a threesome in the next room, rather than taking part in it myself.

I felt the head of a penis knocking at the door and knew it would not take much for him to slip inside me, as wet as I was. I gave a single grunt as, after only a couple of little thrusts, his penis pushed all the way in with a humiliating squelch. Oh, but how I needed it. I must have felt so wet and soft to the head of his rod as he ploughed me, slow and deep at first, gradually quickening until I rocked with each jab and cried out with pleasure.

He continued, expressing his enjoyment with throaty cries and reminding me with colourful language what a tart I was. I did not complain about my treatment, I was still a prisoner of my blissful sexual trance and had no desire to escape it. The first cock withdrew as its owner became fatigued and I barely had time to breathe before the second, smaller and curved, was pushed inside.

'It's a good pussy,' said the larger chap as he withdrew. 'It likes to be fucked fast, I think.'

I felt a tightening spasm in my tunnel in reaction to his tactless evaluation of me. It was liberating to be seen as a sexual object just this once in my life and my sex was responding to it.

The same machine-gun-style fucking began again. The curve of this penis was the perfect complement to its predecessor, scratching the itches that the first had not reached. The friend swore and cussed in disbelief at how good it felt to fuck me, and the thrusts became so hard that I let go of my legs and reached out to put my hands on the grass to hold myself steady. By the time he withdrew for his breather, I was feeling another spasm and knew that this one marked the way to orgasm.

They switched again wordlessly, and one of them spanked me as they swapped position. Soon I was again being fucked at one hundred miles an hour with a pair of firm hands holding my buttocks and rocking me back and forth to facilitate my seeing-to. He was hitting the spot now and I begged him not to stop, for I needed every inch of him to take me there. I felt more admonishing spanks on my succulent arse.

He was gasping for breath now but responded to my needs, pushing himself to maintain the pace and take me over the edge. I came as quietly as I could, through gritted teeth and with one hand over my mouth as waves of ecstasy rippled through my pussy and then up into my abdomen. I felt his penis make a single, spiteful jab into me and then withdraw.

They changed places again, and I barely had time to savour my climax before again I was being pummelled by the skinnier man's cock. It was plain now that he wanted his orgasm – his thrusts went into me at a slightly steeper angle and with more attitude, usually a sign that a lover is getting close. I braced myself for a load as his voice rose in pitch to the near-scream of a man coming, but was surprised when he withdrew to rub his member in the groove between my buttocks. I felt sprinkles on my anus and then two or three hot strings of semen on my cheeks.

I was still hypnotised by my lust and found myself reaching up with my finger to scrape the deposit from my skin and shamelessly suck it all up. The first man stepped up to the plate again, his mission the same as his sated friend's, to come all over me.

I enjoyed the jerkier thrusts of his cock as he used my pussy for his pleasure and satisfaction, spanking me at regular intervals. I always suspected he would take longer than his friend, who seemed less experienced and more excited than the cooler character I had met at the bar.

The moment arrived and, again to my surprise, he withdrew to shoot his globules of spunk over my stocking-tops. It takes something to make a man forgo an orgasm inside a smooth wet pussy, and I guessed that the vision I had given them on bending over had had such a tremendous effect on their psyches that they felt compelled to shoot their seed all over it, rather than orgasm hidden away inside me. He stroked the tip of his penis over the reddened flesh on my arse as he savoured the moment. Again I cleaned up with my finger. I felt much better.

I said my goodbyes in the beer garden as the two went inside to return to their pints, and no doubt to discuss their luck. I went out on to the street to look for a taxi.

In the back of my ride I did my best to straighten my belt and stockings and with a wet finger I removed any flaky spatters of semen I could find. This time I cared not if the taxi-driver saw me, it was too late for modesty. I arrived at my destination and the thought of surprising my man began to turn me on again. Nervously I climbed the stairs, knocked on the door, opened my coat, and adopted the winning pose that I knew would draw him away from his football.

– Mandy Gayle, Glasgow, UK

Extra Curricular

I met her at a parent-teacher meeting, of all places. Not the sort of venue where you'd normally expect to meet the woman who becomes your mistress. I know calling her that sounds . . . well, downright weird, to be honest, but that's what she is. Lover, girlfriend, partner and all the other conventional terms we use to describe the woman we have sex with are OK as far as they go but the only word in the English language that really sums up what she is to me is mistress. She's in charge and that's just the way I want it. I'm her servant, her follower, her obedient puppy. There's nothing more powerful or erotic than kneeling before her in total surrender, knowing that what most turns her on is exactly what I'm giving her.

I fancied her the moment I walked in, but I never dreamt she'd be interested in me. I'd been held up by a meeting at work so I arrived a little late. I let myself into the school hall and sat quietly at the back. I tried my best to come to all the PTA sessions. I still took my responsibilities as a dad seriously even though, since the divorce, I only saw the kids at weekends.

I settled myself down and focused on the stage, hoping I hadn't missed too much. Standing alone on the centre of the stage talking about budgets and targets was a strikingly beautiful, statuesque woman.

Her hair was the colour of a raven's wing and tumbled to her shoulders. Her lips were dark and full and looked as though she were on the edge of an amused smile. Having missed the beginning of the meeting I had no idea who she was but I did know that my cock was stirring inside my trousers at the sound of her rich, deep voice.

I leaned over to my neighbour and whispered:

'Who is she?'

'She's the new headmistress; took over at the beginning of the term. Isn't she wonderful? Such a strong woman, you can't imaging her taking any nonsense from anyone, can you?'

And I certainly couldn't. She was a woman who knew her own mind and expected to get her way and, given the opportunity, I'd be first in the queue to make sure she got it. I knew the school had appointed a new head and I vaguely knew it was a woman, but, if I'd thought about it at all, I'd pictured a middle-aged schoolmarm. A spinster with bifocals, a bun and a tweed skirt.

But Ms Godfrey was nothing like that. She was unusually tall for a woman: several inches taller than my own 5'11", I estimated. She was curvy and solid without being fat. Dressed in a fluid summer frock that clung to her curves, she was impressive, imposing and leg-tremblingly sexy. She reminded me of an Amazon, a female warrior as conscious of her power as she was of her beauty and capable of using both as the most deadly of weapons. Inside my underwear, things were growing distinctly cramped.

She was wearing a pair of high, strappy sandals which would look more at home on a woman who rents hotel rooms by the hour than on a spinsterish headmistress. There was a soft little curve in the front of her skirt that I knew must be the slope of her belly.

22

I closed my eyes and imagined embracing her from behind, my hand cupped over that womanly belly as my erection pressed up against her buttocks.

She strode around the stage as she talked and the sound of her stiletto heels against the bare wood echoed around the hall like a series of gunshots. My cock was hard and tingling. Sweat prickled in my armpits.

In spite of my erection I just had to get a better look at her so I stood up, covered my offending area with my coat and moved to an empty seat a few rows from the front. Up close she was even more beautiful. I could see the pink flush of her cheeks and her sparkling white teeth. I could see the intelligence and playfulness in her eyes together with the confidence and authority of a woman in complete control.

Her dress was made of a clingy flowing material. I wondered if it was some kind of silk. It clung in all the right places and emphasised her curves. I imagined the feel of the dress against my naked skin, her body heat reaching me through the fabric and the scent of her body in my nostrils. My balls were aching and uncomfortable and my cock was having its circulation cut off by my restrictive underwear.

A woman like that would never even look at a man like me, let alone get naked for me. Still, I could dream, couldn't I? And let's face it, dreaming about sex was as close as I got these days. If it wasn't for imaginary sex I'd have no sex life at all, and fortunately my imagination had always been more vivid than most.

The rest of the meeting passed in a blur. I didn't listen to any of the other speakers and I sat through the question-and-answer session in a daze, my eyes focused on her. If only I had the courage to speak to her. But even if I did, what then? I might pluck up the courage to introduce myself as Sam and Carly's dad but how did you bring up the subject of sex – let alone the kinky, forbidden sort of sex I dreamed of – with their headmistress? As far as she was concerned I'd be just another parent, someone she'd be polite and professional with, but she'd never even think of me as a man, let alone a potential lover.

And, what's more, I didn't fool myself that she'd share my interests anyway. My wife had tried, for my sake, to dominate me, but it hadn't come naturally to her and had never been entirely successful. I'd come to the conclusion that naturally dominant women, if they did exist outside of my own fantasies and the pornography I occasionally resorted to, were as thin on the ground in my neighbourhood as the unicorn.

At the end of the meeting I nipped into the loo to adjust myself. I had considered having a quick wank, relieving myself of all that pent-up sexual tension, but I thought better of it. No, I intended to make it last. When I finally allowed myself to come, I'd be aroused beyond measure and would probably have the most intense orgasm of my life. So I leaned against the partition in the cubicle with my cock in my hand, waiting for it to deflate sufficiently for me to relieve myself.

It took a while, but eventually I was able to pee. I washed my hands and walked through the corridors to the exit. I must have been in the loo longer than I'd thought because the school building was deserted. Outside it had grown dark and rain was falling in huge drops. I buttoned up my overcoat and headed for the gate.

There was a car parked beside the gate and, as I drew closer, I realised that the owner was having trouble starting it. It was too dark for me to see who it was, but the long hair and the dark shape made me think it was probably a woman. Under normal circumstances, I'd have offered my help, but these were very far from normal circumstances. I was overloaded with testosterone and I had an urgent appointment with my right hand. I put my head down and headed purposefully for the school gate.

There was a loud exclamation from inside the car which confirmed its occupant was a woman, though I'd never before heard a woman use such foul language. The door opened and a figure stepped out and bent over the bonnet and I instantly realised it was Ms Godfrey. I stopped dead in my tracks, torn between my desire to help and my urgent need to get home and satisfy myself.

But I was too much of a gentleman to ignore a lady in distress, so I walked over to the car. Hearing my footsteps, she turned and smiled.

'A knight in shining armour . . . I don't suppose you're a car mechanic, by any chance? I can't make it start no matter what I do.'

Close up, she was even more beautiful. Her skin was creamy and flawless and her lips were dark and plump.

'I'm not, but I restore classic cars as a hobby, so I know my way around an engine. Let me have a look.' Under the bonnet everything obvious looked fine. I pulled out a spark plug and held it up to the light of a nearby street lamp, but it looked clean and new. 'I suppose you're sure you've got petrol and oil in it and you're battery's not flat?

We bent over the bonnet, our heads almost touching. She was at least six inches taller than me. Our legs were practically touching and I could smell a hint of her perfume. She laughed, a rich trill of notes that turned my legs to custard and my cock to granite.

'It had its 10,000-mile service last week and they replaced the battery and spark plugs. I filled it up this morning. I know I look as though I have no idea what goes on under the bonnet but I did a course in car maintenance. I even know how to fix the fan-belt with a pair of tights in an emergency.'

'It's not the fan-belt.' I could barely keep the disappointment out of my voice. The prospect of her taking off her tights and handing them to me all warm and scented was heavenly.

'I'd worked that out for myself. Any ideas?'

'Why don't you try starting it again?'

She climbed back into the car and turned the key. There was a dull clunk and then nothing.

'It's the starter motor.' I leant an elbow on the roof of the car and bent to talk to her through the open window. 'You'll need to take it into the garage so they can fit a new one, but I'm pretty sure we can get you moving. Start the engine again and I'll rock the car. Count to three.' By this time, it was raining in earnest. Water was trickling down my neck and my hair had begun to cling to my face.

She did as instructed and I leaned against the car, rocking it. This time, the engine sprang into life. She smiled at me through the open window with such gratitude and triumph in her eyes that I practically came on the spot.

'Thanks. You've saved my life. I don't know what I would have done if you hadn't come along. Where's your car?'

'I walked. I only live ten minutes away.'

'But you can't walk in this, you'll get soaked. Get in. I'll give you a lift.' Her tone was commanding and warm in equal measure and, though I was fairly certain that the short journey home would be delicious torture for me, I just couldn't disobey her. I climbed into the car and fastened the seatbelt.

As we drove, the silence in the car seemed enormous and frightening and I felt compelled to say something, anything, to fill it.

'I'm Ben James, Sam and Carly's dad.'

'Of course. I knew you looked familiar. Sam looks just like you. He's very good at Maths, isn't he? I don't know Carly very well, I am afraid, but she seems a nice girl.'

'Do you know all the kids in the school by name?'

'I try to, but I haven't been here long, as you know. I'm Jo by the way, Jo Godfrey.'

'Oh, really? My wife's called Jo. My ex-wife, I should say.' I felt a fool once the words were out of my mouth, but finding out she had the same name as my ex somehow threw me. I don't know what sort of name I expected her to have, but something exotic like Madeline or Anastasia. Somehow Jo, that single, short syllable, seemed rather inadequate. She laughed again, and my cock gave an involuntary little leap.

'You sound . . . I don't know . . . somehow disappointed.'

I squirmed in my seat. The last thing I'd wanted to do was draw attention to myself yet I seemed to have done just that. I looked at my lap. Ms Godfrey (I still couldn't think of her as Jo) pulled over to the kerb and stopped the car.

'Why are you stopping?' I spoke without thinking again, which seemed to be becoming a habit, and instantly noticed the tone of panic in my voice.

'Because you haven't told me your address . . . You look terrified. What's the matter?'

With my peripheral vision I could see that she was smiling at me, a look of concern on her handsome face, but I dared not look at her directly. I kept my eyes focused on my hands in my lap.

'Sorry . . . I can't help it . . .' I knew I was sounding even more idiotic by the second. I owed her some sort of explanation yet the truth was unthinkable and I couldn't seem to come up with anything that sounded plausible. 'The truth is ... well, I find you a little intimidating.'

She laughed again, tilting her head, making her dark hair tumble over her back.

'Oh, there's no need, I assure you. I'm quite human. I take my knickers off one leg at a time, just like everyone else.'

My traitorous cock instantly responded to the word 'knickers' by growing an inch and I was so concerned she'd be able to tell that I crossed my hands over my lap and, without thinking about it, glanced up at her to see if she'd noticed. The moment I'd done it, the idiocy of it dawned on me and I realised that she now knew beyond doubt that I had an erection and was trying to hide it. I felt my face flush and grow hot and, without needing to look in the mirror, I knew that I'd gone bright scarlet. I kept my eyes on my lap, stunned into silence and immobility.

'What's wrong? ... Oh, I see.' Her voice grew deep and slow as realisation dawned. 'I take it that's an erection you're trying to hide?'

I glanced up at her, ashamed, but was unable to read her face, other than that she didn't appear to look angry. I didn't know how to answer but no answer at all seemed preferable to one that might incriminate me further.

'Come on, I've asked you a question. You owe me the courtesy of a reply, don't you think?' The authority and impatience in her voice somehow got to me and I answered without thinking.

'Yes, Ms Godfrey, I'm afraid it is.' My voice was small, quiet and ashamed. Humiliation burned inside me yet I was aroused beyond measure, practically trembling.

'Look at me,' she commanded.

I instantly obeyed. I gazed up into her eyes, conscious of the difference in our heights. Somehow the awkwardness of the position seemed to make me even more aroused and helpless. She must have seen the shame and excitement in my face because gradually hers seemed to change and soften. Anger became recognition and her mouth began to curve upwards in a knowing smile. When she finally spoke, I realised I'd been holding my breath.

'Well, Ben, you've obviously been a very naughty boy and I think we both realise that you need to be punished.' Her voice was throaty and low and with a slight but unmistakable quaver of excitement.

'Yes, Ms Godfrey, I've been a bad boy and I deserve to be punished.' My voice was practically a whisper. I gazed up at her, full of awe and arousal.

'Then I think it would be best if I drove straight to my house where I have all the equipment we'll need. Does that sound suitable, Ben?'

I could only nod my agreement. She started the engine and drove off. As she manoeuvred back out into the road she shot me the sweetest of smiles but I was too stunned and happy to smile back. I opened my mouth to speak but before I could get a word out she said:

'Don't say anything. Let's save all that for afterwards. We don't want to spoil the moment. My house isn't far, so perhaps you can spend the journey thinking about your bad behaviour and the punishment to come. How does that sound?'

'It sounds like heaven, Ms Godfrey.'

'Good.' She smiled at me again. 'But perhaps it would be better if you referred to me as "Mistress". What do you think?'

'Yes, mistress.' I was so excited I could barely speak.

As promised, her house was close by. She parked in the street and got out of the car without even looking at me. I trotted along behind her like an eager puppy and waited as she unlocked the door. Inside she turned to look at me.

'I think we'd better start by taking your clothes off.'

When I didn't begin undressing immediately, she gave me a look that left me in no doubt that she expected instant obedience and I began ripping my clothes off.

'Not like that, fold them. Put them on that chair.' She watched me undress.

I folded each item and laid it on the chair and soon I was wearing just my trousers and underwear. I was aroused beyond measure but, for some reason, actually exposing my erection for her inspection seemed shaming – as if the evidence of the effect she had on me was an acknowledgement of her power over me and my resulting helplessness. I went to turn my back on her to cover my embarrassment but she shook her head so I had no choice but to lower my trousers and pants in one movement, in the full glare of her appraising gaze.

My cock was rigid, its exposed tip purple. She allowed her eyes to travel up and down my body then turned on her heel and headed for the stairs. Without looking back she said:

'I'm going to my bedroom. Wait five minutes and come up after me. Second door on the right. And don't forget to knock.'

I watched her undulating rear as she disappeared up the stairs. Waiting five minutes was agony. I dared not go upstairs before the allotted time so I stood there gazing at the hands of my watch ticking off the seconds. After four and a half minutes I headed upstairs, then waited outside the door until exactly five minutes had passed.

I knocked at the door and then walked inside, certain that nothing in my life would ever be the same again. As I entered she walked past me on to the landing, pausing only to tell me to put on the clothes she'd left on the bed and then get on my knees and wait. She shut the door behind me, leaving me alone with nothing but my erection for company.

When I saw what she had laid out on the bed for me to wear I couldn't believe my luck; it was a school uniform and, when I lifted up the shirt, I noticed that underneath it what I'd assumed was a pair of short grey trousers was actually a pleated gymslip. My heart turned over in my chest. It was as though she'd seen into my soul, identified my deepest, darkest fantasies and made them live. I picked up the gymslip and held it in front of my body. I spotted a full-length mirror at the other side of the room and my first instinct was to go over and look at myself, but she hadn't given me permission and I guessed that she expected me to do what I was told and nothing more.

I laid the gymslip back on the bed and picked up the underwear she had chosen. There were white knickers with rows of frills across the back and a simple white bra. There was even a pair of black self-supporting stockings. I pulled on the knickers with trembling hands and had considerable trouble arranging the gusset so that it covered my swollen manhood.

When I put on the bra the cups bagged a little in the absence of breasts and, though I didn't fully understand why, my inability to fill out the bra was arousing and humiliating in equal measure. I sat down on the edge of the bed and pulled on the stockings, smoothing out the elastic tops over my thighs. Then I put on the white shirt and tie and finally the gymslip. There was even a pair of school shoes which buckled across the instep. I sat down again and put them on. They pinched a little, but they fitted well enough.

When I was dressed I resisted the temptation to sneak a look in the mirror and knelt down at the foot of the bed. Before I'd even had time to think about what would happen next, the door swung open noisily and she came into the room. I wanted more than anything to look up at her, but instinct told me to keep my eyes on the carpet unless ordered otherwise. Her legs and feet came into view and I could see that she had changed her sandals for a pair of tight-fitting lace-up ankle boots with pointy toes and vicious heels.

'Look at me.' Her voice was soft, but the tone of authority was unmistakable. I raised my head slowly. She was wearing black stockings and her legs seemed to go on forever. I saw the stocking-tops come into view attached to thick suspenders, then a froth of dark hair at her crotch. As my eyes travelled up her body I saw that she was wearing a black Victorian corset which fastened with hooks up the front. It flared at the top and finished across the fattest part of her breasts, but there weren't cups as such and I knew that with the slightest movement, I might catch a glimpse of nipple.

I was shaking with excitement. My eyes drank in every detail, feasting on the glorious vision.

'Now, I think it's time for your punishment. You've been a very naughty girl and need to be taught the error of your ways.'

For the first time I noticed that she was carrying a black leather riding crop in one hand. She trailed its tip across my lips then moved it down to the hem of my skirt. She slipped it under the fabric and flipped it upwards, momentarily exposing the straining crotch of my school knickers.

'If you haven't worked it out by now, I expect instant and unquestioning obedience. It's a simple enough arrangement, but I find it works. Do you understand?' She lifted my chin with the tip of the crop.

'Yes, mistress.' The final word came out in one sibilant rush.

'I'm glad we understand each other. Now, I want you to stand up and bend over and grab your ankles. You will stay in that position until I give you permission to move, no matter how much it hurts. Is that clear?' She swung the crop through the air, making it swish.

'Yes, mistress.'

'Well? I'm waiting . . .'

I leapt to my feet and bent over as instructed. I felt her lifting my skirt and folding it back, exposing my lace-clad rear. I could hardly breathe. My legs seemed possessed by some manic quiver I couldn't control.

'Have you ever been whipped before?' She ran the tip of the crop up along the cleft between my buttocks.

'No, mistress, not really.'

'Then this should be interesting. Feel free to express yourself; my walls are soundproofed. I must admit I find the sound of a man in pain extremely arousing.' The crop swished through the air and made contact with the fattest part of my buttocks. I gasped. It stung. The pain was much stronger than I had anticipated but, to my surprise, it turned instantly to the most exquisite pleasure. She hit me again, the crop slashing noisily through the air on each stroke. Each time the result was the same: a second

33

of burning agony that transformed into delicious pleasure almost before I'd had time to register the pain.

My cock stiffened inside my tight knickers, stretching the gusset uncomfortably. I heard the crop again and stiffened my muscles in readiness. This time it struck me across the back of my thigh and I was so surprised I almost toppled forward. I spread my legs a little wider, making my position more stable. She whipped each thigh in turn in a never-ending torrent of slashes. My rear end was on fire, stinging from a mixture of pleasure and pain, the one indistinguishable from the other.

Then she started on my buttocks again, whipping me in a ferocious frenzy. She let out a little grunt of exertion on every stroke. I could hear her feet against the carpet as she moved around behind me. Her breathing was loud and rapid and I was willing to bet that she was sweaty and dishevelled. Maybe one of her breasts had escaped the confines of the corset and was swinging freely, wobbling a little each time she swung the crop.

The thought of her naked breast excited me so much that I couldn't help moaning next time the crop made contact, and before long I was groaning in satisfaction and pleasure with each stroke. My cock was rigid, my balls hard and tight. As it lengthened, my cock had half escaped the confines of my school knickers and I was pretty sure that, from her vantage point, mistress was getting a full view of my shameful arousal.

She must have noticed because the barrage of slashes ceased and she ordered me, in a voice that was throaty with lust and exertion, to remove my knickers. I stood up and removed them, pausing to extricate my erection, and tossed them aside on the floor, then bent over again. She whipped my naked buttocks for several minutes. This time the sweet agony was much more intense.

I was pretty sure that my behind must be criss-crossed with a lattice work of red slashes. There might even be a few bruises. The idea of her punishment having left marks on my body aroused me so much that, without thinking about it, I raised a hand to grip my cock. Mistress gave me several hard slashes across the meat of both buttocks, leaving me in no doubt as to her disapproval. Ashamed and disappointed by my own disobedience, I whipped my hand away and replaced it on my ankle.

After delivering another twenty or so strokes with more ferocity than I would have imagined any woman capable of, she ordered me to stand up and hold out both hands. In my new upright position I saw her for the first time and the signs of excitement were obvious. Both breasts had escaped from the corset and her nipples were swollen and berry-dark. There was a scarlet flush of arousal across her beautiful décolleté and her chest rose and fell visibly. My own arousal was equally visible. My erection tented my skirt, huge and obvious.

She dropped the crop on the bed and went over to the dressing table. She removed something from a drawer. It wasn't until she turned around that I saw it was a school cane with a curved handle like a shepherd's crook. As she walked back over to me she tapped the tip against the palm of her open hand.

'You obviously need to be taught how to keep your hands to yourself. This –' she ran the tip of the cane along the underside of my straining erection, making me gasp – 'belongs to me now, and you're not allowed to touch it without my permission. Do I make myself clear?'

'Yes, mistress. I'm sorry, mistress.'

'Now, you will hold out your hands while I deliver your punishment and you will not move them until the punishment is complete.'

I offered her my hands, palms upwards as if in supplication. She brought the cane down on my right hand. The pain was so intense that it bought tears to my eyes and I was pretty sure that it would be tender for a week. She gave me two more strokes across my palm before turning her vicious attention to my left hand.

When she'd finished she lowered the cane and looked at me. She walked slowly around me as I stood there with my hands extended and I felt her hands on my buttocks. Then gentle fingers touching my weals. She stroked them with a fingertip, exploring them like a blind man reading Braille.

I heard a dull thump as she tossed the cane on to the bed and she came back into my field of vision again, walking over to the dresser drawer. She took out a leather contraption that looked like a garment, but not one I recognised. It wasn't until she began to strap herself into it that I realised it was a harness. Inside its crotch it was fitted with a small dildo and I watched, captivated, as she slid it inside herself. She put the harness on slowly, tightening straps and adjusting buckles until it was comfortable. Then she reached back into the drawer and retrieved a black silicone dildo.

She fitted it to the harness, pressing it through a ring at the front and adjusting it until it stood out in front of her in parody of an erection. She walked over to me slowly, caressing the fake cock with one hand, just in case I was in any doubt as to her intention.

'Have you ever been fucked, little girl?'

I could only shake my head in answer.

'But you'd like to be?' She unbuckled a little pocket on the side of the harness and took out a bottle of lube, swinging it in front of my face, taunting me.

This time I nodded, signalling my consent and eagerness.

'Excellent. Then get on your knees and bend over.'

I was on all fours in an instant, hoisting my rear end like a bitch in heat. She knelt behind me and I heard a squelch as she squirted lube into her hand. I felt her cold, slippery fingers circle my puckered opening. I was helpless, vulnerable, ashamed and unspeakably aroused. I let out a deep moan and I knew that, if she ever allowed me to come, I'd practically explode.

The tip of her finger pushed inside me and a shiver of excitement shot up my spine. My cock was painfully hard. She fucked me slowly with her finger then turned it and located my prostate. She stroked it firmly and my whole body began to quiver. Soon, she was fucking me with two fingers and the pleasure was so intense that it was all I could do to keep still.

She withdrew for a moment and I felt pressure against my opening and I knew she was trying to enter me with the dildo.

'I've lubed it up so it's nice and slippery. Just relax and let me do all the work. If it hurts when it goes in take some deep breaths and use your muscles to try to push it out – that should end the spasm that's causing the pain. OK?' Without waiting for an answer, she pushed the tip of the dildo hard against my slick opening and I felt pressure as she used her body weight to push it forward.

It slid past my muscles, stretching and filling me. Soon, I could feel her warm thighs against mine and the front of the cold leather harness against my buttocks. She pushed forward in one long thrust, holding my hips for leverage, and for a moment there was an intense, cramping pain. But I did as she had told me, pushing back with my muscles and it quickly dissipated, leaving behind it indescribable pleasure.

Mistress waited for me to get my breath back, circling her hips. When she was sure I was OK she began to fuck me slowly, sliding her cock unhurriedly in and out. As the dildo slid into me I experienced a pleasure and fulfilment I had never dreamed of. I felt unbelievably submissive and vulnerable and somehow open and my cock was as hard as I could ever remember. I longed to handle it. I was pretty sure that a couple of tugs would be all I needed to take me over the edge, but she'd already punished me for that infraction and I had no intention of disobeying her twice.

She began to fuck me harder. She gripped the straps of my gymslip where they crossed at the back and pulled on them hard, riding me like a horse. I could hear her panting as she fucked me. She tugged on my straps, making them cut painfully into my shoulders and jerking me backwards, but I didn't care.

She was in a frenzy now, grunting and growling as she fucked me, thrusting into my hole with aggressive satisfaction. My knees were getting grazed by the carpet and my sweaty hands kept slipping from under me, but none of it mattered. I was helpless, totally without power and she was using my body solely for her own pleasure. She thrust into me hard, knocking me forward until I was half sprawling on my front but somehow I managed to keep my arse in the air and her cock where it belonged. Then it hit me that the power dynamic was completely reversed and she felt as powerful and aggressive as I felt helpless and passive. I'd never imagined it could be like this, yet it felt so right, so natural, so necessary.

Mistress was snarling and grunting like a wild animal. Her thighs slapped noisily against mine. I could hear the sound of her leather harness straining under her onslaught. She gripped hard on my straps and the buttons gave way. My gymslip came apart and the bib fell forward over my cock and the waist gaped open. I just couldn't help it, I gripped my erection in my fist and began to stroke.

I could feel her body trembling behind mine. She was keening and wailing, thrusting her hips hard, filling me with her cock. My ruined gymslip hung around my waist, flapping uselessly as she fucked me. My cock was slippery in my hand, my balls clenching beneath it ready for orgasm. But I wanted to wait for her. I gripped it tight, holding myself back until I was sure that she had come.

She gave a long deep thrust, holding on to my hips, pulling me on to her cock. She let out a long, deep groan and I knew she was coming. Her body quivered, her fingers dug into my flesh and she was gasping for breath. I pulled my foreskin down hard and that was all it took. Spunk pumped out all over my hand and the carpet. I didn't think it would ever end. Volley after volley of hot cream shot over the carpet. One of them even hit me in the face.

Mistress was screaming now, rotating her hips, wringing out the last aftershocks of orgasm. Gradually, her movements slowed and her cries subsided. She fell forward over my back and I felt her hair on my neck, her hot breath against my ear. Her sweat-slick cheek pressed up against mine and she whispered:

'I don't remember giving you permission to come.'

'Sorry, mistress, I couldn't help myself. Please forgive me.'

She laughed into my ear then kissed me on the cheek.

'Sorry, Ben, you should know by now I'm not the forgiving type . . .'

And she wasn't, but I'm sure it'll come as no surprise that I wouldn't want it any other way.

– Ben J., Cambridge, UK

Fancy Dresser

When Louise confronted me with the letter, I felt a sudden, gut-wrenching sickness and the most intense helplessness. There really was no escape from admitting my affair with Liz. All I could do was say yes and beg forgiveness.

Strangely, Louise had expressed little emotion during that first terrible conversation. Indeed, the only real sign of it came when, standing in the dining room, the letter on the table before me, I tried to apologise.

'I can't explain why it happened. It meant nothing. I couldn't –'

A loud, bitter laugh cut into my pleading and suddenly there were tears in her eyes.

'You couldn't what? Help it?'

I nodded weakly, ashamed and humiliated.

'Isn't that what you all say, you men? You couldn't help it? As if your cock was some kind of independent entity? And isn't that just an excuse for the real truth: that you can't take responsibility for your actions?'

There was nothing else I could say. I stared at the floor and felt my face burn with embarrassment and a deeper, helpless anger. The truth was, I was forced to endure this because to resist was impossible.

'And it doesn't matter what I say either, does it? You'll just stand there and suck it up. Because if you tell me what's really going on in that little head of yours, you know I'll kick you out. And then I'll speak to mummy and you'll be finished. No big job, no big house, no big car and no fancy clothes.'

I felt a sudden anger wash over my body as she mocked my taste for the good things in life, especially my taste for expensive designer clothing. Yet I fought an indignant explosion, knowing every word she said was true. Her mother, thanks to the death of her husband, was now in complete control of the company. One wrong word from Louise and I was well and truly finished.

'Well,' she continued. 'Let's see how much you can suck up.'

With this she suddenly spun round on her high heels and fled the room, leaving me shocked, angry and very confused.

Shaking from this encounter, I looked at my watch. It was 3.30 p.m. I swallowed hard and cursed my bad luck. The annual company fancy-dress ball was due to start in four hours. I thought about ringing Liz and warning her. She would be coming to the party. But if I phoned her now, she would be in an intolerable situation. The best thing was to go underground for a little while: I would drive out to the cottage and spend the rest of the weekend there. This would give me time to think through a strategy for saving my marriage and my lifestyle.

I stood in the vast sun-soaked living room, with its long, elegantly framed French windows, that overlooked the very considerable family estate. I stood there for what must have been twenty minutes. The massive expanse of perfectly maintained lawn stretched out before me like a desert of despair: I was looking into the oblivion of my future. Now, I was sure, everything I had so carefully prepared for was about to be flushed down the toilet by my own stupidity. Then my mobile phone rang. I answered it hesitantly. It was Louise.

'If you want to stay with me, then come to mummy's bedroom. Now.'

The phone went dead before I could say a word.

I listened to my heart pound against my chest. Feelings of anger and fear washed over me in equal measure. Her tone had been detached, cool, brutal. Her mother's room: the large, overly ornate bedroom that, following her husband's death, my mother-in-law Mary had turned into an office and general living space: a space I had never before been allowed to enter.

I made my way through the large elegant house, my mind spinning with possibilities, my mouth dry with nerves. For a year, I had been deliberately sidelined. When her husband had died, Mary had 'restructured the upper management tier' and I had found myself in a minor role, outside the core decision-making elite. Since then, my job in the company had become quietly ridiculous, a pointless invention to keep the boss's son-in-law in fancy clothes and fast cars. I felt my anger renewed, then destroyed by fear and humiliation.

By the time I knocked lightly on Mary's door, my stomach was turning and my heart pounding.

It was Mary's voice that told me 'come in', her hard, precise, aristocratic voice cutting into me like a cold, sharp knife.

I took a deep breath and opened the door.

The room was huge, even by the standard of the mansion. Mary had divided it into three sections: an office space, a living room and a bedroom. In the living area was a white leather three-piece suite that surrounded a long narrow glass-topped coffee table.

On the table were fashion magazines and a book of erotic art. Before the suite was a large top-of-the-range home entertainment centre. Behind it was a wall hidden by a series of tall white bookcases filled with books and magazines.

The living area faded into the office and a large circular dining table upon which was placed a bottle of golden-coloured Chablis and three freshly chilled glasses.

The office merged into the bedroom space. And it was here that I saw Louise and Mary and had the first hint of the fate they had planned for me.

The women were standing side by side before a large double bed. To their right was a mobile clothes rack.

'Come here, Will.'

Mary's blue, crystal-hard eyes were filled with a mixture of contempt and excitement. She was clearly enjoying herself.

I walked nervously across the thick white carpet that lined the entire floor of the room to within a few feet of the two beautiful, but now also rather sinister women.

I couldn't help appraising Mary's striking form with obviously desiring eyes. She was, as always, impeccably dressed and stunningly beautiful. Today she was wearing her golden blonde hair in a very tight bun held in position by a diamond clasp. Although in her mid-fifties, she had managed to maintain a shapely if somewhat buxom figure, the extra weight adding to a general air of ample beauty. This was emphasized by a tight white silk blouse with a wide, open neck and long, tapered collar.

Around her slender neck she wore a band of white pearls. The dark and teasing valley between her large, still firm breasts was clearly visible above the last sealed button of the blouse, and I found myself staring into it with wide, tormented and fearful eyes.

The blouse was tucked tightly and neatly into a long black velvet skirt that shimmered in the soft light and reached down to her black-hosed ankles and her feet elegantly encased in a pair of very beautiful high-heeled Gucci court shoes.

Her cherry-painted lips curved into a contemptuous smile as she saw my eyes betray my always too obvious desire. I tried to avert her withering gaze, but then found myself looking into the accusing, angry eyes of my betrayed wife.

'I can't say I'm surprised,' Mary snapped. 'I've always known this was all about the money. You managed to wiggle your way into Frank's affections without even trying. For a clever, powerful man, he could be surprisingly weak. Perhaps he saw you as some kind of son. God knows. And I don't care. What I do care about is the simple fact that you have wounded my daughter, very badly, and mocked this family. And I will not stand for that.'

Her words were delivered with a precise and deeply intimidating aggression. I felt them strike against my body like physical blows and cringed. I felt small and pathetic and then, again, angry. I wanted to lash out at her as she mocked me so bitterly in front of my wife. But I said nothing: things had changed too much over the last few months. Mary had the power now, and if I wanted to retain the lifestyle to which I had become so obviously accustomed, dignity was a luxury I could not afford. So I stood there and endured this awful telling-off. Yet as she became angrier, she also seemed to become more beautiful. There was a fierce, carefully applied power in her words and in her physique that, as so often during our past encounters, I found myself helplessly drawn

45

towards. Yes, my simple confession: I had always been deeply attracted to her, and she knew it.

'Louise has told me everything,' Mary continued. 'And she has sought my advice. Initially, I told her to leave you. I could have you removed from this house in a second. You would be back on the streets where you came from with nothing but your physical charms to survive on.'

I blushed at her reference to my almost helpless good looks, another tool I had used cynically to get where I needed to go.

'But I didn't advise her to kick you out. I advised her to take advantage of the situation in a more fitting manner.'

My eyes widened with unease. I looked over at Louise, who was now smiling slightly.

'You're at your best when looking after me,' said my beautiful wife. 'Always so attentive, so caring. And all a sham, of course; but you make me feel looked after, pampered. Even served. It's almost like having a personal maid.'

My eyes moved between Louise, her mother and the clothes rack. As she spoke, a much darker feeling of fear gripped my stomach. This wasn't my marching orders – this was something much worse!

As my gaze darkened, the wicked smiles on the faces of the two women widened.

'So we decided to give you a choice,' Mary said. 'You can go, and I for one won't miss you. Or you stay and continue in your role as Lou's servant. But in a slightly more formal manner.'

There was a dress hanging from the rack, an elaborate black silk dress with thick, fetishistic frills at the sleeves and a very high button-up neck. A sea of thick petticoat netting exploded from beneath its wide, short skirt. Hanging by the dress was a white silk pinafore. The word 'maid' had lodged in my mind as soon as it had eased its way past Louise's lips.

'If you want to stay,' Louise said, 'then it's on my terms. And my terms are simple: you stay as my maid.'

'We'll start tonight, at the ball,' Mary added. 'You will go dressed as the classic French maid. At the ball, you will confess a long-hidden secret: you have been a transvestite since your teenage years and tonight, after years of struggle, you have finally found the courage – with the loving support of Louise and myself – to come out of the closet suitably attired. Then you will join the catering staff and serve the guests. While we don't necessary intend you to stay permanently in this particularly exotic costume, you will remain fully feminised until such time as you decide to leave us, something you may do at any time. However, if you do leave, you will be required to sign a formal declaration waiving all rights to any financial settlement or future support. If you want to be a man, then I am afraid you'll have to live with the responsibilities of masculinity. If you want to stay with us, then it will be as a feminised male employed, formally, as Louise's assistant. We will have the marriage quietly annulled, but as long as you conform to our terms, you will be guaranteed, in a legally binding contract, a reasonably generous salary and suitably stylish quarters in the grounds of the house. You will also receive a significant severance package if, at any time, *we* decide to terminate the arrangement.'

I looked at them both and, perhaps to their surprise, burst out laughing. Yet this wasn't the laughter of arrogance or contempt. This was the laughter of complete and utter defeat, laughter in the face of truly overwhelming odds. For I had, as they well knew, no choice. I would do anything to stay here, to be part of this life, to be a member of a privileged elite.

Then, rather suddenly, I stopped laughing. I stared at them and at the dress. Yes: this was my well-deserved punishment.

I nodded weakly and barely whispered, 'Yes. I'll do it. On your terms.'

Mary's smile widened. 'Yes, of course you will,' she sneered.

'Get undressed,' Louise said, her voice filled with cruel excitement. 'Everything.'

A flicker of anger passed across my eyes and Mary snapped, 'Now. Quickly.'

This was to be the first humiliation of many. My heart pounding, a thin, sticky sweat of fear and despair covering my forehead, I slipped off the expensive Armani jacket and placed it on the carpet. Then, with shaking hands, I began to unbutton my white silk shirt.

The women watched without comment as I stripped before them. I saw Mary's eyes widen slightly as I revealed my bronzed and carefully maintained torso. The house contained a fitness suite and an indoor swimming pool, and I had made full use of them. And as I saw clear attraction warm her cool blue eyes, I felt an unavoidable narcissistic pride and the stirring of my already semi-erect cock.

I kicked off my slip-on shoes and unbuckled the belt of my chinos, my hands suddenly calmer, my nerves replaced by a strangely soothing indifference. Actually knowing their plans, as perverse and disturbing as they were, seemed to reduce their impact. Then, in a rather melodramatic gesture, I hauled the trousers down over my underpants and thighs and let them fall to the floor around my ankles. My tight red cotton underpants made clear my increasing physical arousal and the slightest moan of surprise slipped past Mary's dark, glistening lips.

I stepped out of the trousers and leant forward to pull off my red socks. Then I stood upright and faced my beautiful captors. Suddenly, at this pivotal moment, I felt no real sense of fear or nervousness at all. Indeed, I found myself holding Mary's fascinated gaze with a renewed confidence and the obvious arousal in her eyes seemed to tilt the balance just enough for me to smile slightly and then begin – with a deliberately teasing relish – to ease the underpants down over my now fully erect cock.

As it popped out from beneath the descending waistband, Louise let out a short, edgy laugh, a laugh that communicated her surprise that I was actually prepared to endure this profound and extended humiliation. I wondered if she really actually wanted me to be feminised; if this idea – so obviously her mother's – was only a way to force me out. Yes, I could imagine her dismissing the possibility that I would submit to enforced feminisation to maintain my lifestyle. Not for the first time, she had misjudged me.

Then I was naked, my hands at my sides, my cock rising up before them, both it and the rest of me standing to a paradoxically proud attention.

The women studied my body in different ways – Louise with knowing yet still impressed eyes, and Mary with a deeper, more sexually infused interest, laced with a hint of surprise, both at the obvious masculine beauty of my body and the significant length of my exposed and excited manhood.

It was Louise who broke into the semi-erotic contemplation.

'Follow me,' she said, heading towards the large en suite bathroom that was attached to the multi-functional bedroom.

Once in the bathroom, I was ordered into the shower, given a large bar of pink soap and told to wash myself carefully and thoroughly. I nodded weakly, making no effort to hide my nakedness or acknowledge it as anything out of the ordinary.

The soap was heavily perfumed and, as I used it to wash my body, I felt the first touch of the truly feminine, and it was far from unpleasant. My mind preyed on the dark details of the strange fate that awaited me and the more I contemplated the future, the more excited I became.

When I returned to the bedroom, a thick white towel wrapped rather half-heartedly around my waist, my cock was pressing against its soft layered surface with a furious, betraying enthusiasm that told Mary and Louise everything they needed to know.

I was ordered to the centre of the room, to stand once again a few inches from the two women. I stared into Mary's eyes and saw triumph laced with arousal. I looked at Louise and saw confusion, anger and – despite her best efforts to repress it – desire. It was then that Mary revealed the red plastic lady shaver. Her smile broadened, her beautiful ice-blue eyes widened and her large, tightly and very exactly restrained bosom swelled with a cruel sexual need.

'Get rid of the towel and put your hands behind your back.'

I obeyed with a gasp of dark masochistic pleasure and she set to work, spending twenty blissful minutes carefully removing every inch of hair from my long, almost feminine legs, including between my thighs and – to my arousal-tinged embarrassment – but-tocks; and then, to my even darker joy, she set to work on my pubes. By the time she had finished, my body was shaven completely and utterly, every speck of hair removed with a ruthless, buzzing efficiency by the teeth of the shaver.

Suddenly, my body was new to the world. As Mary climbed back on to her high-heeled feet to admire her expert efforts, I stared down at my strangely infantilised form and beheld the body of a sissy stranger. The sense of transformation and alienation from something that was me and other than me was immediate and powerful.

Then the changing started in earnest. Almost immediately, my denuded form was covered in a sweet mist of powerful perfume. Then I was led by Mary to the vast ornate dressing table, an elaborate Georgian antique upon which had been set out the dainty tools of my feminisation.

I was made to sit before the large, intricately framed oval mirror and stare at my stunned but still recognisable reflection. My eyes were wide with shocked arousal and my carefully maintained body seemed to vibrate with the aura of impending transformation.

Mary stood directly behind me, her substantial bosom only a few inches from my face. I smelt my perfume and hers, plus, on the very edge of this delightful sensory torment, something else, a more fundamental and intimate scent.

Despite Mary's clear leadership in this strange and erotic ordeal, it was Louise who proceeded to apply the various items of make-up set out upon the table before us. As she leant forward to take up a jar of pale foundation cream, our eyes met once again. But now the confusion seen earlier was gone, replaced by determination: she had put the inescapably erotic fact of my body and its impending transformation out of her mind to get on with the job at hand.

I surrendered to her expert touch with a sense of aroused expectancy, my aching cock pressing into my stomach with an angry desperation. I watched my face change and not change; a most peculiar and exciting alteration that became more pronounced with each careful intervention by my cool-eyed wife.

Once my face was covered in the film of soft-toned foundation, the true confession of my feminine potential became apparent. With the masculine edges of my closely shaven face drastically softened by the cream, a heart-shaped visage of helpless feminine beauty appeared before me. I gasped with surprise and saw the look of cruel fascination on Mary's face deepen.

Yet this was nothing compared to the impact of the cherry-red lipstick that Louise then carefully guided across my lips, leaving a pretty, bloody bow that wiped away any doubts about the striking truth of my changing. And this truth was made further and rather shockingly apparent by the careful application of sky-blue eye shadow, dark eyebrow pencil and a hint of peach-coloured rouge dabbed carefully on to each cheek.

Suddenly, I was facing a beautiful not-quite-woman, a disturbingly attractive vision of a half-revealed femininity. I stared at myself with fascinated arousal, drawn by the pull of a black hole of intense narcissism. Louise broke this powerful spell by helping me up from the stool and leading me back to the clothes rack. It was then that I noticed a collection of female underwear had been laid out on the bed and I felt my swaying, pleading cock beg for an impossible and unwanted mercy.

As I looked down at the undies and then over at the dress hanging from the rack, I felt as if I were fading out of focus, that I had stepped into a thick, scented fog of the Feminine that I could leave only when I was fully and finally transformed. This was the ecstatic and painfully erotic moment of no return.

The dressing began with an intimate and terribly arousing gesture of submission and true feminine consumption. A cruel smile lighting up her beautiful, soft-featured face, Louise took a very sheer black nylon stocking from the bed and held it before me.

'First, a symbol of your future, my pretty.'

Her words were delivered with a calculating melodrama, the exaggerated discourse of a professional dominatrix, a role that she clearly considered appropriate for our new relationship.

She wound the stocking into a wide bowl and then told me to put my hands behind my back. I obeyed and she then, to my surprise and undisguised pleasure, began to slip the stocking over the hot, hard length of my cock. And as the endlessly soft, electric nylon material brushed against the intensely agitated flesh of my sex, I let out a low, angry moan of paradoxically fierce male pleasure that inspired a chuckle of cruel delight from Mary.

Louise pulled the stocking down the complete length of my cock and wrapped it tightly around my balls, using a narrow length of pink silk ribbon and leaving a fat, humiliating bow dangling from the base of my scrotum. Then she held up a long, narrow, elastane-panelled snow-white panty girdle.

'To give you a more feminine shape and hide that naughty little man,' Mary explained. 'It's one of mine, but I'm pretty sure it will fit you.'

And so it did, drawn up my legs with a careful determination by my wife and pulled into position with one surprisingly powerful tug. I found myself subject to a taut but not unpleasant figure discipline that also very effectively flattened and half-concealed my betraying male sex. However, before I could fully appreciate the true impact of the girdle's deeply erotic embrace, Louise ordered me to sit down on the bed. As I did do, I immediately became aware of the new level of restriction and the inherently feminine movement this restriction demanded. My sex seemed to grow even harder and longer within its panty-girdle prison as I lowered my petite elastane-wrapped bottom on to the bed's expensive silken sheets.

After the girdle came a pair of black nylon tights and the assurance of my complete surrender to this intensely sensual feminisation. Louise held the tights before me. The soft light of the bedroom revealed the legs as shimmering, semi-transparent flowers. I stared at the tights, my eyes wide with erotic expectation, my delicately painted lips curved into an O of helpless arousal. I looked over at Mary. She smiled slightly, her own excitement obvious.

'Let me,' she said.

Louise handed the tights to her mother, then the gorgeous, buxom beauty, in a gesture of paradoxical submission, knelt down before me.

I stared down at her generous shapely form and felt a dizzying wave of desire wash over my changing body. Her large, sado-erotically restrained bosom rose and fell with an increasing rapidity. The tight black velvet skirt traversed her long legs, which I knew were sheathed in the same sheer, all-embracing nylon, and created a gorgeous mermaid's tail that ended in the pair of gleaming black patent leather court shoes with their teasing stiletto heels.

Then she looked up at me and I felt my heart skip a beat of furious, helpless desire. My responding gaze was a simple confession not only of my obvious sexual excitement, but of something much more important for my future in this house: my masochistic surrender to her ultimate authority, a desire informed by a long and often poorly suppressed craving for this lovely mature beauty. Suddenly, I realised that, while I might be Louise's feminised assistant, I would be Mary's maid and slave. And the thought inspired a slight but clear moan of very powerful pleasure.

She smiled and I knew we understood each other perfectly.

As she carefully pulled the tights up over my feet and ankles, I began to experience a new, deeply sensual and wholly physical pleasure: the kiss of scented ultra-sheer nylon against my freshly shaven skin. Words cannot describe the tactile power of this first envelopment in hose. I found myself barely stifling a girlish squeal of pleasure as Mary guided the delicate material up to my knees and then told me to stand and take the waistband in my hands. Under her expert instruction, I then very carefully pulled the tights up over the silken front panel of the panty girdle and around my tightly restricted waist.

My breathing hard and fast, my cock harder, my heart pounding with a furious desire the like of which I had never experienced, I found myself looking down upon my legs and feeling a savage renewal of the narcissistic arousal that seemed to be at the heart of this increasingly exciting cross-dressing 'ordeal'.

My hands ran helplessly and desperately over the sheer, electric nylon fabric. My eyes were filled with the striking shape of my long legs. The hose stressed and celebrated the feminine truth of my form with a shocking honesty.

I felt the dryness of nervous desire in the back of my mouth and surrendered to the next stage of the transformation. I stared at Mary and fought back tears of painful sexual arousal. Her smile was both cruelly teasing and maternal. I was hers without reservation. Her victory was total.

Louise held a beautiful white silk bra before me, its wide cups filled with two silicon-padded rubber breasts. She slipped the narrow silken straps over my tanned shoulders. The anger had left her eyes now, replaced by something like happiness. She seemed to have moved beyond the disgust inspired by my weakness, by my betrayal, towards something more practical and more positive.

As I considered and frankly revelled in the physical impact of the bra, Louise retrieved the final item of feminine underwear from the bed – a pair of ornate white silk cami-knickers, whose relatively short legs and elastic reinforced waist had been frilled with expensive white lace. She held them out to me and I took them without hesitation. As I stepped into them, I felt the delicate black nylon hose caress my legs and knew that every movement I made in the tights would be an ecstasy that would be hard to endure. My tormented cock strained in its own delightful nylon prison and I moaned with a helplessly feminine yet also fiercely sexual need.

Once the knickers were in place, we progressed to the most striking and potent symbol of my feminine submission: the elaborate French maid's dress, a shimmering confection of black silk that betrayed a very significant amount of forethought on the part of Louise and her gorgeous mother. As Mary took the dress from the rack and held it before me like a proud parent, I knew that she was confessing a carefully thought-through plan that most probably predated my infidelity.

I looked at the dress and said, 'It's beautiful.'

Mary smiled. 'I designed it myself. My first effort.'

'Mummy's rather talented,' Louise said.

'When did you think this up?'

It was a simple but telling question, and Mary smiled coyly when I asked it.

'I must admit I've been thinking about a suitable role for you since I decided to play a more direct part in the business.'

It was just a matter of the right moment, and my affair had surely been that moment.

The dress had a high lace-frilled neck secured by a row of white pearl buttons that ran all the way down the back of the dress. The very short skirt rested on a thick sea of white net petticoating and an almost invisible pattern of black silk roses ran through the core fabric of the dress. It was an elegant erotic masterpiece and as Mary helped me inside it, I knew I was becoming Mary's first work of true fashion art.

As Mary gently secured each of the twenty-odd buttons, I felt myself consumed, devoured by the Feminine. It was as if I was disappearing and being replaced, my body and soul snatched by the most delicate and inescapable of sado-erotic changes. And I was, undoubtedly, loving every beautiful, fetishistic second of it.

Once the dress was firmly and very tightly secure, Louise helped me into the lovely, shimmering white silk pinafore, tying it in place at the base of my back with a particularly fat and elaborate bow.

The women then stood back to consider the results of their kinky labours and I stood before them, nervous and so very dreadfully aroused.

'Perfect,' Mary whispered, clearly very impressed by her handiwork.

'But not quite,' Louise said, moving back towards the dressing table, her movements fluid, elegant, confident; her beauty undeniable and almost transcendent as the soft light of the bedroom poured over her long white dress.

Beneath the table was a large circular pink box. She brought it to the bed and removed the lid. From inside she took a startling blonde wig resting on a plastic stand, a dazzling collection of thick, expertly sculpted waves in the style of a fifties film star that inspired a helpless quiver of intense, electric sex pleasure to pass across my feminised body.

As she slipped the wig over my head and very gently eased it into the optimum position, I was bathed in her sensual French perfume and in her appraising, darkly promising gaze. For the first time, I felt truly comfortable in her presence.

She considered the wig, her eyes confessing increasing surprise, and then Mary revealed the final exquisite touch: my shoes. From beneath the bed, she had taken a pair of black leather court shoes with stunning five-inch stiletto heels. Each had a small silver butterfly buckle set into each toe for purely decorative purposes.

I beheld the shoes with a shiver of anticipation. I remembered the pleasure I had always taken in witnessing shapely, nylon-wrapped legs completed elegantly and sensually by beautifully shaped high-heeled court shoes or mules. I had always encouraged Louise to wear heels to show off her undoubtedly attractive legs and she had always been more than willing to oblige.

Mary placed the shoes a few inches from my hosed feet and I stepped into them with a gasp of gorgeous trepidation, my heart pounding, my cock burning desperately in its delicate but inescapable nylon prison.

Immediately, I was elevated into the realm of feminine perfection. My obviously attractive and feminine legs – made so beautiful by the soft, sheer, pervasive film of black nylon – were finally and stunningly completed by the sensual angles of the shoes. I swayed nervously. Mary took me by the hand. She smiled and encouraged me to take a step forward.

'Be brave. Be bold,' she whispered, her eyes burning with an icy determination.

I nodded weakly and took a cautious step. My entire body seemed to tilt and at the end of the first step I fell uselessly forward. Louise rushed to my side and the two women succeeded in saving me from falling flat on my so carefully made-up face.

For the next ten minutes, I practised walking in the shoes, at first helped by Mary, and then, gradually, unsupported. I was told to take short, careful steps, to find balance through the counterbalance of the heels and my upper body. And, with each tiny step, I did indeed become more confident and, to my deepest delight, more feminine. And soon I was tottering before these two beautiful women with an almost brazen confidence; yet not just the confidence of balance, but also the confidence of the Feminine. Each step confessed a simple truth: my inherent femininity, my natural womanly grace.

Mary and Louise watched with fascinated, excited eyes. Their expectations had clearly been exceeded.

Then I was led to the walk-in closet and brought before the long mirror built into the inner door. Now I was suitably amazed; now my own expectations were well and truly exceeded. For I was facing a tall, rather buxom and very beautiful young woman, a sexy blonde attired in the teasing costume of a French maid. My eyes sparkled with arousal. With my legs pressed together, with my nylon-enveloped thighs rubbing helplessly, with the erotic counterweight of my striking realistic bosom, I was quite astonishingly convincing. Their art and my inclination had produced a vision of genuine feminine beauty.

I was allowed to practise wiggle walking for a few

more minutes. Then there was a light knock on the door. Mary looked up at the clock and smiled.

'Bang on time,' she said, stepping forward to open the door.

My eyes darted between the door and Louise. A darker, harder light now framed my beautiful wife's gaze. What on earth was going on?

When I found out, my jaw dropped open and a sense of utter embarrassment and humiliation washed over me. Suddenly, I was no longer the beautiful maid but a man forced into a dress by his vengeful wife and her gorgeous, scheming mother. For standing in the doorway was Liz, the woman I had risked everything for, the woman who had shown me care and affection when everybody else had appeared indifferent or contemptuous.

I faced Liz, astonished and appalled. She came into the room, her eyes wide, her beautiful peach-red lips curved into a smile of disbelief.

'Is it him?' she asked. 'Is this pretty creature really him?'

A wave of humiliation struck me and washed away the strange, liberating confidence that had been growing since the beginning of this deeply erotic transformation

To make things worse, Liz was in her fancy-dress costume, the costume she had promised to wear just for me with the same teasing smile she was now employing so ironically.

A tall, full-figured brunette, with particularly large yet still firm and shapely breasts, her eyes a dark brown, nearly black, she was dressed – or rather sealed – in a semi-opaque black nylon body stocking covered in glistening silver silk stars. Her height was strikingly emphasised by a pair of truly sado-erotic black patent leather ankle boots with striking six-inch stiletto heels. Her thick shining hair was bound in a very tight bun that was held in place by a black metal clasp and a matching plastic frame holding two black velvet cat's ears. This erotic feline theme was further stressed by a long black tail that hung down from just above her plump yet particularly shapely backside.

'I can't decide who's sexier,' Louise said, a lighter and crueller irony in her voice. 'You or . . . him.'

'Him?' Mary said, faking incredulity. 'Surely not him.'

'Oh, definitely *her*, Lou,' said Liz, her eyes glowing with pure sex tease.

I felt my cock stir in its unbearably erotic nylon prison. I felt the scented hose of the tights torment the warm, silken skin of my thighs with a thousand gentle, loving kisses. A terribly arousing sense of complete submission to this ultra-femininity flooded through my mind.

'You were in on it,' I said to Liz. 'From the beginning.'

This halted the teasing joviality almost immediately. Liz looked surprised, Louise angry, and Mary vaguely amused.

'You're clever as well as pretty,' Mary said, her voice cool, edged with sex. 'Yes, she was. Bait for my weak-willed son-in-law. Bait you swallowed eagerly.'

I nodded, seeing it all in an instant, realising how Mary had seen me as a competitor from the beginning and arranged for me to be permanently moved to one side, understanding how she had set the trap by arranging for Liz to seduce me at the very moment my self-confidence was – thanks to Mary – at its weakest.

I stared at her regal, strikingly beautiful form and knew I would obey her without question, that the genius of her plan was not just to sideline me but to make me desire the very thing that ensured I remained sidelined.

My initial humiliation at being exposed before lovely Liz faded quickly as she tottered around me, her tail waving teasingly in the electric air, examining every inch of my expertly feminised form with fascinated eyes.

'It really is astonishing, Mary. How did you ever know he'd make such a gorgeous girl?'

I swooned as she teased and Mary laughed.

'I saw it in his eyes.'

It was then that Louise went to the bedside table and retrieved a circular tray.

'Go to the dining table,' she said to me, a simple, confident order. 'Pour the wine and serve us. And do it properly.'

I looked into her determined eyes and felt my knees weaken with an almost overwhelming masochistic arousal.

I nodded, took the tray from her hands and tottered over to the table, feeling more deliciously feminine with each step, and also feeling their eyes burn into my long, nylon-wrapped legs. I found myself deliberately wiggling my bottom and taking the tiniest of steps in the testing stiletto heels. And as I did so, I surrendered to a pleasure I never thought possible.

I poured the drinks with careful, delicate movements, no longer nervous, no longer afraid. Tonight, at the ball, I would pour and serve many more drinks as I was revealed as a transvestite slave; tonight I would confess a desire I never knew existed within me, but which Mary had clearly recognised as she had peered into my tormented soul. Perhaps when I spoke there would be laughter. But I had seen my astonishing reflection and I knew any laughter would be hiding helpless fascination and maybe desire.

I returned to the three beautiful women. Tonight Louise would dress as a whip-wielding dominatrix, a costume she had suggested and I had encouraged her to design and wear. And Mary planned to go as a warrior queen.

I minced up to my gorgeous mistresses, smiled sweetly and then, before serving the drinks, performed a bob curtsey that displayed both my lovely silk knickers and my absolute acceptance of my new role in this elegant, privileged household.

– *S. Page, Buckinghamshire, UK*

Cock

There's so much bullshit talked about sex. What you're supposed to like, who you're supposed to like, why women like this and don't like that. I know what I like, and I don't need some prissy cow from a magazine or a shrink with a shiny new degree to tell me. I like cock.

Best of all, I like to suck cock. There's something about it, to feel a guy swell up in my mouth, and the way men taste, and get so horny for me. I just love it. Sure, I want a caring man and a house of my own and kids and everything, eventually. It's not going to stop me anyway, because I aim to find a husband who'll take me out in the evening, maybe to a restaurant or a film, sure, but after that, to some car park where he can watch me take three or four strangers in my mouth, or a club where I can get bukkake from ten guys.

OK, so I'm a slut. You can call me what you like, but once you're in my mouth you'll be thankful for it, because believe me, I suck like an angel. I should, because I've had enough practice. I know all the tricks too, like running the tip of my tongue up and down on the underside of a guy's foreskin when he's fully erect, or making a pussy with my lips and suddenly pushing down. I've known guys to come like that, just from doing it once.

Let's start from the beginning. I won't say how old I was, only that I was old enough. He was a PE instructor at the convent of Our Lady, and he shouldn't have been allowed near girls. Not me anyway – I dare say he was safe enough with the ones who did what the penguins said and believed the bumf we got in chapel every morning.

Mr Moore, he was called, and he believed in what he taught, all muscle and sweat, and a big bulge in the tight shorts he used to wear. I used to fantasise about pulling him out of those shorts long before I had the guts to do anything about it. It's just nature, I suppose, but it's so compelling, the need to take out a man's cock and put him in my mouth and just suck and suck and suck. Maybe it's not so natural to want it in my mouth while I stroke myself off instead of up my pussy, but that's just the way I am.

I used to imagine myself going down on Mr Moore, and all the ways I could do it. The changing rooms were my favourite. He never did, but I would imagine him trying to peep at us in the shower and getting horny over what he could see. I'd hang back until everyone else was gone, so that he would catch me drying myself, and one way or another I'd end up sucking on that big bulge in his shorts. Another was for him to catch me playing with myself, which I used to do a lot, and blackmail me into giving him a blowjob in return for not reporting me to the penguins.

He was far too careful of his job for the first, and far too nice for the second. Looking back, I can't understand how any guy can be in a job like that without going off his head, unless he's gay maybe. For all I know Mr Moore did prefer boys, but he didn't mind girls either, I can tell you that.

I did think of doing it for real, and used to work out little schemes for how to get him alone long enough, not that I really knew what long enough was, and I used to imagine spending hours down on him. I even made an excuse for calling at his house, meaning to ask him straight out, but I lost my nerve. Maybe he realised, but he didn't show it, not until the end of that term.

With Dad in Nairobi I had to stay on another night for my flight, so it was just me, the penguins and Mr Moore. He was leaving, and it was my last chance, but I still wouldn't have done it if I hadn't met him down by the river. He was walking his dog, and I fell into step beside him, walking away from Our Lady. I knew I wanted to do it, or something, and I was hoping he'd stop and kiss me, or make a dirty suggestion, anything to set the ball rolling.

He didn't, and I couldn't, not right out, so I started to flirt, going on about how we all wanted to wear short skirts, even telling him about a friend who'd had an accident and ended up sitting through an exam with no knickers. I didn't know what he'd like. I didn't really know anything, only a little bit I'd picked up from books and other girls, and what went on in my head. Something must have got to him though, because when we'd got right out into the fields he gave this sort of strangled laugh and said something about me not understanding what I did to him.

As he said it he adjusted his cock in his trousers, with his body turned away from me so I wouldn't see, but I did. I got the words out before I could think better of it: 'Let's see then,' just that, an open invitation to take his cock out for me. His answer wasn't at all what I expected, really quite aggressive as he told me not to say things like that when I didn't mean it. I told him I did.

Still he hesitated, as if he couldn't quite believe that I was making a genuine offer, but then he seemed to reach a decision. I suppose he decided I was safe, or maybe he just couldn't resist, but he climbed the low fence we were walking beside and beckoned for me to follow him into the wood. I'd imagined it so many times, but I didn't know what to do, except to follow and hope he'd teach me.

We went in behind this thick bush, just a few feet from the path, and it was quite funny really, because he still looked as if he expected me to scream and run away, even as he took it all out. All I'd ever seen before were Greek statues and medical diagrams, so he looked pretty impressive. He must have already been half hard, but I didn't realise. I knew what I wanted to do, though, and when he invited me to touch I only hesitated a moment, then did it.

He felt warm and rubbery, good, but I had no idea what to do until he put his hand on mine and began to tug up and down. The moment I got the hang of it he let go, and I reckon if I'd just pulled him off he'd have been happy, but that wasn't what I wanted. I wanted him in my mouth. It took a bit of courage, even then, but I was telling myself I had to do it, and not to be pathetic after I'd thought about it so much, and I did.

I squatted down, still pulling at him as he got bigger, right in front of my face, pointing at me and just needing to be sucked. My mouth had come open before I really knew what I was doing, but it took an effort to make myself go forward and put it in. It felt so weird, lovely, but weird, only it wasn't so much the feel of him, or the taste or anything like that which really turned me on, it was just having a man's penis in my mouth and knowing how rude that was.

That's what got me, and still does, the pleasure of being rude. I reckon if I'd been brought up to believe I ought to suck men's cocks I'd think it was a bit of a chore, just one of those things you do so you'll get your own pleasure in return, like letting some weirdo fuck my feet because it's the only way he can get hard. As it is, sucking cock is more than just plain sex. It makes me feel like a bad girl, a rebel.

Anyway, it felt seriously rude to have Mr Moore in my mouth, and even better because he was telling me what to do, how to use my lips and tongue, to wank him into my mouth and gently squeeze his balls. I was being made a dirty girl, which was exactly what I wanted to be, and most of all, a cock-sucker. I love that, just to know that I regularly allow men to put their cocks in my mouth and suck them off, such a deliciously dirty thing to do, or to hear one guy say to another, at a dogging car park maybe, 'She's a great little cock-sucker' or just 'She'll suck your cock.'

Mr Moore didn't take long, in the end. If he'd wanted, he could have had me, I was soaking wet, and it wouldn't have taken too much to persuade me to touch my toes and let him stick it in. A combination of riding and those deodorant cans with the rounded tops had already disposed of my hymen, so although he'd have been my first I could have taken him without any pain. Instead I got a mouthful, just as I was starting to rub the front of my knickers and thinking about sticking a hand down them. It was a bit of a shock, and I hadn't realised it was going to be like getting a mouthful of snot, but I'd read somewhere that bad girls swallow, so I did, not very nice maybe, but so rude.

Afterwards he was furtive and guilty, while I wanted to celebrate what we'd done, so it wasn't the greatest success, but that didn't put me off. I'd had a taste and I wanted more, while I knew it could be better. Most of all I wanted to come while I was doing it, because I knew that would be special. Even the orgasm I had that night, lying alone in my bed and thinking of how it had felt to have him in my mouth, was one of the best I'd ever had.

That was the start, but I spent a long time with just the memory of Mr Moore to keep me company before I did it again. My parents were very protective, perhaps because Dad was involved in security and always saw the downside of people, but he seemed convinced that if I was on my own for five minutes I'd either be lured into a drug den or raped and murdered, maybe both. In Kenya I even had body-guards, always two, because he didn't trust them.

He was right, although it was really me he shouldn't have trusted. Then again, what was I supposed to do, with two big, powerful guys with me all day? I think Dad imagined I wouldn't be interested because they were blacks, but that just made the idea of sucking them all the more rude. It still took a lot of courage to proposition them, especially after dropping a hint and getting turned down flat, but when Joshua and Luke took over the winter after the incident with Mr Moore I knew I was on to a good thing.

At the start they were very formal and respectful, but as soon as they realised I wasn't going to play the high lady with them that changed. They were brothers, and very close, always joking together and commenting on passing girls, in Swahili, which they didn't realise I knew, until I answered them back and told them not to be cheeky. After that it was easy, just a matter of a few carefully dropped hints before they took me out into the bush and had me suck them both off.

I did it on my knees, with the two of them seated side by side on a big yellow-wood trunk and their trousers around their ankles. Being hard in front of each other wasn't a problem for them, and they had great cocks, big and jet-black and glossy, so good to suck on I wanted both in my mouth at the same time. They kept competing in what they wanted me to do as well, so when Joshua made me suck on his balls I had to do the same for Luke as well, and when they came they took turns to do it in my mouth.

What they'd have done to me if I hadn't been my Dad's daughter I don't like to think, probably spit-roasted me or fucked my bottom hole or something, which I couldn't have handled. That didn't matter, because I was my Dad's daughter, and they had to keep me happy. So I got what I wanted, and I can be a bossy little madam when I need to.

The first time it was all too urgent and I was nervous too, but the second time I took my trousers down and stroked myself off while I sucked, after telling them firmly not to go any further. That was so good, one of the rudest, most thrilling things I've ever done, kneeling there with my trousers down and one hand between my thighs, sucking two beautiful black cocks turn and turn about while I handled the other.

I had my top up too, because they'd asked to see my tits, and that added one more rude detail to the whole experience. When I came it was electric, like I was getting shock after shock through my whole body. I had Joshua's cock in my mouth as deep as it would go and I was tugging on Luke, with the other hand pushed down my knickers to rub at myself, and I swear I was so wet that if a rhino had come up behind me I'd have taken it, no fuss.

What I got was both men, not in me, but over my face, first Luke while I was still sucking his brother, then Joshua, who held me by my hair while he jerked himself off into my open mouth and just about everywhere else. I was still coming, just about, and it felt great, again not physically so much, but just because letting a man spunk up in my face is such a wonderfully rude thing to do.

I can't remember how many times they took me into the bush, but it was quite a regular thing. They never pushed it either, knowing they could count on me for blowjobs as long as they respected my limits, while I could have spent forever just feasting on those two huge black cocks. I rubbed myself sore I liked it so much, not just while I was doing them, but in bed at night too.

All good things come to an end, and when I got back to England and Our Lady I hadn't felt so homesick since my first ever night away. I'd never really felt I belonged, now it was far worse, but I only had to close my eyes and I'd be back on my knees in front of that big yellow-wood trunk with two gorgeous cocks to play with. I was hooked, and I have been ever since, but it wasn't until I'd left university that I really got into it.

Other than with Joshua and Luke it had always been boyfriends or one-night stands, but one cock was never really enough for me, while after theirs most of the men I met seemed a bit inadequate. They say size doesn't matter, but that's bullshit. Not when the guy's in you, 'cause a really big one can hurt if you're not ready and otherwise it doesn't make much difference. It's the aesthetics of size that matter. Who wants to see some weedy little pencil dick? It just doesn't look good.

I like big ones, long and thick and straight except for that slight upwards curve that can make a cock look so proud and so suckable. I like veins, and a big ridge underneath where the tube comes up, so it's like a tree trunk. There should be plenty of meat on the foreskin too, and a big, round helmet, so shiny with pressure when he's erect it looks like he's going to pop. A really well-shaped, shiny helmet makes me want to kiss and lick and nibble until he just can't hold back any more and spunks up right in my mouth.

Sometimes I like to imagine a ridiculously big cock, so big I can climb on and wrap my arms and legs around the shaft. That way I could rub myself off on him while I licked and cuddled and just held on. One variant is for me to be the priestess of a religion with an animate god two hundred feet tall and with a cock in proportion, which I can worship and make him come all over me. Silly, maybe, but it gets me there.

Back to my naughty behaviour. I came out of uni into a city job, well paid, but a real pain when it came to indulging my fantasies. Everyone in the building knows everyone else, and pretty much in the square mile too, so God help the girl who gets a reputation. I know it shouldn't be that way, but a lot of men just don't seem able to cope with full-on female sexuality.

For about a year I contented myself with a string of so-so boyfriends, but they either seemed to want to control me or were too wet to take advantage of me properly. I even had one guy tell me he respected me too much to come in my face, even though I wanted him to, and he seemed to think I should 'sort myself out'. That didn't last long.

Then I discovered a dirty little secret, dogging. Maybe I sound naïve, what with the internet and everything, but it had simply never occurred to me that people would behave like that. I found out completely by chance too. I'd been to the wedding of a guy from my firm, a really fancy do in a village in Lincolnshire where he'd bought a house. On the way back I quickly realised I was too tired to drive, so I pulled in to a lay-by to sleep. I was in my car, with

73

the doors locked, so I felt safe enough, and I was having trouble keeping my eyes open anyway, so it was that or crash.

I only meant to snatch half an hour, but it was more than three hours later when I woke up as bright light washed over my face. Another car had pulled in, and parked across from me. I was going to move on, but I was still shaking the sleep from my head when the interior light of the other car came on and I saw that the occupants were a couple.

Obviously they were there for sex, which was intriguing, but they weren't the sort of teenage couple with no house to go to I'd have expected. She was maybe thirty or thirty-five, pretty in a soft sort of way, and maybe a housewife or working in an office, definitely not a pro. He was a little older, and obviously fancied himself because he was in a black leather jacket and shades.

I assumed they didn't know I was in the car, although looking back they obviously did, and I never even realised they were putting on a show. I even felt guilty for watching! Not that it stopped me, because she'd quite clearly taken out his cock, and while I couldn't see it I could imagine it growing in her hand and I was hoping she'd go down and suck him.

What she did instead was open her blouse and pull up her bra to leave her breasts bare while she tossed him, so that he could see and play with them to help get him off. So I thought, anyway, until I heard a rustle from the bushes directly beside my own car and turned to see a man step out, only his silhouette visible in the darkness, but with his fully erect penis sticking up out of his fly like a flagpole.

It was completely unexpected, and I nearly jumped out of my skin. I didn't stop to find out what was going on either, but left at full speed, with so much adrenalin flowing I barely slowed down until I hit London. Only back at home did I begin to wonder if rather than having had a close call with a rapist I'd actually witnessed something completely consensual, and very, very rude.

I began to dig around on the net, and soon found out how it works, with people deliberately going to lonely lay-bys and car parks to indulge their love of exhibitionism, voyeurism or whatever it might be. Clearly most of those involved were single men, and not necessarily very attractive ones, but there seemed to be plenty of couples involved, and even some who went in small groups. By the time I'd finished my research I was wishing to God I'd had the courage to stay, let my window down and offer the guy in the bushes a nice leisurely suck while we watched the others get off.

It was irresistible, and just what I needed, no names, no consequences, no bullshit about me being loose, just a nice cock to suck on while I played with myself, and in such a rude situation. I could see there were risks, unpleasant characters and police snooping around, but I had to at least give it a try.

For a month or so I just thought about it, masturbating over the same fantasy with only subtle variations, of leaning out of my car window to suck on a complete stranger's cock while I played with myself. Only then did I begin to get my act together, working out where it was best to go and what I would need to bring.

The most important thing seemed to be a boy-friend, for the sake of my security and to make sure that at the very least I got one cock in my mouth. Unfortunately no ordinary man would do. I needed somebody who would let me take control but be there to support me when I needed him, and not get possessive or demanding, more of a bodyguard really. The other thing was lots of tissues.

It took me months to find Stephen, and to go out dogging for the first time, but I've never looked back. He understands exactly what I need, no more and no less, just as in return I provide what he needs. Just as I don't want to feel tied down or controlled, so he doesn't want to leave his wife, even though they haven't had sex for years. We're having an affair, I suppose, in the conventional sense, but what we really are is dogging partners.

My first encounter was at a notorious place off the M1, which had better remain nameless. I was full of nerves, and probably wouldn't have gone through with it on my own, but he was so calm about it I managed to cope. He'd been there before too, as a watcher, and knew the ropes. We parked, turned the engine off and locked the doors, then flashed our interior lights to signal that we were doggers and not just a couple out for sex. We left the light on.

It felt weird, a little scary but very exciting, sitting there with absolute blackness outside the windows, but it was very easy to do what Stephen told me. First I was made to lift up my top and bra, showing my bare breasts and playing with them until my nipples were hard. He played too, holding me and teasing me until I was seriously aroused. Only then did he take his cock out, making me wank him as I played with my nipples.

He said there were people watching, but I nearly jumped out of my skin when somebody tapped on the window. It was a man, just some ordinary bloke, a businessman I suppose. I wouldn't have given him a second glance in the street, but there, in that sleazy car park, I took his cock in my hand, then in my mouth, and sucked him off.

Just the memory makes me want to touch myself. It was all so beautifully rude. His polite, rather shy enquiry to know if I would touch. Stephen's assurance that I did. Watching the window come down and seeing him pull a podgy, white cock and balls out of his trousers. Touching and feeling him start to swell in my hand. Taking him in my mouth and bringing him slowly to erection as Stephen looked on and toyed with my breasts. Tossing him off into my own mouth and face, tasting his spunk and feeling it hot on my skin, a man whose name I didn't even know. I've been doing it ever since, and more, once or twice a week, always with Stephen, and I love it.

Like anything else, there's good and bad, and if you ever meet me when you're out dogging there are some things you should know if you want your cock sucked. There are two things I insist on, that a guy is clean, and polite. I don't mean when we're at it, once you're in my mouth you can call me a bitch if it gets you off, but beforehand. I hate guys who just assume they're going to get theirs, even if I'm taking bukkake in a club and there are eight guys around me with stiff pricks. If number nine wants to join in he'd better ask permission. Then you can spunk in my face, but not before.

That's the other thing Stephen got me into, bukkake. If dogging is rude, then bukkake is filthy. Basically we go to a special club, our favourite is near Coventry, where everyone knows the rules and I can be safe. After talking to people for a while and a few drinks any girl who wants it can strip off and go into the middle of the floor, where she can take as many men as she likes.

Stephen likes me to do a striptease first, and to go completely nude, which is just as well, because any clothes you leave on are going to get filthy. Once I'm naked I go out on to the floor and kneel down. It's a great feeling of power, having twenty or thirty blokes all wanting it and being able to choose as few or as many as I like. The funniest thing is when you get guys who really think they're it and don't choose them, especially after making them show their cocks. Generally I prefer the guys who're less full of themselves, the younger ones, or those who've never been to a swingers club before, just as long as they have nice cocks. I do have a soft side though, and sometimes I'll let someone join in just because they look so pathetically desperate.

Generally I choose in advance, and Stephen always keeps an eye on the men for me, while they know that bad behaviour means they'll get banned. Bad behaviour from our perspective, that is, because in an ordinary club what they do would be considered very bad behaviour indeed.

There's only so much a girl can do, so I have them wank themselves and take my time choosing who has the nicest cock before I start sucking. I try to be fair, at least at first, and I always make sure that anyone I've said can join in gets a go in my mouth. If somebody's having trouble getting hard I may give him extra attention too, perhaps a rub between my tits or something, because I find the thing that turns men on the most is to feel wanted, sexually.

Whether it's dogging or whether it's bukkake, I like to come my own way, playing with myself while I suck cock, or with my face spunked in. Having just one guy do it is great, but when it's a dozen or more and my whole face is plastered and my mouth's full of it, and it's running down my tits and in my hair and on my back and my legs and my bum, that really gets me there, like nothing else.

I've learnt to deep throat, practising with a banana and Stephen's cock, and just occasionally I like him to fuck my head, even though it makes me gag. It's one of those weird things. Nobody actually likes to gag, I don't suppose, and if a guy makes me gag during a bukkake session I have to stop and take a break. Afterwards it's different, when I'm alone in my bed with my vibrator or in the car with just Stephen after a dogging trip. I like to close my eyes and remember how it felt to have a cock jammed down my throat, the way he gripped my head or pulled my hair, how helpless I felt, even how I choked when he spunked up.

So there it is. I suppose you think I'm a dirty slut, but I don't care. I like myself the way I am, and when Stephen takes me out tonight I'll enjoy every minute of it, and I'll come, maybe more than once. If you're there, well, be nice and you might just get your cock sucked.

– Julia, London, UK

Ukrainian Au Pair

The au pair had lived in our home for three weeks when it first happened. She was good with the children, friendly and helpful, and her quaint use of mangled English always made me smile. Pretty, enthusiastic and competent, Sofiyko was a joy to have around the home. And I never worried that John might have any interest in her because he's out of the country so often he barely finds time to show any interest in me.

'Please I have one of carrot, Mrs John?'

I shrugged and passed her a carrot, quietly reflecting that it was nice to see young people eating so healthily. Raw carrots have never had a great appeal to me but I know they're a good source of vitamins and nutrients. By the time I'd selected a second carrot, and started washing it ready for our dinner, I'd forgotten about Sofiyko's request. If I was thinking of anything I was probably trying to find a way of having Sofiyko call me Margaret rather than Mrs John.

A week later she asked for another. This time, when I offered her the one I'd been about to cut, she shook her head and pointed to a different one from the bunch. 'Please, that one, Mrs John?'

'Sure.' I passed her the largest carrot from the packet. It was vibrant orange: thick and long. Her eyes glittered as she held it and I thought: *that young lady really does like her health food*. I put it down to her home country having strong agricultural roots. And then I was asking her if she missed the Ukraine and her family in Chemihiv.

Sofiyko was polite and answered my questions, stroking her fingers slowly around the fat carrot as we spoke. Her husky Ukrainian accent had deepened slightly and I thought she was suffering a touch of homesickness. When she asked to be excused for half an hour I guessed she would be in her bedroom composing a letter to her family.

Two bananas, a courgette and three carrots later, and still the proverbial penny hadn't dropped. It wasn't until Sofiyko had taken a whole cucumber from the fridge that anything untoward crossed my mind. And even then I hadn't completely made the connection. I went to Sofiyko's bedroom, intending to ask her if she'd taken the cucumber. I wasn't angry. I just wasn't sure if the first signs of dementia were taking their hold on me. I thought I'd bought a couple of cucumbers but there was only one in the fridge where I expected to find two. I approached her room quietly, not because I intended sneaking up on her but because the children are restless sleepers and I knew Sofiyko had not had an easy job putting the pair to bed that evening. I crept stealthily to her bedroom door, thought about knocking and then decided the noise might carry and wake the children. I entered without making a sound.

The sight inside amazed me.

Sofiyko was sprawled out on the top of her single bed. She was naked except for her white knee-high socks, which accentuated the beauty of her long slender legs. One hand was entwined in her hair, pulling so hard on a fistful of blonde curls that she had her eyes squeezed shut in pain. The other pushed the cucumber between her spread legs.

I gaped at the vision before me. She was young and slender. Her chest was flat and unremarkable but that wasn't where I was looking. My gaze had travelled lower, beyond her flat stomach, to the sight of the cucumber entering her body. Her sex was a neatly trimmed triangle of blonde curls without any hairs near the lips of her pussy. The thick girth of the dark green cucumber spread her wide. I could see the tendons in her wrist straining from the effort of working the vegetable back and forth. Her sex lips were engorged to a dark purple as they struggled to accept the mammoth offering. Sofiyko pushed herself against the vegetable with an urgency that was both frightening and exciting. I was amazed to see she had managed to accept more than half of the eighteen-inch cucumber. I could even see the ring of glistening cream around the length, like a dipstick mark showing how deep she had already forced it inside.

Quickly and quietly, I stepped out of the room.

I was shaking.

And very excited.

I tried to busy myself in the kitchen but I couldn't do a thing properly that evening. My thoughts were constantly returning to Sofiyko and the sight of her masturbating. The memory made me dizzy. My nipples were hard. My entire body tingled. And my pussy was hot and dripping and desperate for attention. If John had been home I would have dragged him to the bedroom and demanded he satisfy me. I don't think I would have told him what I had seen. I wouldn't want my husband getting excited by the image of a nubile Ukrainian blonde masturbating two doors down from our bedroom. But it would have been Sofiyko's face that I saw while John was thrusting between my legs. Because he was spending another week in Washington, though, John's involvement was a moot point. All I had were my fingers, my imagination, and the entire evening to indulge the most delicious and torrid fantasies.

It was a fantastic night.

I urged myself to come three times.

I had hoped my night of self-indulgence would clear images of Sofiyko from my mind. But it didn't happen that way. The following day, whenever I saw the au pair, I remembered the way she had looked sprawled across the bed with the cucumber in her pussy. She usually dressed in a short skirt with long white socks and, each time my gaze fell on those knee-highs, I remembered they had been the only things she wore while masturbating. The vision repeatedly stirred my excitement and, by the time she had put the children to bed, I was a shivering wreck of nerves and arousal. I knew I had to do something about it and so I planned our evening accordingly. I asked Sofiyko if she intended watching a little TV with me and, seeming pleased by the invitation, she said, 'Please, yes, Mrs John.' I opened a bottle of red, poured us a glass each, and for an agonising hour we watched boring soaps.

The wine was slowly depleted and, although Sofiyko seemed a little reluctant, I opened a second bottle to make sure we were both beyond our inhibitions. The sight of her impaled on the cucumber had stirred a powerful hunger inside me and I was determined to do something about that. While the TV chattered inanely in the background I asked, 'Do you have a boyfriend in Chemihiv?'

Her shy smile stirred butterflies in my stomach. 'I have boyfriend. Yes. He is name Artem.'

'You must be missing him.'

She looked briefly pained, and then smiled as though we shared a burden. 'You also miss Mr John, yes?'

I was shocked by that question and surprised by her sharp observation. I shrugged in reply and tried to move the conversation back to her. 'Is it frustrating being away from Artem?'

Sofiyko frowned. 'Please? I not understand frustrating.'

'You're a young woman,' I said carefully. 'I assume you and Artem were lovers?'

She glanced shyly away and nodded. 'Very much lovers.'

'Aren't you missing that side of your relationship?'

Her smile was suddenly knowing. It was the sort of wicked glint I had hoped I would see in her eyes. She leaned forward in her seat, conspiratorial. 'I sometimes pretend Artem with me,' she whispered. In the muted lighting from the TV set there was a faint blush colouring her cheeks.

I refilled her glass and asked innocently, 'What do you do?'

Her blushes were no longer faint. Her cheeks had turned scarlet. 'I use vegetable,' she admitted. 'With my eyes closed it like with Artem.' There was the hint of a smile on her lips. 'You do same too, Mrs John? When Mr John away long time?'

It was my turn to blush. I'd wanted to talk to her about what I had seen. I didn't plan to specifically say I'd been in her bedroom while she'd been wanking, although I was prepared to admit as much if I'd thought the conversation needed the impetus. But I hadn't expected to be confessing anything so personal as my own masturbation techniques. I squirmed against my seat and stammered to find the words.

'You use vegetable, Mrs John?' Sofiyko suggested.

'No,' I said quickly. I struggled to escape her questions and realised I was already in too deep. 'I just touch my clitoris,' I said eventually. It was mortifying to confess that much. My embarrassment was complete. Worse than that, Sofiyko stared at me in a way I'd already come to know very well. Even before she asked the question I knew what she was going to say.

'Please, what is clitoris?'

I rolled my eyes and tried valiantly to think of an explanation. There was no point in searching through my English/Ukrainian phrasebook because it had already proved hopelessly inadequate for the simplest translations. I snapped my fingers, impatiently trying to conjure up a way of describing the clitoris.

'You not know other word, Mrs John? Can you draw?'

I felt a moment's relief at her suggestion, and then floundered again. How can you draw a picture of a clitoris? I tried miming, using the index and middle finger of my right hand to suggest a pussy, and pointing at the top of them with my left.

Sofiyko continued to look perplexed. Even when I cupped the fingers over the crotch of my jeans, and then licked at my left index finger and pretended to rub the top of my right hand, Sofiyko still appeared confused. 'Please, can you show me, Mrs John?'

My heartbeat raced. I don't know if it was the excitement of the moment, the heavy tension in the air, or if I was just feeling extremely adventurous. But when Sofiyko asked her question, I realised I was nodding and slipping out of my jeans before I could stop myself. It felt strange to be undressing in front of another woman. I'd stripped in changing rooms before, and never thought anything of carrying on conversations with other women at the gym or the swimming baths while I was naked. But I'd never uncovered myself to another woman while we were discussing sex. And I'd never done anything as daring as what I planned to do with Sofiyko. It was exhilarating.

I peeled my panties away with the jeans. I was embarrassed that the crotch was already sodden with musk. Sofiyko watched me without saying a word. Her expression was polite and expectant. She sipped at her wine as I kicked the jeans from my legs. The hem of my blouse went down to the tops of my thighs but that didn't stop me from feeling exposed and extremely daring.

Sitting in the seat facing her, somehow finding the strength to force my legs apart, I took a deep gulp at my own glass of wine before pulling the hem of the blouse aside.

Sofiyko's large, pale-blue eyes grew wider. Her gaze dropped from my face to the tops of my open legs. Her lips had opened into an expectant pout.

I reached down to my pussy and used my left hand to pull the lips apart. The flesh was already warm and dripping with moisture. When I spread the labia I knew my clitoris would be swollen and engorged. It had been that way throughout the day. Licking the index finger of my right hand, I traced a gentle circle against the pulsing nub and shivered. 'That's the clitoris,' I explained. My voice sounded as husky as Sofiyko's delightful Eastern European accent. 'That's where I touch.'

'You only touch there?' She leant forward to study me more intimately. I wanted to pull away from her examination but I didn't dare break the spell building between us. 'You never use vegetable?'

'Never,' I admitted. Excited, and no longer embarrassed about the show I was giving the au pair, I stroked a second circle against the throbbing bead of flesh. Shivers ran through me. Arousal made my bowels quiver. The sensation was so satisfying I groaned.

Sofiyko watched me for a while and then stood up from the settee. Reaching for the clasp of her skirt she unfastened it and then removed her panties. She shrugged off her blouse, revealing herself nearly nude save for her white knee-high socks. They looked incredibly sexy on her young, slender legs. 'Please, show me my clitoris, Mrs John?'

I blinked in mild surprise. 'You've never touched your clitoris?'

'I no think so.'

She stepped closer and I realised her pussy was on the same level as my face. It seemed unthinkable that a girl as sexy as Sofiyko – a girl whom I had watched pleasuring herself with a fat cucumber – had never discovered her own clitoris. But to my mind it explained why she was resorting to stealing vegetables when her fingers could have satisfied her needs. I stared at her neatly trimmed pubic curls and the shaved flesh around her closed pussy lips. The scent of her sex was strong and I figured we were equally excited. 'You want me to . . .?' I couldn't bring myself to finish the question. Instead, I lifted a finger and held it close to her pussy.

'Please, yes, Mrs John.'

Not allowing myself to think about my actions, knowing I would have backed out if I'd given myself any other option, I reached for her and touched Sofiyko's pussy. The skin was moist, warm velvet against my fingers. When I eased her lips apart, reaching for her clitoris, I couldn't distance my thoughts from the excited knowledge that I was touching another woman's sex. The warm mouth of her pussy suckled at my fingers as I stroked between the split of her labia. 'Here,' I said gently. 'Here it is.' I traced a light circle against the pulsing nub.

Sofiyko gasped and then pulled away. Her expression was momentarily startled and she glared at me with enough intensity so that I felt guilty.

'I'm sorry,' I began. 'I didn't mean to upset –'

'That was good, Mrs John,' she gasped. 'Please, how you do that?'

It was as much as she needed to say. I spent the remainder of the evening sitting by Sofiyko's side on the settee, idly touching her pussy and then allowing her to touch mine. We explored each other fully, all under the guise of my finding Sofiyko's clitoris and teaching her how to properly masturbate. Once she was sure of the location she tested her new discovery on me. Within half an hour of our impromptu lesson beginning, Sofiyko had teased my clitoris until I almost screamed with relief. If it hadn't been for the fear of waking the children I would have yelled so loudly that John might have heard my cry on the other side of the Atlantic.

She giggled as she watched my climax, and then began teasing herself to the same state of ecstasy. It was a thrill to watch her nubile young body writhing under the paroxysms of pleasure. When she finally came I knew she was battling against the same struggle to contain her screams. She collapsed against the settee, her bare body touching mine, and we settled comfortably together. I glanced at the clock and was shocked to see how late it was. We had been playing together for the better part of two hours. 'We should be getting off to bed,' I said quickly. The words made me blush when I realised they sounded like a crude invitation.

'You have show me how the clitoris,' Sofiyko said quietly. 'But I no show you vegetable, Mrs John.'

As soon as she said the words I remembered how I had seen her the night before. Her naked body had been racked with tremors of pleasure. Her climax looked like it had been incredibly strong. The thought of witnessing that scene again ignited a hot rush of adrenalin through my body. We were both tired, and school for the children meant neither of us could afford to oversleep, but I wanted to see Sofiyko climax again and the thought of her using a vegetable made me willing to suffer the penalties of a late night.

She hurried out of the room, towards the kitchen. When she returned with a fresh cucumber my stomach lurched with rekindled excitement. 'You can't be serious?' I whispered.

Her grin shone with delight.

'Please, Mrs John. You have show me clitoris. I show you this.'

I needed no further encouragement. I sat back against the settee while Sofiyko stroked the end of the cucumber against my pussy. It had been in the fridge, and felt incredibly cold against the wet lips of my sex. But that didn't stop me from being thrilled by its pressure. She stroked it back and forth against my labia, teasing me with its shape and silently promising to plunge it between my legs. The width of the vegetable was intimidating, and because I had seen Sofiyko violently forcing a similar weapon into her own pussy I was more than a little apprehensive. But we had been so gentle with each other so far that I had faith that she wouldn't abuse my trust.

'You are ready, Mrs John?'

I drew a deep breath before nodding. 'I'm ready,' I whispered. Sofiyko's smile shone momentarily brighter. And then she thrust the cucumber into my pussy. The icy girth filled my hole and stretched my pussy impossibly wide. I wanted to tell her it was too much but, as she continued to urge the length deeper, I couldn't find any words to stop her. She continued to push it inside, nearly splitting me with its vast width. When I did manage to speak the best I could manage was: 'It's very big.'

'It is like Artem,' Sofiyko explained.

The thought pushed me close to the point of orgasm. If I had been trying to find something in the kitchen that resembled John's penis my first port of call would have been the baby sweetcorn. Sofiyko's boyfriend was clearly more well endowed than my ill-equipped husband and the idea that I was experiencing something like the penetration she regularly received when at home made me feel bolder and more daring than ever. It was almost as though I was experiencing her boyfriend. I moaned as another ripple of pleasure flowed through the inner muscles of my sex.

Sofiyko worked the length in and out of my pussy with slow and unhurried thrusts. My inner walls were stretched far apart and the sensation of fullness was overwhelming. I remember reading somewhere that penetration is seldom enough to make most women orgasm. But, on this occasion, I could have happily climaxed just from the sensation of the cucumber filling me. I was close to coming and I hissed as much so that Sofiyko knew the effect she was having on me.

'Touch my clit,' I grunted. 'I want to come.'

She didn't respond at first.

Impatience and arousal mingled inside my chest making me desperate to be touched where I needed it most. 'Please, Sofiyko,' I begged. 'Please, touch my clitoris.'

'Later, Mrs John,' she assured me. Her wrist continued to work backwards and forwards. The cucumber had quickly warmed and as it slid in and out I could only think of how satisfying the sensation was. Sofiyko reached for my hand and placed it around the girth of the cucumber. 'Please, you do this now,' she encouraged.

I had been on the verge of touching my own clitoris, impatient with waiting for Sofiyko to do as I had asked. But when she passed me control of the massive length, I was denied that pleasure and had to work the cucumber back and forth. The motion made my wrist ache.

Admittedly there was a wealth of pleasure to be had from the sensation of being penetrated. And each time I forced it forward I could feel my sex accepting a little bit more of the thick shaft. I glanced down at Sofiyko and saw the pretty Ukrainian grinning at me. Her obvious enjoyment, caused by my pleasure, added another dimension to my enjoyment. As we smiled at each other I felt the rush of a powerful orgasm preparing to burst from my body.

'Artem do other thing when he fill me,' Sofiyko murmured. 'Please, I do to you?' She stroked a finger against my cheek as she asked.

I couldn't imagine what else Artem might do to make Sofiyko's pleasure more exquisite but I was more than willing to learn. I nodded, watched her grin, and then felt her tug at a fistful of hair. The pain was immense. I squeezed my eyes shut and got ready to tell her it hurt too much.

And that was when I realised why I had been able to watch her masturbating without her knowing I was there. More than that, as Sofiyko pulled harder, the pleasure and pain combined to make my satisfaction meteoric. I was no longer alone in the room with my beautiful Ukrainian au pair. Her huge and powerful boyfriend rode me while he filled my sex and tugged on my hair.

That was the thought that made me climax. The explosion was so strong it threatened to push the cucumber from my hole. It was only because I was holding it firmly in place that I was able to feel my inner lips convulse around their prize. I was close to squealing from the pain of having Sofiyko pulling at my hair but that agony only added to the ferocity of my release.

'Now I touch your clitoris,' Sofiyko said with a laugh.

I tried to tell her that my body couldn't take any more pleasure but, by that point, she was lowering her face to my pussy. The warmth of her breath, the wetness of her tongue and the breathtaking sensation of her lips against my sex were too much. She lightly kissed the tortured flesh of my sex. When she started to use her fingers, testing the shape of my wide-open labia, I knew she was going to easily tease another orgasm from my sex. The cucumber continued to fill my hole and I climaxed with a fury that almost left me unconscious. How I suppressed my scream is still a mystery but I know the orgasm was enough to make me finally pull away from Sofiyko. I closed my legs and drew the huge cucumber from my sex. Turning away from her, embarrassed by the way the vegetable had left me feeling so used and open, I breathed deeply as I tried to regain my composure.

'Please, I do no good, Mrs John?' She sounded concerned.

'You did it very good,' I said with a laugh. I pushed her back on the settee and insisted she spread her thighs. Treating her to the same delightful punishment she had made me endure, I got the pleasure of working the vegetable into Sofiyko's sex and then tasting the sensational flavour of her

93

cucumber-flavoured pussy lips. Also, to make sure it was like Artem was riding her, I pulled long and hard on her hair until the tears she shed told me she was close to screaming.

We spent the remainder of the night (and most of the hours that led into the early morning) licking, lapping, sucking and fucking each other. By the time we staggered off to bed my pussy felt sore and Sofiyko staggered as she tried to mount the stairs. We didn't speak about the incident until the following evening. Red wine gives me heads, and Sofiyko looked as though the excess alcohol had taken a toll on her usual exuberance. We washed and dressed the children together in the morning, Sofiyko organised their breakfasts and I drove them to school. Neither of us said much when I returned, except to agree that we needed more sleep, and we retired to our respective bedrooms.

That evening, after the children had been fed, bathed and put to bed, Sofiyko and I met in the kitchen. I saw her glancing at the open bottle of red left over from the previous night and was torn between revulsion at the thought of ever drinking wine again, and wanting her to suggest we share the remainder of the bottle. Then she went to the fridge, and when she closed the door I saw she had a carrot in her hand. 'Thanking you for last night, Mrs John,' she said warmly. 'I now not miss Artem so much.'

I smiled, pleased I had been able to help banish a little of her homesickness but disappointed that my own situation had become slightly less bearable. Whereas I had once looked forward to John's return every month, and always hoped he would be staying a little longer each time, I now hoped to spend more time alone with the au pair.

Walking past Sofiyko, and removing a second carrot from the fridge, I smiled at her and said, 'Perhaps we should do it again some time?'

Her wicked smile was all the answer I needed.

– *'Mrs John', Hertfordshire, UK*

Illicit Night Work

When the letter arrived, I was devastated. I hadn't got the job. From fifty or so applicants, they'd whittled the list down to just three people. With my qualifications, I honestly thought that I'd win hands down. How was I going to tell my husband? Steve was relying on my landing the position as personal secretary to a managing director. My hands trembling, my stomach churning, I screwed up the letter and dropped it into the bin. How the hell was I going to tell Steve?

After his redundancy, Steve had tried for one job after another and had failed miserably. He'd finally taken a job as a van driver until something worthwhile came along, and he hated it. At least he was earning. But his wage didn't even cover the mortgage, let alone food and other bills. We were heading for financial disaster, and it seemed that there was nothing I could do to save us. Steve was only thirty-five and had done so well. A qualified accountant, he'd earned a good salary until ... It was no good looking back, I decided. I was going to have to do something, but what?

'Any news?' Steve asked me hopefully when he got home that fateful evening.

'Steve, I ... yes, I got the job,' I replied, immediately wishing I hadn't.

'Chrissy, you're brilliant,' he said, punching the air with his fist. 'You're amazing, you're wonderful . . . God, what a relief. When do you start?'

'Next Monday,' I breathed softly.

As he praised me and talked about the future, I felt terrible. I must have been mad to lie to him. But he'd been really down over the last few weeks, close to depression, and I couldn't bring myself to tell him the bad news. What on earth was I going to do now? I wondered anxiously. I'd have to tell him the truth at some stage. I'd have to tell him that I'd lied to him and we were facing financial ruin. We'd lose the house, that was certain. And we might even end up losing each other. I had exactly one week to find a well-paid job.

I spent several days answering adverts and going to interviews, but I had no luck – until a small classified ad caught my eye. I rang the number and the man told me to go along to his office that afternoon. This wasn't what I wanted, but I had no choice. I found the place above the Indian take-away in the high street and climbed the narrow stairs to a tatty door. The so-called office looked like a seedy bed-sit, and I didn't like the man at all. He was fat with greasy hair and a worn-out grey suit. His beady eyes grinning as he looked me up and down, he finally pointed at a chair and told me to park my bum.

'You done this before?' he asked me as I removed a pile of magazines from the chair and sat opposite him.

'No,' I replied softly. 'No, I haven't.'

'Well, you look the part. Blonde, nice body, nice tits . . . How old are you?'

'Twenty-five,' I said, despising him more by the minute.

'Fifty quid for an evening, OK?'

'Fifty?' I echoed. 'Is that all?'

'Take it or leave it, love. Whatever you earn on top of that is yours, of course. If you get my drift?'

'I'll take it,' I said with a sigh. 'And, for your information, I'll not be earning anything on top of that.'

'It's up to you. OK, be at the Raven Hotel at seven o'clock this evening. You know where it is?'

'Yes, yes, I do.'

'The guy's name is Alan. He'll meet you in the bar.' He took a cheap bracelet from a drawer and tossed it on to the desk. 'Wear that so he'll know who you are. What name do you want to go by?'

'Angela, I think.'

'Angela it is.'

'And, the money?' I asked him.

'Tomorrow, I'll pay you tomorrow. OK, good luck.'

'Aren't you going to tell me anything about the job?'

'There's nothing to tell. You accompany the man for the evening, and that's it. He might be meeting friends and want to introduce you as his girlfriend or whatever. Just play it by ear.'

'How long do I have to stay with him?'

'The punters expect two or three hours. After that, it's up to you.'

Leaving his office, I couldn't believe that I'd taken a job as an escort. Steve had never wanted me to work, and I'd never had to work – until now. I'd had a university education, I was qualified ... Fifty pounds for a couple of hours was better than nothing, but what was I going to tell Steve? I couldn't go out every evening without giving him an explanation. I was in a mess, I knew, as I headed home. If I worked five nights each week, I'd only get two hundred and fifty pounds. At least it was tax-free.

Steve was more than happy when I said that I was meeting a girlfriend in town. He said that I deserved a night out and passed me a ten-pound note. That was all he had in his wallet. Awash with guilt as I dressed in a miniskirt and white blouse, I didn't think I'd be able to go through with it. Lying to my husband, working as an escort and going out with another man . . . I had to force myself to do it, I decided. We needed the money and, after all, I'd only be spending the evening with someone.

Alan was in his forties, and not bad looking. Wearing a dark suit and crisp white shirt and tie, he had black hair swept back from his suntanned face. He was well spoken, and I decided that the evening might not be so bad after all. To my relief, he said that he wasn't meeting friends and simply wanted some company. He bought me a drink and we sat at a secluded corner table, and I felt a lot easier. But I still felt extremely guilty. Steve was at home, no doubt relaxing now that he thought our future was secure. And I was working as an escort girl.

'Is this your first time?' Alan asked me.

'Yes, can you tell?'

'It's just that you seem a little nervous. I guessed that you're not used to this. So, tell me about yourself.'

'Well, I'm . . . I'm just doing this to fill in. I have a job lined up at a university and . . . I don't start until next month.'

'I suppose this is easy money. You're a very attractive girl, Angela. The best the agency has come up with.'

'Thank you.'

I noticed that he kept looking at my breasts as we talked, and I wished that I'd worn something a little less revealing. But he seemed all right and I quite enjoyed the evening. He'd bought me several drinks and, at ten o'clock, I decided that it was time I went home. I finished my drink and Alan insisted on giving me a lift, which made me feel a little uneasy. I'd planned to get a taxi, but finally accepted his offer.

Not wanting him to find out where I lived, I asked him to drop me off by the common. He parked the car and switched the engine off and asked me whether he could see me the following evening. I agreed but I wasn't sure how the agency worked. Alan said that he'd arrange it with the fat man, as he aptly called him, and meet me in the hotel bar at seven.

'OK,' I said. 'I'll see you tomorrow.'

'Do you give extras?' he asked me as I was about to get out of the car.

'Er . . . no, no, I don't,' I replied.

'Most of the girls offer a little something. How about a handjob?'

'Alan, I don't . . .'

'They usually charge twenty,' he persisted, pulling a note from his wallet. 'Just a handjob, nothing more.'

'I'm not a prostitute,' I returned.

'I know that, Angela. I just thought that you might like to earn a little extra cash.'

I'd vowed not to go down this road, I reflected apprehensively. Although I needed the extra money, I wasn't a prostitute and had no intention of becoming one. There again, Alan was a nice man and it wasn't as if I was going to have sex with him. I tried to convince myself that it would be all right and it would only take a few minutes to wank him and . . . I didn't know what to do.

I couldn't shatter Steve's happiness by saying that I'd lied about the secretarial job. But I had to earn some real money if we were going to survive. Fifty pounds from the fat man, and twenty from Alan. If I gave a handjob each night . . . three hundred and fifty for five nights? Finally taking the cash, I watched as Alan unzipped his trousers and hauled out his erect penis.

As I held the warm shaft of his cock in my hand, I thought about my husband. Our sex life had fallen by the wayside since his redundancy. What with our financial worries and a bleak future, the last thing we'd thought about was sex. I'd read somewhere that money troubles were the biggest cause of divorce, second to adultery. Was I committing adultery? I wondered as I ran my hand up and down Alan's solid cock. No, this was a business arrangement. And I was determined to sort out our finances and keep the marriage going.

Alan didn't try anything. He didn't attempt to kiss me or touch me as I pleasured him. I felt quite safe with him. Besides, if he did try anything, all I'd have to do was leap out of the car. This was easy money, I mused as he breathed heavily and trembled as I rolled his foreskin back and forth over his swollen knob. If this was all I had to do to the clients, then it would be well worth the extra cash. And the extra guilt?

Alan let out a low moan of pleasure as his sperm jetted from his knob and bathed my hand. Another man's cock, another man's sperm . . . strangely, I didn't feel too guilty as I sustained his orgasm. Again reminding myself that this was purely a business arrangement and it wasn't as though I was having full-blown sex with another man, I finally released Alan's deflating penis and opened the car door. I'd done it, I thought with some relief. I'd earned the extra money and could now go home to my husband.

'See you tomorrow,' Alan said as I climbed out of the car.

'Yes, I'll be there,' I replied.

'Thanks, Angela. You were great.'

'I'll see you at seven, Alan.'

I opened my bag and wiped my hand on a tissue as he drove off, then walked the short distance to my house and took a deep breath before opening the door. I'd thought that I'd conquered my guilt, until I came face to face with Steve. He smiled and kissed me and asked me whether I'd had a good evening. He then poured me a glass of wine and told me how much he loved me. That's when my guilt really hit home. I'd been out with another man, I'd masturbated another man and his sperm had run over my hand and . . .

'You've saved us from ruin,' Steve said, sitting next to me on the sofa. 'You're beautiful and very clever, do you know that? I have the best wife in the world. You're amazing, Chrissy. I knew you'd get that job. I had every faith in you, and I was right.'

'I'm not that good,' I breathed. My hand was sticky with another man's sperm. 'Steve, I . . .'

'You're an angel, and I love to you to bits.'

'Steve, if it's all right with you . . . I'm going out again tomorrow evening.'

'Of course it's all right with me,' he replied with a chuckle. 'For goodness sake, you're the breadwinner. You go out with your friends whenever you want to. Once I get a decent job we'll plan a holiday and . . .'

As he talked about the future, our future, I pondered on my new line of work. Would Alan want me to wank him again? How many clients would I see each week? And what the hell was I going to do on Monday morning? I'd have to be out of the house all day, make out that I was working as a secretary, lie to Steve again and . . . He often called in between deliveries. I'd have to find somewhere to go every day. Although I was earning some money, things were a total mess.

'There you go,' the fat man said, passing me the money as I walked into his office the following morning. 'Alan rang me earlier.'

'Yes, he wants to see me again this evening.'

'I want you to meet Mr Johnson this evening.'

'But Alan said –'

'I run the agency, just remember that. I don't like my girls seeing too much of one client. And I don't like arrangements being made behind my back.'

'It wasn't behind your back,' I returned indignantly. 'Alan said that he'd check with you first.'

'I wasn't accusing you, I was simply pointing out the rules. You're to meet Johnson in the Dog and Duck at six o'clock, OK?'

'Yes, OK.'

'You know the pub?'

'Yes, I do.'

'Good, that's that settled. By the way, the girls sometimes do me a favour, if you get my drift?'

'I do get your drift and I'm not interested,' I returned coldly. 'I'll see you tomorrow morning.'

Leaving the seedy office, I couldn't imagine touching the greasy little fat man. And I didn't want to meet Johnson in a backstreet pub. The Dog and Duck was a dump. I'd been there several years previously and had sworn never to set foot in the place again. I knew where I stood with Alan, and I felt safe with him. The hotel bar was nice, and I'd enjoyed the evening. But I was an escort, I reminded myself. And I had to see more than one client.

I got to the pub at six and was immediately approached by Johnson. He was a balding man in his late fifties, and he was a lecherous old bastard. He bought me a drink and almost dragged me to a secluded table in an alcove well away from the bar. Gazing at his creased shirt straining to contain his fat stomach, I wondered how he could afford to go to an escort agency. Slurping his beer, he spilled it down the front of his shirt as he stared at my breasts. I'd have walked out if I hadn't been so desperate for the money.

'You're a bit of all right,' he said, winking at me. 'I'm rather partial to blondes with hard little tits.'

'I'm sure you are,' I breathed dismissively, sipping my drink. 'So, are we staying here for the evening?'

'Yes, we are. Now then, tell me what you offer and how much you charge.'

'I don't offer anything.'

'Nothing at all?'

'I'm an escort, not a prostitute.'

'It's the same thing, isn't it? Perhaps this will tempt you,' he said with a chuckle, pulling out his wallet. 'Twenty, if you let me put my hand up your skirt.'

I'd been spoilt by Alan, I reflected as the man pressed the cash into my hand. I'd enjoyed his company and had almost been looking forward to seeing him again. I'd certainly been looking forward to the extra cash. But now I was sitting in a seedy pub with a dirty old man who wanted to put his hand up my skirt. At least none of my friends would walk into a backstreet pub like this, I thought. Twenty pounds, I mused, gazing at the crumpled note in my hand. No one could see us and I needed the cash, so I agreed.

'Tight little knickers,' Johnson said, pressing his fingertips into the warm mound of my white panties. 'I'll bet you're wet.'

'No, I'm not,' I replied softly, wondering how I'd plunged this far into the depths of filth.

'I'd like to push a finger into your tight little cunt.'

'No,' I said through gritted teeth, closing my thighs and crushing his hand.

'I'll give you another twenty if you let me finger your sweet little cunt.'

'You must be made of money.'

'I am, and it always gets me what I want.'

Retracting his hand and passing me another twenty-pound note, he asked me to slip my panties off. Fifty pounds from the fat man, forty from Johnson . . . this was prostitution, there was no other word for it. But Johnson only wanted to push his finger into my vagina. There was no harm in that, I consoled myself. He had plenty of money, so I might as well take what was on offer. Allowing another man to finger my vagina wasn't adultery. Not technically, anyway.

I felt like a common whore as I made sure that no one could see me as I lifted my buttocks clear of the seat. I slipped my panties off and stuffed them into my handbag. I hated the pub, I hated the dirty old man . . . but I desperately needed the cash. Besides, he was only going to push his fat finger into my vagina. Again consoling myself that I wasn't having sex with him, I took a deep breath and allowed him to part my thighs.

'You're very tight,' he said, sliding a finger between my soft inner lips and driving it deep into my vagina. 'And nice and wet. You're far more attractive than the other agency girls. They're dirty little sluts who'll do anything for a few quid. You're more of a challenge, and I like that.' Easing a second finger into my sex sheath, he chuckled. 'What's a nice girl like you doing in a place like this?'

'Earning money,' I breathed as he massaged my inner flesh.

'I've got what you want, and you've got what I want. I've got money, and you've got a tight little cunt. Do you like me fingering your tight little cunt?'

Trying not to listen to his vulgar words, I sipped my drink and checked my watch. The evening had only just begun. I had to endure this for at least two hours, but I'd already earned ninety pounds. As he managed to push a third finger into my vagina and massage my clitoris with his thumb, I wondered how I was going to explain my evenings out to Steve. If I said that I was going out with friends five nights a week, he'd soon become suspicious. I'd be far better off seeing clients during the day, I mused, deciding to ask the fat man about it.

'Do you masturbate?' Johnson asked me. 'Do you frig yourself off?'

'No, I don't,' I returned. 'Are you going to buy me another drink?'

'All in good time. You're getting wetter. You obviously like having your little cunny fingered. When were you last fucked?'

'I don't want to talk about my sex life.'

'As you wish. How about giving me a nice wank?'

'No, I . . .'

'Another twenty, OK?'

It occurred to me that, once he'd come, he'd probably leave me alone. And I might even get away earlier if I quelled his libido. He slipped his fingers out of my vagina, passed me the cash and I decided to go for it. One hundred and ten pounds, I thought happily as he unzipped his trousers. That was more like it. If I managed to earn that sort of money every day, our financial worries would be over. But I still had to explain my nights out to Steve.

Grabbing the man's solid cock, I wondered where on earth he got his money from as I ran my hand up and down its length. He was obviously loaded and, although I didn't like him, I hoped that he'd want to see me on a regular basis. This was the second man I'd wanked, and I was beginning to look upon it as a means to an end. Wanking a man and bringing out his sperm only took a few minutes, and was well worth the extra cash. And my guilt was fading, at last. Adultery, prostitution ... this was a job, a business arrangement, and I had to keep that firmly in mind.

'I want to come in your panties,' Johnson gasped as he neared his orgasm. 'Put them over my cock and I'll spunk in them.'

I took my panties from my bag, wrapped them around his cock and continued to wank him. I wasn't bothered about losing a pair of panties. With the money I was earning, I could easily afford more. Again hoping that I'd get away early as he reached his orgasm and filled my panties with his sperm, I reckoned that he was more than satisfied as he moaned softly and shuddered. Finishing the job, I downed what was left of my drink and smiled at him.

'OK?' I asked him as he zipped his trousers.

'Perfect,' he breathed shakily. 'May I keep your panties?'

'I certainly don't want them,' I returned with a giggle. 'You hang on to them.'

'I collect stained panties,' he said, stuffing them into his jacket pocket.

'Now, why doesn't that surprise me?' I quipped.

'Would you like another drink? Or would you rather go now?'

'I'll go, if it's all right with you?' I said, trying not to show my relief.

'OK, I'll be in touch with the agency and, hopefully, meet you again.'

'I'll look forward to it,' I breathed, leaving my seat and tugging my skirt down to conceal my naked pussy.

Leaving the pub, I couldn't believe that it was over so quickly. Freedom, I thought happily as I headed home. Freedom, money . . . and no guilt. I was doing well. But I still had to come up with an excuse for my evenings out. I could tell Steve that I had a part-time evening job, I mused. Perhaps doing typing or some sort of office work. He certainly wouldn't mind if he thought that I was earning money. Which I was.

'You're early,' he said as I wandered into the lounge.

'Sally had to go,' I lied. 'So I thought I'd come home.'

'Sally?'

'Oh, you don't know her. We met ages ago and . . . I might see her tomorrow evening.'

'Oh, I see,' he sighed, obviously not happy with my going out yet again.

'I'm seeing her about a part-time job. Her office has a lot of work on and –'

'You start full-time on Monday, Chrissy. You don't have to work evenings as well.'

'It's only until we get on our feet again.'

'I suppose you're right. I just hope that I can find something decent before long.'

It was ironic to think that I *was* doing a part-time evening job. Not the sort of thing that Steve had in mind, of course. But I didn't feel guilty any more. Going out with other men, wanking them, lying to Steve . . . I was doing it for us. I'd allowed Johnson to push his fingers into my vagina, but I'd been paid well and it couldn't be called adultery. I felt no guilt because I was earning money. I was saving us from ruin. I also reckoned that I was saving our marriage.

The way things had been going, it wouldn't have been long before huge rows had started. Lack of money and adultery. The two main reasons for divorce.

The fat man paid me the following morning and I asked him about working during the day. He said that very few punters wanted escorts during the day but he'd bear me in mind. At least he had someone lined up for me that evening. I'd been hoping that I was going to see Alan again, but I was to meet a Mr David Groves at a private address.

'At his house?' I asked the fat man. 'I don't like the sound of that.'

'It's up to you,' he returned. 'There's nothing else for this evening. Besides, he's a regular. He won't give you trouble.'

'If that's all you have, I suppose I'll do it,' I said with a sigh. 'Will he be taking me out?'

'No, he likes the girls to spend time with him at home. According to Johnson, you were pretty good last night.'

'Yes, well . . .'

'Groves will want the same treatment. He's quite free with his money, so you should do well out of it.'

'I don't like the sound of it, but I'll do it.'

I felt apprehensive when I called at the client's house that evening. It was one thing meeting men in pubs or bars, but I didn't like the idea of home visits. I took a deep breath as Groves answered the door and invited me in. I should have been at home with my husband, I reflected as I stepped into the hall. What the hell was I doing calling at a stranger's house? Hopefully, all I'd have to do was wank him and I might get away early.

'Very nice,' Groves said, looking me up and down

before leading me into the lounge. He was in his thirties and not bad looking. 'I'm David, by the way.'

'Angela,' I breathed softly, looking around the expensively furnished room. He obviously had money.

'Would you like a drink?' he asked me, opening a cabinet and pouring himself a scotch.

I opted for vodka and tonic and made myself comfortable on the leather Chesterfield. Although I'd wanked two men and allowed one to finger my pussy, this was the first time that I really felt like a prostitute. What was I going to do if he wanted full sex? If he offered me a lot of money to open my legs and take his cock into my vagina . . . What was I worth? I found myself wondering as I sipped my drink. How much would it take to entice me to commit adultery?

'I won't waste time,' David said, standing before me. 'Tell me what you do.'

'What I do?' I murmured, fearing the worst.

'Perhaps it would be best if I told you what I want. Have you shaved?'

'Shaved?' I echoed, wondering what sort of man he was. 'Er . . . no, no, I haven't.'

'Not to worry. OK, if you'd like to take your panties off –'

'I'm not a prostitute,' I cut in.

'I know that. The man at the agency said that you didn't offer extras. That's why I asked for you.'

'But . . . I don't understand.'

'Everyone has their price, Angela. And I want to find out what your price is.'

'I don't have a price.'

'Don't you? Slip your panties off and open your legs, and I'll pay you one hundred.'

'Just for opening my legs?'

'For starters, yes.'

He took his wallet from his trouser pocket and tossed a wad of notes on to the coffee table. Did I have a price? I pondered. He wanted full-blown sex, that was pretty obvious. And I needed money. Johnson had pushed his fingers into my pussy, so what did it matter if I allowed a man to push his cock there? As I pondered on slipping my panties off, I realised that I was changing. Although I'd vowed not to entertain men sexually, I'd already wandered a fair distance down that sleazy road. All I had to do now was allow my client to slip his penis into my vagina and . . .

'You're not a slut,' David said, smiling at me. 'Sluts are easy. You're refined, and I like that.'

'Thank you,' I breathed, eyeing the money. 'I suppose you want sex?'

'Yes, of course.' He pointed to the cash on the table. 'That's just for starters. There's more where that came from.'

Lifting my buttocks clear of the sofa, I slipped my panties off and sat with my thighs parted slightly. He was right, I wasn't a slut. But I had what he wanted, and he had what I wanted – money. Steve would be none the wiser, so what the hell? All along, I'd tried to delude myself, tried to convince myself that I wasn't committing adultery. Wanking a man *was* committing adultery. Allowing a man to finger my pussy was an act of adultery. Whether I liked it or not, I was a prostitute. The time had come to stop kidding myself.

As he knelt before me and pushed my thighs wide apart, I tried to drive all thoughts of Steve out of my mind. It wasn't as if I was going to leave my husband and run off with another man. All I was doing was earning money, and there was nothing wrong with that. As David lifted my skirt up over my stomach and kissed my fleece-covered outer lips, I closed my eyes and relaxed. As his tongue ran up and down my sex crack, I realised how long it had been since Steve had licked me there. Two years? More like three years.

Parting my outer lips, David swept his tongue over the sensitive tip of my pink clitoris. I could feel his hot breath against my most intimate flesh, his saliva running down my gaping valley. Unable to drive thoughts of Steve from my mind, I imagined that he was licking me, loving me. In the darkness behind my eyelids, I pictured Steve between my thighs, his tongue working on my erect clitoris. Why didn't we enjoy oral sex any more?

David spent some time licking and sucking my clitoris, but I couldn't come. I didn't want to come with another man. He finally slipped his shirt off and lowered his trousers. I stared at his huge cock as he retracted his foreskin and exposed the swollen bulb of his purple knob. I had time to put a stop to this, I knew as he moved forward. I didn't have to have sex with him. Noticing my apprehension, he took another wad of notes from his wallet and tossed them on to the table.

No words passed between us as his knob parted the pink petals of my inner lips. Watching his purple globe disappear as he drove his cock shaft slowly into my vagina, I knew that there was no turning back now. I'd done it, I thought uneasily. I'd lied to my husband, cheated on him, committed adultery, sold my young body for sex . . . I was now a fully-fledged prostitute.

Watching his pussy-wet penis sliding in and out of my tightening vagina, I felt my clitoris swell. I couldn't deny that my arousal was heightening. He opened my blouse, lifted my bra clear of my firm breasts and leant forward and sucked my nipple into his hot mouth. I let out an involuntary gasp as he sucked hard on my milk teat and increased his shafting rhythm. What was Steve doing? I wondered, closing my eyes as David closed his mouth over my other nipple and sucked hard. He was no doubt wondering about my part-time evening job, thinking what a good wife I was to bring in money. I was a slut.

'You're tight,' David breathed, my nipple slipping out of his mouth as he smiled at me. 'Tight, hot and very wet.'

'And you're big,' I said. 'Almost too big.'

It was true. He was far bigger than Steve. I'd only had one boyfriend before meeting Steve, and his cock was small. Perhaps I should have played the field? I mused. The squelching sound of my vaginal juices resounding around the room, I wondered how many men I'd have sex with, how many cocks I'd take into my vagina. Unless a really good job came up, I couldn't see myself leaving the agency.

David gasped as his sperm jetted from his throbbing knob and bathed my cervix. My solid clitoris massaged by his thrusting shaft, I reached my orgasm and cried out as my young body shook uncontrollably. The sad thing was that I couldn't recall the last time I'd come. It was a shame that it took another man to take me to a climax, I reflected. Perhaps, now that our financial situation had improved, I'd enjoy sex with my husband again.

David finally slowed his thrusting rhythm and massaged the nub of my clitoris with his thumb. My orgasm receding, my vagina flooded with another man's sperm, I lay writhing and whimpering on the sofa in the aftermath of my incredible coming. With fifty pounds to come from the fat man and two

114

hundred from David, it wasn't a bad evening's work. An evening of adultery, prostitution . . . but I'd saved my home and my marriage, hadn't I?

The fat man paid me the following morning and said that I was to meet Johnson again that evening. He was the last man I'd wanted to see, but at least he paid well. Thinking that it would have been nice to see Alan again, I was about to leave the office when the fat man gave me the good news. He'd arranged for me to have lunch with a client. Not only would I earn more money, but I'd be out of the house when Steve went home for lunch.

I met Mike Burrows in the restaurant at one o'clock and was pleasantly surprised by his manner. As the waiter showed me to the table, Mike stood up and greeted me. He was in his fifties with greying hair. Dressed in a three-piece suit, shirt and tie, he was a businessman, and a real gentleman. Far removed from the likes of Johnson.

'I don't like eating alone,' Mike said, smiling at me as the waiter poured the wine. 'It's nice to have company, don't you agree?'

'Yes, I do,' I replied. 'This is a nice place. I've never been here before.'

'I come here once or twice a week. It's expensive, but the food's good.'

As we chatted, I wondered whether he had a hotel room lined up for the afternoon. A nice meal followed by an afternoon of sex . . . He'd no doubt go home to his wife and tell her that he'd had a hard day at the office. After the meal, he asked me about myself. I found him easy to talk to, and blurted out my tale of woe. Steve's redundancy, our financial disaster, the secretarial job I'd hoped to get . . .

'I'm sure something will turn up before long,' he said.

'Maybe,' I breathed softly.

'You're an intelligent girl. Working as an escort shows that you're also resourceful.'

'So, where to from here?' I asked him as we finished our coffee.

'Back to the office, I'm afraid. It's been really nice, Angela. I've enjoyed your company immensely.'

'Oh, right,' I murmured. 'So, you don't want anything else?'

'I'm a happily married man. My wife travels quite a bit and . . . All I wanted was some company, and you were delightful company.'

'That's very nice of you, Mike. I'm also happily married. As I said earlier, I'm having to do this sort of work because . . .'

'It's all right, I understand. The job you went after. What was the company?'

'Combined Chemicals. I was on the shortlist but . . . Well, not to worry.'

'Yes, I've heard of them. Would you excuse me for a minute? Only, I have to go to the small room.'

'Yes, yes of course.'

As he left the table, I again thought what a nice man he was and I hoped to meet him again for lunch. I'd enjoyed the meal, but I now had to think of the evening. Why had the fat man arranged for me to meet Johnson in the backstreet pub? Johnson must have asked for me. He liked blondes with hard little tits, and must have asked for me. Back to reality, I mused as Mike returned. Back to the seedy world of prostitution.

'Sorry I was so long, Christine,' he said, sitting opposite me. 'I had to make a phone call.'

'Christine?' I echoed, frowning at him. 'How . . . how do you know my real name?'

'The MD of Combined Chemicals is an old friend of mine. I just rang him and it seems that the position

116

is still vacant. They're very interested in seeing Christine Woods again. If you're interested, that is?'

'Really?' I breathed.

'Are you interested?'

This was incredible, I thought, holding my hand to my head. After all I'd been through with the vulgar fat man and acting like a common whore with Johnson in the back street pub . . . personal secretary to the Managing Director of Combined Chemicals? Eyeing the cheap bracelet adorning my wrist, I smiled. Johnson would be waiting for me in the Dog and Duck that evening. He'd buy me drinks and give me hard cash in return for crude sex. He'd want to finger my pussy and get me to wank him off in my panties and . . .

'Well?' Mike breathed, breaking my reverie. 'Are you still interested?'

'This is amazing,' I said, toying with the bracelet. 'I can't believe it.'

'It's true,' he said with a chuckle. 'Shall I ring him and –'

'No,' I cut in. 'Thanks anyway, Mike. But I have a client to see this evening.'

– Christine, Sussex, UK

A Girl Goes Dogging

I'm twenty-four years old and live in South London. I've been working as a florist since leaving college and plan to open my own shop within the next five years. I've had three steady boyfriends since I lost my virginity and a few one-night stands. Jeff was one of my steadies, though I'm not with him any more. We lasted nearly a year together. He was a chemist, which wasn't as dull as it sounds, and the sex was pretty good. But we actually broke up in the end because the sex was so good. That's how it felt at the time, anyway. We were quite adventurous, tried different positions and oral sex on each other, and even had anal sex a few times. But eventually I could see that Jeff was getting restless, in spite of all the stuff we were doing. He kept making off-the-wall suggestions like partner-swopping or joining a swingers club, so he could have sex with other people. One of his previous girlfriends had been into threesomes and all that, and he kept comparing me to her, which made me feel annoyed and a bit inferior.

I didn't want us to split up, so in the end I agreed to try at least one new thing a month. As soon as I said that, he went off browsing on the internet and came back with his first suggestion: dogging. I had a good idea what that meant – having sex in a car park while others watched or joined in – and wasn't really comfortable about it. I mean, you never know who's going to be there, who you might end up having sex with, or even if the police might turn up. It sounded dangerous. But Jeff was clearly excited by the risk, so I reluctantly said yes.

Jeff found what sounded like a discreet dogging site from his online contacts and we drove up there one Thursday night in late spring. It was a small car park next to an area of woodland and common ground, only a few hundred yards from the main road but well hidden by thick bushes. I'd expected to see loads of cars there, with people shagging everywhere, but of course that wasn't how it happened. It was getting dark by the time we arrived and the small car park was deserted.

I wanted to go straight home but Jeff said we should wait at least half an hour before giving up. 'This is the right night. I left a message on the website. Someone will come, we just have to be patient.'

I had dressed up specially for the occasion in a very short skirt and black stockings, new high heels and a bra top in see-through white lace. Sluttish-looking, in other words, which is how Jeff liked me to dress when we were getting dirty together. I didn't mind too much, it always made me feel very feminine to wear stockings. But my friends would have a fit if they knew the sort of outfits he made me wear.

It seemed a shame to waste such a sexy outfit, so I took his hand and put it under my skirt, let him feel the flimsy white lace thong that matched my bra top.

'We might as well make ourselves comfortable,' I said jokingly, to lighten the mood, 'while we wait for someone else to turn up.'

Jeff didn't need much encouragement. One of his fingers nudged past the lacy thong and pushed right inside me. I was already wet up there – had been wet for hours actually, imagining what was going to happen to me – but Jeff didn't start masturbating me, which is what he usually did whenever we started fucking. He always liked me to come first, so he could take his time and concentrate on himself after that. That time, though, he pulled his finger straight out again after a few strokes and unzipped his jeans instead, pulling out his cock.

To my surprise, he was erect already. Jeff must have been fantasising about the whole thing as much as me, because I hadn't seen his penis that stiff or swollen in a long time. He pushed my head into his lap and told me to suck it. I liked the way he said that, very domineering, so I did what I was told and started licking and sucking his cock. It always turns me on when men get bossy like that, though I wouldn't like it if I couldn't refuse. He put his hand on the back of my neck. Again, a bit domineering of him, but I quite enjoy that when I'm going down on a man.

I must have been down there about five minutes, with Jeff well on his way, breathing hard and pushing his groin into my mouth, when headlights swung across the windscreen. He swore and told me to stop. I sat up and stared about the place, my face damp and my hair all mussed-up, which is the only part about fellatio that I hate.

Sure enough, another car had arrived. It had parked right opposite us – maybe two cars' lengths away from our bonnet – and the driver was just sitting there, engine running and the main headlight beam shining right into our faces. I thought it was the police and was a bit panicked, wanting to leave, but then whoever it was flashed twice – some sort of coded signal, according to Jeff – and dipped their lights.

Jeff gave a sigh of relief and pushed my head back into his lap. 'Go on, keep sucking. First they watch, then they join in. That's how it works in these places.'

After that, everything changed. Before, the 'dogging' idea had been a game, not real. But now someone had actually turned up for sex and there I was with my head in Jeff's lap, lips working up and down his shaft, feeling like a prostitute and aware that at any minute some strange man could be ogling me through the car window. The odd thing though was that I was actually excited by the idea of being watched while I sucked my boyfriend's cock. Maybe that makes me a pervert. I don't really care now, but I did wonder that night, feeling my pussy go damp at the thought of being watched and perhaps fucked by some random stranger in a car park.

I must have groaned a bit when I was sucking, because he wriggled his hand between my legs again and rubbed at the white lace thong. 'You're soaking,' he said. 'What are you thinking about?'

I tried to say 'cock' through the cock in my mouth but it came out wrong, like a choking sound, and he just laughed, pushing my head further down into his lap.

My pussy was quite wet and it was embarrassing, knowing that he knew it wasn't just for him but for this other bloke: the stranger in the car opposite, watching us and probably wanking himself at the same time.

'Better give him a show, then.' Jeff told me to take my bra top off, helping me with it. 'Bit too late to be shy.'

My tits sprang clear of the white lace bra top, which Jeff threw deliberately on to the top of the dashboard, so the bloke opposite could see it in the headlights. It was a cool spring evening and my nipples were quickly erect, hard as buttons. I sat upright for a few minutes, cupping and squeezing my tits in plain sight, pretending they were someone else's hands, a hot flush on my cheeks as I tried to imagine what this bloke was thinking, what he must be able to see now. Jeff stroked his penis while he looked at my bare tits, nodding with approval. He would have been perfectly happy to watch me get fucked by dozens of men, I think. But I was a bit shaky at that point. I wasn't quite ready to fuck another bloke and not even sure I wanted to continue, when suddenly the driver's door of the other car swung open and it all seemed to be happening for real.

'Here he comes now,' Jeff said, his voice slurred with excitement. Then he frowned, staring ahead. He stopped touching himself and even drew his coat over his lap to hide his erection. 'Jesus, it's a woman.'

I stared too, astonished. I couldn't believe it at first, having been completely geared up to expect a man, or at least another couple like us, looking for sex. But it was a woman. And a woman on her own.

She was dark-haired, tall, with long slim bare legs, wearing a short black skirt to accentuate them, and a transparent blouse in red chiffon. Underneath the blouse, I could see her bra as she drew closer to the car, a smooth-cupped red bra that peeped over the edges of her low cleavage, very sexy and inviting. Definitely not a man in drag! I remember thinking how beautiful her tits were, and how they looked far too big for her neat waist and slender hips. Then hurriedly trying not to look, because it didn't feel right. But I'd never had a relationship with a woman then and I didn't understand about sexual attraction between women, except that it was something I ought to avoid.

The woman tapped on the window and Jeff wound it down halfway. 'Hello,' she said, and even her voice was sexy, very low and suggestive. 'Mind if I join you?'

She was wearing this gorgeous red lipstick, a rich shade of scarlet to match her blouse, and I suddenly imagined it smeared all over Jeff's cock as she sucked him off, down on her knees in the dirt and leaves. 'Dogging' had been a fun idea when it was me that would be shared between two or more men. But I didn't like the idea of sharing Jeff with another woman, however horny we all were. That hadn't been part of the plan.

Jeff was clearly up for two women though. He was staring at her red bra and he'd uncovered his penis again, grasping it in his hand. 'You want to climb in the back or shall we get out?'

The brunette said she preferred to fuck outside, because she liked a lot of space. Jeff got out immediately and followed her back to her own car, where she lay back over the bonnet and pulled up her skirt without saying another word. I felt a bit awkward, following them both with my bare tits bouncing and hoping nobody else would pull into the car park before we had finished. But if I'm honest, I was feeling quite curious and turned on by the situation too.

She had red silk knickers on, not a thong but those old-fashioned knickers, the sort that go right up to the waist. Jeff watched with his mouth open as she began to unpeel them, revealing a flat stomach and a well-trimmed dark-haired pussy. When she stepped daintily out of them, he positioned himself between her legs and tried to insert his penis, not even looking back at me for permission. The woman immediately said no, pushing him aside, and beckoned me over instead. I think Jeff was quite annoyed at that, but he didn't say anything, just stood there wanking while he watched us.

She played with my bare tits for a moment, smiling at me when my nipples ached and stiffened with pleasure. Then she leant back and opened her pussy lips with the fingers of one hand, showing me her clitoris. 'Have you ever licked another woman out?'

I shook my head, feeling embarrassed but rather hot and horny after having my breasts handled like that. So the woman told me how to do it, the long strokes and the quick strokes, then how to suck her clitoris until she came. Jeff was looking uncertain but it was too exciting an opportunity to miss, even if it did make him angry.

I knelt down on the filthy ground of the car park and put my mouth between the woman's legs. She tasted of almonds at first, and then a sourish sort of cream as my tongue explored her deeper. I was dizzy with excitement, my own pussy wet and aching. But I remembered everything she told me and think I did a pretty good job of licking her out.

Her clitoris and pussy lips were soon gleaming with saliva; it was the most amazing thing I'd ever seen. And we were right out in the open air too, where anyone could have seen us, with the constant hum of traffic from the main road, which was only a few hundred yards through the bushes behind her car. We'd have been arrested if anyone had caught us. Two half-naked women having sex over the bonnet of a car. Well, cunnilingus anyway.

After a few minutes of this, she made an odd noise and grasped my hair, tugging on it cruelly. It hurt and I nearly stopped, then realised it just meant she was on the verge of orgasm. So I ignored the pain and licked even harder, sucking on her clitoris the way I like it to be sucked, pressing it against my tongue until it stood out like a hard shiny button between her pussy lips.

125

She cried out and came, sagging against me. I had to hold her up, standing to kiss her on the mouth with my hand still moving between her legs while she moaned and writhed. It was fantastic.

She wanted to taste me too and I was only too eager to oblige, lying on my back across the bonnet for my turn. Feeling her push my skirt up to my waist, I held it up so she could burrow her face into my cunt, nuzzling the white lace thong aside and going straight for my clit. There was something rough and insistent about her hands on my body, like she'd paid for me and I had no choice but to obey. It was the dirtiest thing I'd ever done. And the best thing was Jeff's face; his eyes were full of frustrated lust, and his cock was very stiff in his hand. Yet there was nothing he could do but watch, perhaps hoping for a few scraps of pussy at the end.

It was total heaven, being licked out by another woman. I felt completely free with her and came several times, whimpering and unable to control the trembling in my legs. When I couldn't take any more, she turned me over, slapping my bare bottom quite sharply. I remember begging her to smack me again and groaning when she obliged. Jeff made an angry noise under his breath somewhere behind me but I ignored him. I was too far gone by then to care what he thought.

She must have realised I needed something more after her spanking, because suddenly her fingers were inside me. Two or three fingers, right past the knuckles, moving in and out with a corkscrew motion.

It was nothing like being fucked by a man, having a cock inside me. There was no way I could forget she was a woman. I could feel her breath on my neck as she leant over me, hear her voice murmuring filth into my ear, and her long slim fingers knew exactly how to move, what sort of rhythm was required to bring me back to the edge. Every now and then her thumb flicked smartly over my clit as she continued to fuck me, and before long I was coming again, with her fingers still inside me, grinding my hips against the car and shouting obscenities.

As I came, not bothering how it looked, I pushed my own hand between my legs and pressed her fingers deeper inside me. 'Fuck me, keep fucking me,' I groaned, loving the feel of her soft body against mine, breasts and hips and damp pussy.

I was shaking with pleasure, with the best orgasm I'd had in years, when she leant forward and kissed the back of my neck, so sexy and tender I was almost in tears. Close behind me, I heard Jeff grunt as he suddenly lost control. I glanced back and caught the white spattering of spunk as he shot his load over the car bonnet right beside us.

As we returned to our car afterwards, both of us feeling a bit shaky and disorientated, the woman came after us with a piece of paper in her hand. It was her email address.

Jeff was furious and wanted me to destroy it, but I refused. Later, I got in contact with her and we agreed to try meeting up again at a local hotel. It turned out her name was Susan and she worked as a holiday rep, so was abroad most of the year. We spent some delicious afternoons together, fucking each other in the bath or sprawling naked across the bed, just licking each other's pussies or taking turns with her strap-on dildo. But Susan kept having to jet off to holiday resorts in Greece and Turkey, and the affair petered out in the end.

I split with Jeff soon after that and I'm living with another man now. We have a good sex life, but he doesn't know anything about the night Jeff took me dogging or about my new-found taste for pussy. Which is how I like it. Rather than change things between us, every few months I slip out to a gay bar and usually end up going back to some woman's place for sex. I try to pick a different girl each time, so they don't get the wrong idea and think I'm looking for a relationship. I'm not a complete lesbian, of course; I still love having a man's cock inside me. But now I've discovered how sexually exciting it is to fuck another woman, I've no plans to stop.

– *Kim, Wimbledon, South London, UK*

Bill's Parties

The snow falling outside seemed never-ending; it had been coming down steadily since early morning. I turned down plans with the girls for an evening surfing 'The Nightline'. I had been on a couple of times since first meeting the gent I fondly refer to as 'The Pussy Eater' when talking to my friend Deb, who is the only one that knows my dirty little secret. I never did bother to see him again after that first time.

Pickings were slim on the line; there were a lot of men on, not surprising considering the weather, but there seemed to be no one whose greeting caught my attention. I had become a pro at manoeuvring my way through the line: one for replying, six to erase, five hear more about the member – a total pro, which really helped me skip past all of the losers.

'Hi. I'm looking for a lady that wants to chat and maybe hook up . . .' whispered another of what I refer to as the 'low-talkers'. A 'low-talker' is a man who is either married or still living with parents, who has to whisper so he is not caught. There were a lot of low-talkers on the line.

'Hi, I'm Bill. This is an open invitation to any clean and safe ladies out there who might be interested in attending one of my parties. I'm a clean-cut, friendly business professional living downtown, and I have regular parties with like-minded people, mostly in their forties and fifties, who are just into enjoying sexy times together. If you'd like to know more, please message me back,' said a much more laid-back-sounding voice, catching my attention right away.

I was definitely intrigued. The idea brought a visual to my mind of a bunch of naked bodies together, intertwined on a big bed. I was immediately aroused and didn't hesitate to message back: 'Hi. I heard your greeting and am interested in knowing more about your parties. Listen to my profile. If you like what you hear, please get back to me.'

He replied quickly, 'Well, your profile sounds great. You are a touch younger than the people that I normally play with, but I'm sure you will fit in fine. We are a great group of people and will do anything to make the experience comfortable for all. Give me a call . . .' He ended with his telephone number.

I sat and thought about it for a minute. I was incredibly aroused, but hesitant, even more so than with the last man I had met from the chat line. I guess the fact that it would be a group of people had me intimidated.

I sent him another message: 'Hi, it's me again. I'm really turned on by the idea of attending one of your parties, but I'm really new at all of this. I've never been in a group situation and I'm a bit nervous. I really don't want to waste your time, thanks.'

I put the phone down for a second to run to the washroom and returned to several messages waiting. I went through about four messages from other members before I reached another from Bill. 'Well, thank you for being so honest. You seem very real and that is exactly the type of person that we like to bring into our group. If you have access to a computer, go to ⟨billsparties.com⟩. You can check out photos from a few of our parties and see how harmless we all really are. If you decide you want to give it a try, you have my number,' he finished. His voice was very soothing.

I went online immediately and searched through his site for the pictures. I was stunned: there were about twenty pictures, not far off from what I had imagined. There was one that particularly caught my attention, of a woman who was, I'd say, in her late forties, with short dark hair. She was quite simple looking, not at all intimidating. She sat naked on a chair and next to her was a white-haired, slightly heavy-set older man – very distinguished-looking, considering he too was nude. She was holding his cock in her hand. Between her legs was another man who was going down on her; he had salt-and-pepper hair and a regular build. They were all so average-looking, like normal everyday people, and they seemed very relaxed. I stared at the picture for a few minutes, aware of the warm tingling between my thighs. I got so wet so quickly I had to call him back.

His number was busy each time I attempted to call for the next hour. I lay on the couch and couldn't get the pictures out of my mind. I imagined what it would be like and couldn't help touching myself. It was just as my hand began to slide into my panties that he answered his phone.

'I knew you wouldn't be able to resist once you saw the pictures.' His chuckle was jovial.

'So how many people would be at one of your parties?' I asked.

'Well, I have had anywhere from just three of us to ten. It depends. If you'd be more comfortable, we could start off with just one other woman or couple.

I do have one woman I play with – she is attached, but her husband doesn't agree with the lifestyle, so he isn't involved. Discretion is a must. You said that you had never participated in group sex, but have you been with another woman?' he asked.

'Nope – up until a couple months ago, I had never had anything other than regular sex with a boy-friend!' I giggled nervously.

'Maybe you'd prefer to come to one of my parties and just watch at first? You can always join in if you feel up to it,' he suggested.

'I think I'd be fine with just another one or two people there. When do you think we could do this?' I asked anxiously, not wanting to lose my nerve.

'How about tomorrow night? I'll give Judy a call – she was in a few of the pictures you saw. We'll leave it at just the three of us then,' he said.

We ended the conversation with his giving me his address and office number, just in case I changed my mind during the day.

That night, I tossed and turned. I struggled with the idea of what I had agreed to. Was I taking it too far? Could I even go through with it? It was starting to become day outside and I was still up, feeling restless. I played it out in my mind, the way I pictured the event going over. The more I envisioned having several hands and lips on my body, the more turned on I became. My fingers kept making their way into my panties. I began playing with my clit and my cunt was so wet that I couldn't help but push my finger in and out of my hot hole. I brought myself to the verge of climax several times, but would stop myself before going over the edge. Maybe I was afraid that once I came and felt satisfied I would lose the urge to follow through. I had been so reserved in the past, at least on the outside, never daring to let anyone know of the things that I fantasised about, or how often I masturbated. This chat line gave me a safe outlet for all of my dirty desires. These people whose greetings I would hear on the line were all looking for the same thing I was: a go-ahead to do the things that were buried in the recesses of our minds and loins without the fear of judgment.

I climbed out of bed and made my through my dim apartment to my computer – I needed to see the pictures again. When they came up, I stood at the desk and stared, examining each one carefully. In one, a close-up of a woman's lips covered in come. The next was a shot of maybe five couples spread nude across a living room's floor and sofa. I clicked to expand the picture for a better view, my cunt dripping into my flannel pants. There were two women, one lying on the floor being eaten out by another woman while a man knelt at her side licking her nipple.

There was another man lying across the couch with a woman sitting on his face while another was giving him a blowjob. On a chair was a woman riding on the cock of a man, while another man stood bent over sticking his finger up her asshole. All of their bodies were less than perfect, to say the least, and they were by no means very physically attractive, but I found myself wanting to be there, naked in the middle of all of them. I slept soundly after that.

My workday seemed to fly by. I kept close guard of the piece of paper with Bill's number on it, but didn't use it. My cunt felt as if it were on fire the entire day and, though nervous, I had no intention of backing out.

After work, I headed home and straight for the bath. My mind raced with visions of Bill's face and how it looked in the pictures when nestled between a woman's thighs. I tried to imagine what it would be like to be with another woman – how she would feel and taste. I resisted the urge to play with myself again; there was no time. I chose my outfit with convenience in mind as opposed to appearance. I knew from the pictures that they really were a very relaxed bunch. Mind you, they were all naked. I threw on a simple brown jersey knit dress and a pair of boots and nothing beneath it but a bra – my tits were way too big to go without.

I called Bill for directions, and his tone calmed my nerves a bit. He seemed pleased that I hadn't changed my mind. As I rang for a cab, I downed a mug of Baileys – it was all I had to take the rest of the edge off. The cab arrived quickly and we were at Bill's in less than ten minutes.

Despite the liqueur, my nerves appeared to be getting the better of me; my hands were shaking so much that I could barely ring his apartment. When the elevator door opened, he was standing right there waiting for me. He looked exactly as he did in the pictures: a full head of grey hair, very light blue eyes and distinguished features. He was much taller than I was, I'd say close to six feet, and he was dressed in a pair of black slacks and a white button-down shirt, as if he'd just come in from the office. His eyes seemed sweet, and there was definitely something endearing in his expression as he welcomed me with a hug.

'Wow. You are an attractive little thing, aren't you!' he said, laughing as we embraced.

'Well, thank you,' I replied flirtatiously, already feeling at ease.

The apartment was tastefully decorated and smelled of pipe smoke. He appeared to be well-off, judging by the decadent furnishings. He led me to his living room, where his coffee table was set up with a vast array of bottles and glasses. 'Drink?' he asked.

'Sure. How about some wine – whatever you have there is fine,' I said, sitting on the couch.

Just as he was about to take a seat next to me, I heard a woman's voice. 'Sorry I'm late!' she called out.

'That's all right. This is Judy,' he said, placing his arm around her and leading her in my direction.

It was the short-haired woman from the photos. She was almost as tall as he was, and seemed equally pleasant, with a warm smile. She wore a patterned wrap dress and large earrings that really stood out against her short, thin hair.

'Nice to meet you.' She smiled as she leant over to greet me with a kiss on the cheek.

When her lips brushed against my face, my entire body seemed to tingle. I was becoming increasingly aroused.

Once served our drinks of choice, we all settled on to the sofa with me in the middle. The conversation seemed to flow easily; they were very comfortable and obviously not new at this. We talked about 'The Nightline' and some of their experiences. The more they recounted, the stronger the pulsating between my thighs became. I could feel my pussy swelling with excitement and I wondered when they would make their move.

'So, Bill tells me that you've never been with a woman. Is that true?' she asked, turning around to face me.

'It's true. I've never done anything like this.' My lip practically quivered.

'Not even a kiss?' she asked, leaning in closer.

'Uh-uh,' I managed before she pressed her lips to mine.

Her lips were cold from the ice cubes in her drink, but so soft and gentle. The kiss only lasted a second, leaving me wanting more. Judy put her glass down on the coffee table and leaned back, at the same time untying the belt that was holding her wrap dress closed. She pulled the fabric off to the sides, revealing her small and slightly drooping breasts.

Her nipples were very dark, much more so than mine, and they were hard. She just sat looking at me, not saying a word, with her milky white body exposed. I froze. I wanted to reach out and touch her, but just didn't know how. Bill then took my hand in his, holding it tight because it was trembling. Slowly, he placed it on her breast, and began to move the flesh about. Her skin felt so soft and so different from a man's. Her nipple seemed to harden even more with my touch, and she began to moan. I loved knowing that I was turning her on, making her as wet as I was. Bill took his hand off mine, leaving me to fondle the breast myself.

As my insides began to tingle with longing for more, I couldn't help but bring my lips down to her breast and begin sucking on it as I would want mine to be sucked. Lapping away at her taut nipple, I became aware of Bill's hand caressing my thigh over the fabric of my dress. I spread my legs apart slightly as a silent go-ahead for more. He took me up on the offer and raised my dress, exposing my naked cunt. I leant into Judy even closer, now devouring both of her tits with my mouth, all the while raising my ass up off the sofa so that Bill could pull my dress up higher. I pulled away from her long enough for Bill to remove my dress completely.

As the dress pulled away, leaving me almost completely naked, the contrast between the cool air and the heat that was emanating from our bodies caused little goose-bumps to prickle all over me. Judy took the opportunity to slip out of the rest of her dress, and then Bill helped her to remove my bra. I was overcome by contrasting emotions: more aroused than ever before, yet vulnerable, sitting there nude in the company of two strangers.

I wasn't sure what to do next so Bill took the lead, placing his hands on my shoulders and leaning me back, and then kneeling between my legs. Grabbing my knees, he pulled me towards him until my swollen cunt was inches away from his face. He used his fingers to pull my lips apart. I could hear how wet I was. Then, looking me in the eyes, he began to run his tongue over my clit. I glanced at Judy who was sitting next to me fingering herself furiously while watching him lap away at my pussy. Bill moaned and grunted into my cunt as he sucked and licked it. I used one hand to hold his head tight against my clit and with the other grabbed at Judy's thigh, pulling her closer so I could touch her sexy cunt. I quickly found my way into the wet, slipping two fingers into her effortlessly. She gasped as I pumped my fingers in and out of her and I could feel her getting wetter.

I wanted to taste her, my first pussy, and said so out loud, immediately causing Bill to raise his face up from between my legs. I leaned over and kissed her before assuming my place on my knees in front of her and finally kissing her moist mound. It tasted a little salty and I recognised the scent; it was similar to the smell of my own sex. She was crying out in ecstasy as I sloppily worked her cunt with my mouth. Bill, who had gotten undressed, moved in close and I glanced up just in time to see him shove his cock into her mouth. The mix of my juices and his saliva ran down my leg as I wriggled about. He reached over and began toying with the crack of my ass while enjoying his blowjob and I felt as if I would explode. My insides were pulsing on the brink of climax; I needed a cock inside me. Almost in unison, Judy and I cried out: 'Fuck me!'

Bill didn't hesitate and pulled his cock out of her mouth. 'Let's go in there where it's more comfortable,' he said, leading us to the bedroom.

He had one of those large cherrywood beds, almost Gothic-looking, with the really high mattresses. Hungrily, Judy and I began to make out, our tongues flicking outside our mouths. I lay back on the bed with my legs dangling off the edge and she straddled me so we could continue kissing. I could feel the wet hairs of her cunt tickling against my thigh, when I felt Bill spread my legs open and enter me. He pushed his fat cock into me so hard that it hurt, causing me to gasp, but I took all of it at once and met his rhythm, pumping against him and taking it like a champ. My tongue darted in and out of Judy's mouth with each thrust, until he pulled out of me. Judy began to rock on top of me as Bill fucked her from behind. I looked over her shoulder and thought I would surely come, seeing his belly smacking against her as he fucked her hard. He saw me watching and seemed to enjoy putting on a show, so while watching me he pulled out of her and plunged his cock back into me.

Feeling his cock all wet with her juices as it pumped in and out of me got me more excited than I thought I could handle. He began to alternate between my hole and hers. The combination of his cock filling me and her warm body rubbing against mine caused me to go over the edge. My insides began to pulse and I could feel my cunt squirting as I came harder than I had ever dreamed possible. Her cries made it clear that she too was coming hard. My head began to spin and my muscles continued to spasm for a moment as Bill continued to thrust in and out of me, finally moaning, 'I'm going to come!'

Judy jumped up and pulled me swiftly up off the bed, down towards the floor. We knelt in front of his swollen dick as he stroked it fast and hard, finally blowing his load into our faces. Our tongues met as we licked up the thick jism that was dribbling from his cock, until it finally stopped pulsating against our faces.

Once he had come, he let out a laugh and bent down, giving us each a kiss on the head. Judy and I collapsed on to each other, there at the foot of the bed, and sat enjoying the afterglow, sharing a couple of delicate kisses.

The three of us celebrated the great night with one last drink before I left, satisfied and exhausted.

– *A. S., Ontario, Canada*

Kelly's First Job

We all start somewhere with our little 'kinks', and for me it was when I began to work at the hotel. I don't work there now and I'm pretty sure that the things I got up to are unlikely to come back and bite me after all this time.

I was very young, just finished college, wondering what to do with my life, and I took the first offer that came along, as something to tide me over. I live in the South, near one of London's three big airports, and you can't really move for hotels here, so I suppose the odds were stacked that I would end up cleaning hotel rooms.

The uniform was pretty bland really – at least compared to my idea of a maid's uniform. In my ignorance, I had in mind something from a French farce, with a short, flared-out skirt, white lace pinny, seamed stockings and high heels. But the uniform I was handed on my first day was drab by comparison: a reproduced plain black dress with an unimaginative cut, a hem to the knee and a shirt-style collar. Very 'respectable'. We were given white cotton tabards to go over the top with big ridiculous pockets at the front and were told to wear sensible black shoes and black or flesh-coloured tights.

I was naïve about the power of alluring clothing back then. I certainly wasn't looking for a glamorous outfit or wanting to take part in any sort of fashion parade along the hotel corridors, but I was still a little disappointed with it.

First few weeks, I kept my head down and concentrated on the work – it was the only way to get through, really, especially given some of the things we were left to clear up by inconsiderate, snobby guests. As you can imagine, with my mind on just getting through the day, it took a little while before I looked up from my work and noticed the guests. Then I saw that, despite the unflattering uniforms, I and a few of my colleagues were attracting attention from some of the male guests. On more than one occasion I noticed men fumbling with room keys as they stole glances at me when I wheeled my trolley or vacuum cleaner along the carpeted corridors. Soon, I began to notice that it happened more often if I wore flesh-coloured tights than if I wore black tights – something to do with the programming of the male eye, I presume, responding to the suggestion of flesh in the same involuntary way it responds to movement or danger. I became amused, intrigued, and so my 'thing' was born.

I started to experiment with all the different shades and finishes of leg coverings, to see which drew the most attention amongst guests and colleagues. I tried dark and light tans, sheer, shiny, glossy, matt, all sorts. But I eventually settled on a pair of flesh-coloured, high-sheen tights that shaped the light beautifully along the contours of my legs. I used to spend at least five minutes every morning just admiring myself in the mirror and running my hands over the smooth finish before leaving for work.

I enjoyed the glances I was getting from colleagues and guests alike and always felt slightly victorious when I noticed an eye flick in my direction and down to my legs. And, yes, even slightly wet.

I began to wonder what other changes I could make to my bland uniform to attract the attention of guests. It was a difficult balancing act as I knew that if I went too far I would attract the notice of management, who might not take too kindly to me going off-beam with my outfit.

I started with the plain black dress, taking the hem up an inch. It sounds pretty meagre but I hoped that even just an inch would make a difference. I stopped buttoning the collar up and added holes to the fastener at the sides of the tabard so that, rather than it giving me the maternity-dress look, I could wear it tighter, at more of a cinch. Suddenly, looking at myself in the mirror in the mornings, I actually felt like a woman.

Next I moved the sexy little experiment to my shoes. It was a delicate process, for again, if I made the change too radical I would incur the wrath of management and be made to switch back to the boring blocky heels. I scoured the airport shops for a pair with a higher, more stiletto heel, and after three lunch-hours trudging around the terminal I came across the perfect pair of court-style black shoes with something approaching a three-inch heel – the highest I dared to go for. They were made of a hard-looking leather, with a finish like beetle-skin. Despite the look they hugged my feet so snugly that they felt like slippers inside. I bought them immediately and wore them that afternoon.

The cumulative effect of these tiny individual changes was amazing. I found myself catching eyes and giving half-smiles to men all day, and soon I was actually enjoying my work. I would invent little games to play in the lobby and corridors, just seeing how wet I could get myself wiggling and strutting around, teasing guests. I started deliberately choosing to clean the rooms of men, of all ages, who had shown an interest in me. I don't know why, I did not even fancy most of them, but their interest, their reaction to me, attracted me. I began regularly cleaning the room of one man in particular.

He was a regular guest of the hotel and always spent the last working week of the month enjoying our hospitality. He was just over forty years old, slim, dark, reasonably tall and always well turned out in a suit and a coloured shirt, open at the collar, with no tie. I would watch out for the silhouette of his long black coat when the end of the month drew near.

To be honest, his reaction to me was a little different from most. His glances at me were not so furtive as the rest; indeed, they were brazen and confident. I would moisten uncontrollably as I vacuumed the carpet in the corridor and observed him deliberately turn his head, look me up and down from head to toe and coolly go into his room without a word or a smile. It might seem rude, it might seem sexist, it might even seem shifty, but I loved it.

After the second month I was desperate to clean his room. I don't really know why, or what I expected, but I felt drawn to him somehow and as the end of the month drew near I made sure I was cleaning on his floor. The minute he left for work one morning, taking an eyeful of me as I waited by the door, I slipped inside.

He had only been in the room for a day, but there was already a slightly masculine smell in the air. I hoped it would get stronger as the week wore on. I flung myself on the bed and squirmed on the quilt, rubbing my covered legs over each other. The thought of him humping me roughly on that bed entered my head, quite unexpectedly, and I banished it, returning to my feet to regain my composure. I started to clean.

144

As I worked my way around the room, I sneaked little peeks at his belongings, his underwear, his expensive shirts and his shoes, smirking to myself that I was getting intimate in some way with this man without him even knowing. I rifled through his bathroom items, his razor and smellies. I smiled at the packet of condoms in the shower bag, opened but unused.

But it was when I came to empty the wastepaper basket that I really became intrigued. I tipped the contents into my bin liner: a newspaper, an emptied coffee sachet – and a single black stocking. I shook my head in disbelief as it fell into the bag, and reached in to pull it out to make sure my eyes were not deceiving me.

It was definitely a stocking, soft and glimmering. I draped the delicate nylon garment over my hands to regard it. I gaped in disbelief and wondered what story might be behind this.

It was a simple stocking, nothing too expensive or fancy, with a plain black band around the top. There was no adhesive band on the inside, so it was intended to be worn with a suspender, I think. I was just making assumptions, though, as I had never worn stockings up to then. Fascinated, I considered buying a pair, and felt all along its soft length as I ruminated. I was getting quite moist as I imagined strutting into work in a pair of stockings and a tight suspender belt.

It was then that I felt the end of the stocking, at the toe, which, unlike the rest of the material, was hard and bendy. I immediately knew why. My first reaction was to drop it into the bin-bag, wiping my fingers on my tabard with an initial shiver of disgust. But I could not get it out of my head and only a few seconds later I was drawn back to it again.

I picked it out, and found myself crumpling the semen-stained end of the stocking between my fingers. I could not believe I was doing it, but I licked them. I did not taste or detect a thing, but I was immediately ashamed of the act and threw the stocking into the bag for the third time, knotting the plastic loops as quickly as I could to remove the temptation of playing with the stocking again. I tried to take stock of my behaviour and refocus myself. Biting my thumb I left the room.

After that incident it was impossible for me to pass the lingerie shop on the way home. I had been thinking about stockings constantly for the rest of my shift and, while my tights felt smooth on my legs and made them look fantastic, I was curious as to how stockings might feel. I wondered if they would feel sexier still than my tights. I had to try them.

The shop had quite an array of hose and it wasn't hard to find a shade that matched the glossy tights I had been wearing recently. There was a choice of a pair with a seam, a pair of lacy hold-ups and some plainer stockings for use with a suspender belt. I had no real idea which to choose and my dithering attracted an assistant.

'Having trouble deciding which to buy?' a slender blonde woman asked me. Her vivid red lips smiled widely, highlighting some very comforting laughter lines on her maturing face.

'I've never really worn these before, I don't know which is best.'

'I remember the first time I bought some,' she said, grinning warmly. 'Are they for an outfit, for a special occasion?'

I did not really know what to say. Should I make something up? Did I need the excuse of a special occasion to justify this purchase? What would she think if I just said I was curious or trying to make myself feel sexy? I did not want to look like a sex-crazed harlot. I weighed up my answer during a breathless pause.

'No, I really just wanted to make myself feel more attractive in this horrible outfit,' I answered bravely, pinching my hotel-issue dress between my thumb and forefinger to show her.

'I don't blame you.' She laughed, placing a warm maternal hand on my forearm. I felt the lightest touch of her red nails as she pulled her hand away. I was calm. 'Although you really don't look bad in it,' she added.

'Thank you,' I said quietly.

'If you want to feel attractive and sexy I would recommend using a suspender belt and one of these two,' she said, putting the hold-ups back on the rack. I took the seamed and the plain stockings.

'Come on, we'll find you a belt,' she whispered. I followed her.

We stopped at a rack arrayed with a collection of suspender belts of all the colours you might imagine suspender belts to be produced in: black, white, red, purple, and so on. She glanced at the stockings I held in my hand and then at my uniform and pursed her scarlet lips as she picked out what she thought might go.

'I think you should start with a black one, with the normal four straps, and perhaps a bow, nothing too fancy,' she said, handing me a coat-hanger with the garter belt described clipped to it. It was in my exact size; her practised eye had picked it out apparently without a thought.

I thanked my lucky stars that I had found someone so understanding (someone whom I now know very well, but I promised not to use her name), and bought

147

the items that she had picked out and hurried home to try them on.

I went to the mirror in my room, kicked off my shoes, which were hot and aromatic from the day's exertions, and peeled off my similarly pungent tights. I unclipped the suspender belt and put it on, first lifting my hem to expose my sleek bare legs in the mirror. It felt somehow – despite the fact it affected my movement in no way at all – restrictive. But it was a good restriction, just as its pressure on my body was a reminder of my true shape, curving in at the waist.

The stockings seemed so small when I first removed the packaging, more like socks than a covering for all but the sensitive upper thigh. I hooked my thumbs inside each in turn to roll them up, put them over my pointed toes and, stretching the fine mesh, pulled them up my leg, enjoying the sensation up to my thigh. I affixed the clasps, clumsily at first, and then took a look at my appearance in the mirror. I liked what I saw. I put my shoes on and pulled the hem of the dress back down.

It felt different from the tights, more exposed, more daring and, yes, more attractive. I was even a little nervous from the excitement of the new experience and I did not want to remove them. I slept in the hose and garter belt that night. I don't really know why.

By the time I got into work the following day I felt almost at one with my new stockings, as if they were just an extension of myself, a second skin, and I truly wondered if I could ever go back to tights now. Catching the eyes of customers and colleagues now had an extra ingredient. Sure, the same feeling of power to turn a man's head was there, and the same feeling of self-satisfaction that having an audience gives you, but I had the added knowledge that I was wearing very special, naughty, jaw-dropping undergarments.

It was an early shift for me that day and I had to wait a couple of hours before the guests began to awake. I made my way to my favourite guest's corridor and, like a lion taking position in the grass, began dusting and polishing within sight of his door.

As I dusted I wondered if he had performed his little ritual of wanking himself into a stocking before he went to bed last night. Was this a regular thing for him? Had I stumbled across an obsession, a fetish? If so, I wanted to be the focus of that fetish. I had only just discovered my fascination, but was being drawn into it.

To some I am sure this gentleman would have seemed to be something of a pervert, but to me he was just an attractive and imaginative man. I had never been near a fetish before and I was finding my first to be irresistibly magnetic.

As I stalled for time I got my first inkling of the problems that must face perverted men and women the world over – how to reach out, make contact with the like-minded. My plan was to wait near the door, hoovering, dusting and polishing the same area two or even three times if necessary, until he emerged. Then, with my duskiest look, flash my green eyes at him suggestively. Pretty daring stuff, I thought at the time.

But I began to doubt the plan. How would that set me apart from any other females that might have come into his orbit that day, or even that week? How would a flash of the mince pies suggest to a man that I was specifically interested in his little nylon thing? It wouldn't.

Whether it was the fumes from the brass polish or not I don't know, but I decided to scrap the plan for a more daring one. I started by leaving a duster in the corridor directly opposite his door and by packing the vacuum cleaner away – if I used that I would never hear any clues as to his movement from within his room, and I would need that sort of warning to take position. I reached under the hem of my dress and adjusted my suspender straps to full length, allowing my stockings to be worn dangerously low. They may have wrinkled a little, but that really didn't matter too much. I then reached under my hem again and, using a couple of hair grips to hold it in place, folded it up by nearly an inch. My stocking-tops were now dangerously close to exposure and my heart leapt at the thought of anyone seeing. My pussy even seeped a little moisture.

It was approaching 8.30 a.m. and I knew he would be leaving soon, so I proceeded to polish his door handle and number plate as slowly as I could and await his materialisation. I'd like to say that the task of polishing and buffing took my mind off how horny I was making myself, but it didn't; gradually, I got wetter and wetter and, by the time I heard a briefcase clipping shut and the scrape of keys being picked up from a table, I was worried that I might squelch as I walked.

But, with no time to worry about that sort of thing, I quickly turned, stepped away from the door and slowly began to bend over to pick up the duster I had left on the floor minutes earlier. The door opened behind me, and my heart skipped a beat; I knew I had to go through with this now and hope for the best. I continued to bend down, reaching for the yellow duster. I felt the hem of my dress rising up and up, making me more and more excited with every inch. I stretched right down – much further than I would normally, just to pick up a duster. And as my fingers grasped it I was confident that my stocking-tops must surely be showing. I heard the door click shut, but nothing to indicate how my show was going down.

I stood upright again, casually adjusting my hem as I turned to look behind me, affecting an expression of innocence and nonchalance. The gent was standing with his hand still on the door handle behind him, frozen like a deer in headlights, with his mouth half open.

'Morning, sir,' I said.

'Morning,' he replied vacantly, before heading away down the corridor. My stare followed him. He turned back before going out of sight, just as I had hoped he would, and I gave him a flirty smile and flirty eyes to send him on his way.

Once he had gone I took my pass key and went inside his room.

I was so horny now I was half-wishing that he had forgotten something and would come back in a second. I wanted to sit him on the bed, unzip his trousers, put my foot on his thigh, unroll a stocking from my leg, place it over his penis and wank him into it. With such thoughts in my head, of course I made straight for the bin, to check for used stockings. I was not disappointed, as he had left another, exactly the same as the previous day's, crusted with semen, at the bottom of the receptacle.

I was really horny now, and my hand kept wandering to my crotch, where the tip of my middle finger rubbed on my clitoris for a few seconds. I had to stop myself on three occasions.

I had wasted much of the morning and I had a lot of work to do to catch up, so I thought I would begin with this room. I fetched my trolley from the hall and flew around the room like they do on the adverts, leaving a gleaming trail of cleanliness behind me, and came to a halt in the bathroom. With the work done, my thoughts were coming back to the handsome guest and my hand wandered again as I stared into the cabinet mirror. I was filled with a drive to leave him a 'calling card' and I thought strongly about leaving behind a pair of my knickers for him.

No, it would be too obvious. I decided against it. Perhaps I could rub myself all over his bedclothes before I left? No. That was too tame. Then, without further thought, I suddenly found myself reaching for his toothbrush and easing the handle up my wet pussy. I moaned to myself and sat on the edge of the bath and fucked myself with it. It wasn't easy at first as the handle is rather thin and did not really fill my pussy, but after a readjustment I found my G-spot and was able to get a rhythm on it. I squelched as my pussy got wetter and wetter until eventually the sound of my voice echoed off the tiled walls. I eased the toothbrush out and, without wiping it, put it back in the glass by the sink. Composing myself, I grabbed my things and left.

The next morning was another anxious wait, but it passed more quickly this time. I had done so few rooms the day before that I really could not afford to waste time loitering in the corridor – I had work to catch up on. I worked like a Trojan until around 8.30 a.m., and then raced to his door ready for his emergence. I didn't really have a plan, other than the same plan as the previous morning: pretend to pick up a duster and give him another show.

Even now I have no idea what I was expecting from him. Did I want him to reach out and cop a feel? Was I trying to get asked out on a date? Did I really think it likely that he would strike up some improbable conversation – 'I see you're into stockings, Miss. Me too, I like to wank into one every night. Why don't you come in?' – just like that? I have no idea. I didn't care. I would have responded to anything, whether reserved or outrageous – even if he'd lifted my skirt up and rammed a wet middle finger up my anus I think I would have let him get on with it. I just wanted my attempt at fetish-wavelength communication to be reciprocated in some way.

I started to get wet again as I gave his door handle and number plate an unnecessary polishing. I had been even more daring with the skirt hem this time and I was a little afraid that I might inadvertently treat him to the sight of a gusset. Not that he would complain, I'm sure.

It was Thursday, and I knew that this was my penultimate opportunity to get through to him, for after Friday morning he would not be back again for another month. The feeling of urgency added a more desperate horniness to my pussy that morning. I heard the tell-tale sounds again from behind the door and took my position, bending right over for the duster, as the door opened. I felt more of my flesh being exposed to the air as my hand pawed for the duster on the floor, and I knew that I had given him his money's worth this time. My gusset must have glistened like a sugar-coated plum between the two stocking-tops, so wet and excited was I. I turned to smile at him. Again he took a good look, but again smiled nervously and retreated down the corridor. I bit my lip in frustration at his apparent reticence. Can this man not take a hint?

I slipped inside his room and wondered if he had noticed any strange and alluring aromas while brushing his teeth the night before, or if my toothbrush rogering had gone unnoticed. I walked over to the wastepaper basket and peered inside. The sight was rather different that morning.

The usual black stocking had been replaced by two flesh-coloured, high-sheen nylon stockings – just like the ones I had recently started wearing. I grabbed them for further inspection: both toes were filled with semen, one of them crusted, the other still wet. With the tip of my little finger I tasted his juice, out of curiosity more than anything, and the clear salty cocktail tingled on my tongue.

My discovery was hugely encouraging. Up to now my attempts to get through to this gentleman had been totally fruitless, with no indication or feedback to encourage me. It is not easy for a lady to maintain her pursuit in the face of apparent rejection or indifference – we're not used to that and don't respond well to it as a rule. So the indication that yesterday's stunt had caused my target to go out during the day, purchase hosiery that matched mine completely and then, thinking about me and me alone all the while, given himself a double dose of stocking-wank fantasy, was just the shot in the arm my ego needed. My hand wandered down to my moist lips again and I used the juice to lubricate a little clit rub.

As I masturbated, I fantasised about bursting in on him while he reclined on his bed with a stocking over his rock-hard penis. It felt good and I became more frenzied. I started to imagine milking him into one of my own musty stockings and how excited that would make me. Thinking about fantasies was one thing – always enjoyable and a great way to improve an orgasm – but I find they really take off when they have an element of realism, when you really believe it could happen. This was one of those fantasies: I knew deep down that if I really put my mind to it I could engineer events to that very end, and now that I knew he was thinking about me, I felt brave enough to try it.

I squirted a little as I came that time, leaving a little sprinkle of sugary syrup on the bed-sheet, and as I wiped myself dry I made a plan. It was based on a lot of guesswork. I really didn't know what his routine was. For example, did he come straight in from work and perform his ritual? Or was it his last act before going to sleep? I guessed the former – I knew what these offices were like, with girls strutting around the place in their pencil skirts, tan tights and sling-backs, and I suspected that after a day of being teased he would be popping to ejaculate by 5 p.m.

So it was decided, then: I would hide myself in the room at around 5 p.m. and see what happened. The more I thought about it, the more I felt it was a good idea. If I caught the little closet pervert at his thing he was hardly going to react badly. I tried to imagine if the man I was fantasising about at home in my bed suddenly walked out of my wardrobe wearing a ripped T-shirt and tight jeans; would I scream for the police or wave him on between my legs? It would be weird, I won't deny that, but the latter, I think.

The kinky gent would be the same: there's no way a man, desperately pumping a frustrated load into a stocking, would react badly to the sight of the very woman he was thinking about emerging from the bathroom. Provided I let him know I did not disapprove, it would go well, I knew it.

There was the possibility that he would find me skulking in the bathroom before he began his little game – say, if I was wrong about his routine and waited until later in the evening – but I decided that if that happened I would just pretend to be cleaning. If that didn't wash with him, I'd say I was waiting for him and propose sex. I'm sure that would turn away any anger he might have at the intrusion. Actually, I was not really thinking of shagging him, but if it was the only way to come up with a convincing story for my presence, then I was willing to fall back on it.

All in all, I knew I was on shaky ground, and I was as nervous and anxious as I've ever been, but the logical part of me had me convinced it would go well, one way or another. Tomorrow was Friday, so it had to be that night.

I just turned up in my uniform – they don't check at the tradesmen's entrance whether you're on shift or not. I casually meandered my way to the room, dusting here and picking up a room service order there to blend in, and just before 5 p.m. I slipped inside his room and locked the door behind me.

My plan was to hide in the bathroom when he came home and then see how things went from there. Meantime I sat in the seat next to the television and with the volume extra quiet I passed the time by watching.

After about half an hour of jittery viewing I heard the unmistakable click of the door being opened and in one swift movement I turned off the television with the remote and swept into the bathroom. I stepped into the tub and pulled the shower curtain around me. I heard the bedsprings go as a tired man relaxed after a day's work by throwing himself down on the soft mattress. My one big fear was that he would do what I always do when I get in from somewhere and go to the toilet, but I seemed to be getting lucky. My heart pounded in my mouth, which was feeling incredibly sensitive suddenly, all tingly on the tongue. My legs were like jelly, which did not help matters, as anyone who has tried to stand silently in a bath in high heels will testify. And my pussy, well, it was running like honey.

I now know, now that I'm a bit more familiar with naughtiness and fetishes and the like, that this was the feeling that aficionados crave, this incredible all-over excitement is what drives them all to do the strange things they do. It had driven me to break into a man's room and hide in his bathroom to spy on him wanking, and only now did I have an inkling of why I was doing it: for this feeling.

I tried to listen over the pounding in my ears. After some silence, I heard bedsprings again and the opening of a briefcase. Bravely I stepped out of the bath and peered through the crack in the door to see what was going on.

There he was! Not three yards away from me, reclining on the far end of his bed with his opened briefcase to his right and a new packet of stockings in his hand. I smiled when I saw the bag, which he put back in his case; it was from the shop where I had bought mine.

This was it, then: I was going to see in the flesh the act which had so fascinated me for the past few days. I flushed at the idea that, as he opened the packet, he was probably thinking about the flash of panty I had given him that very morning.

He was very delicate and very tender towards the stockings as he removed them from the packaging, carefully placing them over his leg as he stuffed the cardboard back in his case and closed it. He ran one over his mouth and nose as his free hand rubbed his bulge through his trousers. My moment was coming near now, and my sides ached with the thundering power of my excited heartbeats as I anticipated it. Typically, I wished for a way out of it, but knew deep down that if there was one, I would not take it.

I saw him place his hand inside one of the stockings, feeling his way inside it, experiencing its sensual gift. The weave stretched, just as it does when one is first worn. He reached down to unzip his trousers and I watched with pouted lips as his firm penis sprang forth. This really was it. I wanted my stockings on that penis, not his, so it was now or never. I took a gasping breath, and stepped out into the room.

'Don't stop, please don't stop,' I said to him, my eyes fixed on his penis. I hoped this would calm him and put him at ease.

'Shit!' he exclaimed and tried in vain to zip himself back up again.

'Don't stop,' I said. 'I like it.' I could barely talk, I was so nervous and excited.

His arms fell to his sides and he just stared at me in disbelief. I realised that if this was going to work, I was going to have to take charge. I was learning fast.

'Would you not prefer to do that into one of mine?' I asked, stepping forward to the end of the bed.

He nodded.

'Keep it hard,' I whispered.

He reached for his cock again and slowly pumped it as he regarded me. I gave him a show to enjoy while he did.

I put one foot on to the bed and made a big show of running my index finger down my calf into my shoe, just behind the ankle, to lever it off. It fell to the floor. I slowly pulled back the hem of my uniform, right back, revealing stocking-tops, suspenders and knickers. His eyes widened. I unclipped the clasps from one stocking and slowly, very slowly indeed, rolled it down my thigh, over my knee, down my calf and off the end of my sweet little foot. I kicked off my other shoe, and took two demure strides to his side. He looked up at me and continued to pump his leaky cock. I felt like a million dollars at that moment, so powerful, so beautiful, really and truly appreciated.

I reached down and allowed my stocking to play over his mouth and nose, giving him a scent of the nylon and my pheromones. The mix was intoxicating to him, I think, as I noticed his hand move faster as he inhaled. Finally, I placed the stocking over his cock and slowly worked the folds down until the head of his penis pressed against the toe of the garment. Holding it at the base of his penis I wanked him into it.

He groaned through gritted teeth – I understand the combination of stimuli from the pumping motion and the play of the film of nylon over the penis head is quite intense – and I quickened the pace in response. He threw his head back against the head-board and scrunched the bed-sheet with his hands as the sensations increased.

I felt the throbbing begin, little twitches at first, then three big thumping throbs in the muscles at the base of his penis as he filled the stocking with spunk. His voice was now very high-pitched indeed, and I knew that this had been a good one. Boyfriends had told me that the head of the penis is highly sensitised after orgasm and I deliberately continued to pump, knowing that the nylon would be stimulating him there. He could barely stand it.

I felt so fulfilled I can barely describe it, and all without any physical sexual activity myself. It was at that moment that I first had any understanding of kinky sex.

I picked up my shoes, grabbed the new stocking from him to replace the soiled one, and smiled. 'See you next month,' I whispered, and left him there. A dramatic exit seemed like the thing at the time, but I've always wondered what we might have got up to if I had stayed.

I'm afraid I was dismissed later that month for breaching the dress code, when I took my hem up another inch and accidentally exposed a stocking-top in the lobby, so I'm afraid I never got another chance to find out.

– Kelly Houston, West Sussex, UK

Venus Wears Red Leather Boots

Venus wears red leather boots. Thigh length. Pointed toes. Four-inch stiletto heels. Secured at the front by a crisscross of black leather bootlace. They are as red as Satan's eyes: an angry shade, made glossy with polish and meticulous attention. Wrinkled lightly at the heel and knee, with the tops folded over to expose a glimpse of milky thigh, they are boots that were made to worship. They complete Venus as a goddess.

'Lick my boots,' she demands.

No mortal man could disobey that instruction.

But it can never be as simple as merely licking.

Homage is properly paid by first lowering one's face over the foot. Leather has mysterious properties. The Spanish fashion leather *botas* to hold water and wine. It is a material used for waterproof coats and all manner of protective coverings, yet the toe of a leather boot can never fully contain the scent of the woman inside. Leather comes with its own distinctive fragrance. It is blessed with a rich musk that, at its most subtle, can still be overwhelming. Yet that sweet perfume can never mask the tantalising tang of the feminine foot it houses.

Even though I lower my face to the boot, it is the leather that kisses my lips.

And so many memories can be stirred by a kiss.

This was the toe that pressed against my naked chest. The pressure was intense, bad enough to bruise skin, hard enough to break a rib, severe enough to stop my heart (if Venus had so wished). This was the toe I had licked a thousand times, knowing my tongue was following the trail of a thousand other worshippers and never caring about their inferior praise as I strove to make my efforts superior to those impostors.

This was the toe that kissed my lips.

My arousal is apparent. But unimportant.

Venus has given her instruction and it is my calling to obey.

Continuing to breathe the perfume of her feet ensconced in leather, trailing my lips against the scarlet hide, I kiss the vamp – the bridge of leather that becomes a tongue on the blucher design of these boots – and let my chin polish the toe. Her fragrance is stronger here. Sharp. Potent.

So close to her foot my world has become crimson.

The temptation is to move higher.

If I glance up I know Venus will scowl down at me. From this position I would be able to see beneath her miniskirt. Venus's body is never concealed by underwear. The sight of her would be mine. Shadows would try to conceal her but my gaze is used to raw crimson. Darkness no longer presents a barrier. If I lifted my eyes I could stare at the sleek, silvered slit of her sex. A mere glance and I would know the detail of those hairs that covered her essence. It would be a shocking intimacy that would fulfil my arousal and complete my experience.

But Venus has not told me to admire her.

Venus has told me to lick her boots.

And I obey this command.

My lips move from the vamp to the inner counter. I am sufficiently belligerent to force my head between her ankles, urging her to spread her legs apart. As I approach the heel – still taking in her scent, quietly mumbling gratitude for this honour – I close my eyes for fear my gaze might inadvertently trail upwards.

The heel evokes the strongest memories.

While Venus has tortured me with the toe of her boot, there aren't words to explain the degradation she has imposed with this heel. I've sucked on all four inches, as though I were a sexual submissive gobbling a master's erection. That memory makes me shrivel with shame. Venus has used this heel to stamp on my penis, flattening it against a hardwood floor while I shrieked with agony and begged her to stop. The stiletto has tattooed dimples on my bare buttocks and crudely penetrated my behind. Its sharp edge has scored red welts down my back from the shoulders to the rectum. This is the heel that exerted an exquisite pressure against my scrotum, while Venus giggled at my pitiful howls of anguish.

I kiss the heel with heartfelt gratitude.

Adulation.

My arousal is close to unbearable. It remains unimportant.

Moving my face back to the tongue, pressing kisses between the black-edged diamonds made by the crisscross pattern of the bootlace, I begin to work my way upward.

Boots are the embodiment of all that is sexual.

In my mind I let the words associated with the footwear trickle through my thoughts. *Vamp, dressing, lace, collar; shaft, girth, tongue; leather, buckle, calfskin; welt; upper, lasting; pinking, piping; foxing, pitch. Lift!* Every word belonging to the boots flows like pornographic poetry. What others dismiss as mere footwear I know is symbolic of all that is sexual.

My fingers cup that hatefully beloved heel.

My other hand circles the back of her calf. It is tempting to caress the taut hide but her instructions did not bestow that privilege. My hand simply holds and I can only wish it were allowed to caress.

I remain on my knees but I have been forced to inch closer. My exposed penis rubs against the toe of her boot. The shaft is hard and the foreskin has peeled back. My scrotum rests against the toe. The purple glans at the end of my length trails a line of silver over the vamp.

Venus notices.

She gently lifts her foot.

Pressing down she catches the end of my erection beneath the toe.

The pain is as sharp as a dagger.

Her foot rolls from side to side, as though she is practicing pronation and supination. My erection refuses to subside. This defiance encourages her to tread more forcefully. Knowing she will not heed my pleas if I beg her to desist, I ignore the suffering and press my penultimate kisses against her knee.

The leather is stretched here. It is as taut as the flesh of an erection, or the swollen skin on an excited areola. The scents of the boot and her foot have become indiscernible. More potent fragrances from beneath her skirt overpower the musk of leather. My nose brushes against the overturned topline. When I deliver my kisses to the rim, I know I will be touching the bare flesh of her thighs. The thought and the pain bring me close to ejaculation.

When Venus snatches her foot away, the relief is so immense I fear I have ejaculated. 'Now do the other one,' she demands. She kicks me backwards to punctuate the instruction. The pain is sharp, unarousing, but makes my ardour perversely stronger. 'You've licked the left one. Now lick the right.'

I pull myself from the floor, apologising for no fathomable reason. I promise I will do as she requests and lower my face over the toe of her right boot. My breathing is rapid. The urge to climax is intolerable. But the need to pay homage to this boot is far more important.

'Lick them well,' Venus cries. 'Worship me as I deserve.'

I stiffen and prepare to disobey her last instruction.

Venus is a goddess.

Venus is worthy of any man's veneration.

But I'm worshipping her boots.

– *M. Walsh, Preston, UK*

Flashing for Fun

'I dare you to!' taunted my friend Pam.

'Only if you do it too!' I giggled.

Pam had been my best friend since we first met in high school four years earlier. She was a tall, thin and uniquely pretty blonde with a penchant for the naughty – in my parents' words, a bad influence. We were actually opposites in every sense: I am a petite brunette, with a curvier figure and more traditional good looks, and like to dress in more feminine and provocative clothing, while she plays down her beauty with more quirky ensembles.

We were spending a weekend at her mother's house up north and were going a little stir crazy; boredom sets in quick in the boonies. We had spent many days there in the past and would fill the time with swimming or with her family, but a whole weekend seemed never-ending.

Feeling restless, we decided to play a game of truth or dare to pass the time. She dared me to flash my tits at the next car that drove past the porch. I agreed only because it was such a rarity for anyone to drive past her mom's place. Then, to my surprise, we noticed a beat-up old Suburban coming up the road. If I had been with anyone else, I would never have even considered doing such a thing, but I had always been envious of Pam's lack of inhibition and wanted so much to be like her. We got our hands ready to pull up our tiny T-shirts, she whistled to get the attention of the two men in the front seats, and we flashed our young and perky breasts. The truck came to a quick stop. My heart was racing – it was a mix of exhilaration at doing something so left-field and fear that they were going to complain to Pam's mom and tell her what we had done. The town was a small one and full of very close-knit religious folk, and word travels fast in a place like that.

'You gals like to play?' the slightly older passenger asked. His skin was tanned and weathered and his hair lightened from the sun.

'Yes sir!' Pam exclaimed, rushing towards the two men, who appeared to be construction workers, judging from their great tans and unkempt clothing.

'What are you doing?' I asked as I hesitantly followed.

As I came closer, I got a better look at the two men, who were obviously older than we were – definitely not college boys! Despite being a bit rough around the edges, they were nice-looking, but again, we hadn't seen anyone at all since being up there, let alone guys. They were holding up cans of beer as Pam leaned into the passenger-side window. 'I'm Pam, and this is Gina . . . got any more of that?' she said flirtily, pointing at the beer.

'Hmm. Got a couple of party girls here, do we?' he asked with a grin. 'Maybe you two would like to go for a ride somewhere nice and have a drink? It's a really nice day . . .' He smiled and his friend nodded in agreement.

Before I could get a word in, Pam opened the door. 'Let's go!' she said, grabbing my hand.

We drove a few minutes before stopping by the riverside park where Pam and I had spent a few afternoons suntanning before college. We learned along the way that the driver was Paul and the very talkative passenger was Robbie. They worked as landscapers for the city and had finished their shift early. They were also, as we'd guessed, in their mid-thirties, and looked at least that up close.

It was too sunny to sit outside for long, so we all made our way into the back of the truck where we sat on a couple of old tarps and blankets drinking beer.

Pam seemed completely at ease in the company of these two grubby strangers, but I felt uneasy; they seemed nice enough, but I'm sure they thought we must be sluts or something, considering how we met. After a couple of beers, I began to feel more relaxed. Paul was telling jokes, and there was something kind of sweet about him and the way his eyes seemed to almost twinkle when he would laugh – or maybe it was just the beer.

'Maybe we can see those nice titties of yours again,' slurred Robbie, the more rugged-looking of the two.

'Uh, I don't think so,' I replied quickly. Should have known that what we did would come up!

'We were playing truth or dare when you guys rolled by, but if you really wanna see them . . .' Pam leaned in, clearly making her claim on Robbie. Then she sat up and slipped off her T-shirt, leaving her bare breasts inches from their faces.

'Pam!' I shouted, horrified at what she had done.

'Come on, Gina! Your turn!' she said, laughing and lifting my T-shirt up over my head.

I tried to push her hands away and struggled to keep my T-shirt down, which just seemed to get them going even more. As the fabric tore away from my skin, I could feel my face flush with embarrassment and unexpected excitement as my nipples hardened into two tiny peaks while they all stared. The two men hooted and howled in their state of intoxication and arousal. Maybe it was their encouragement that kept me from struggling further and allowed me the nerve to just sit there in front of them topless.

'Mmm. Beautiful,' Robbie moaned as he reached over to Pam, ran his hand along her breast and squeezed her nipple. To my surprise, instead of stopping him, she just sat back and watched as he tweaked her nipples with his grubby fingers. Though shocked, I was getting excited watching the two of them as he groped her and then finally leaned in and began making out with her, never taking his hands from her little tits.

I took a gulp of my beer and glanced over at Paul, who had inched his way closer to me and my rock-hard nipples. I could feel my pussy beginning to tingle and I tried to reason with myself why I should do like my friend. Finally Paul said, 'Come on, hon. If you're showin' me your titties, you must be up for some fun too,' his words slurring, making him seem almost dirty.

I don't know what had come over me – he wasn't my type at all – but when he leaned in and crammed his tongue down my throat I didn't try to stop him.

I was getting wet as I let him kiss me and grope my bare breasts. His beer-drenched kisses began at my mouth and inched downwards to my neck. It felt so good. I looked over at Pam and couldn't believe it: she was on her back with her shorts off and Robbie naked on top of her. He had one of her tits in his mouth and I could see she was loving it.

I had only ever been with one guy before, and had always been very guarded when it came to sex, but watching Robbie as he began fucking my friend right next to me got me so hot that my clit ached. He was already dripping with sweat, and every hard thrust into her caused drops of sweat to fall on her naked body. He was fucking her so hard I was surprised that she seemed to be enjoying it so much. I couldn't help but stare as his chubby cock shoved its way into her little cunt. She was so tiny compared to him, but was taking it like a champ.

My eyes were still on them when Paul's mouth made its way down to my chest, sucking hard on my nipples. He proceeded to take off my shorts and at first I hesitated, but another glance at Pam getting fucked was all I needed to change my mind. I yanked at his shorts, pulling them down quickly and exposing his swollen, purple head. His cock was definitely the biggest I had seen.

'You like to play, huh? You are a dirty girl, aren't ya!' Robbie grunted as he pumped in and out of Pam, now from behind. I was hornier than ever watching my childhood friend take it doggie-style.

I lay back and spread my legs for Paul, revealing my hot juicy cunt and my clit, so swollen that it stuck out. He seemed giddy with excitement as he stared at my pussy, dipping his fingers in and feeling the wet. Just his fingers felt so good, but, I knew his huge cock would feel even better. He was pumping his fingers in and out of me, watching intently, when I grabbed his hand and stopped him. 'Fuck me!' I begged. 'Please!', pulling him closer.

'You are a horny little thing! I'll fuck you, but first you'll suck my cock!' he said, grabbing hold of his dick with his dirty hands.

I had never had a cock in my mouth before, but I wanted his bad. He lay on top of me, his balls hitting my chin as he stuffed his cock into my mouth, almost causing me to gag. I got the hang of it quickly and slid my mouth up and down his stiff shaft, sometimes stopping to lick the head. I could hear Pam and

Robbie's moans as they came and it made me hotter. Paul was pumping in and out of my wide-open mouth, really fucking my face, when I felt someone rubbing my clit. I knew it wasn't Paul, but I didn't care. I spread my legs, pushing my dripping cunt towards what I assumed was Robbie's hand. Paul's cock started to tremble in my mouth and I thought he was about to come when he pulled out. It was then that I got a glimpse of Pam – grinning as she played with my cunt. I couldn't believe it was her. But it didn't matter at that point, it just felt too good.

Robbie was cheering on in the background as Pam moved away from my glistening slit to make room for Paul and his throbbing cock. He plunged into my hole, deep and fast, pumping in and out of me like mad. I went lightheaded for a second as his cock tore into me, filling me like I had never been before.

'Fuck her, Paul! Fuck her!' Robbie chanted, with Pam looking on, her nipples still hard.

And fuck me he did. He raised my legs up into the air and slammed into me so hard that the sound of his balls slapping against my ass echoed in the back of the old truck. 'Oooh, I need to come so bad!' I cried. And before I knew it, Pam reached over and began rubbing my clit again while Paul's dick flew in and out of me. My whole body convulsed as she stroked me to the most intense climax ever.

I could feel my juices dripping out of my pussy and down my ass and she kept rubbing my clit, almost as if to rub all the come right out of me. Paul's cock began to shake again, and with a quick movement he pulled it out of me and spewed his hot load all over my belly and some even on to Pam's face. It turned me on so much that I leaned over to her and slowly licked the jism off her cheek. I think they were all in disbelief as even I was; this was all so unlike me. My tongue inched slowly towards her lips and I began licking them softly. She squirmed and let out a pleasurable sigh. I had never imagined that kissing a girl could feel so good. There was an 'Oh yeah!' from one of the guys as Pam and I began to feel each other's tits.

Her small breasts felt amazing between my fingers as I squeezed and rubbed them, wanting to savour every inch. I don't know what had happened to me – I was insatiable. I had just had the best orgasm possible, but was ready again for another.

Taking charge for a change, I guided her on to her back, barely letting go of her sweet lips and beautiful breasts. I couldn't help but smile as I started covering her body with kisses, tracing downwards over her stomach and then finally down to her pink fold. I had never seen a pussy that close up and had never thought that I would want to, but as I inched my face closer, taking in its sweet scent, all I could think of was how badly I wanted to taste it. It was still wet and swollen from her romp with Robbie as I began to play with it. My finger ran slowly over her clit, and then back around her hole, lingering there to tease her just for a second. The guys were in heaven as they watched me push my forefinger into her waiting pussy. 'Mmm . . .' I could hear Pam moaning softly, spreading her legs for me.

My clit was hard and my cunt hungry again as I got down to give her what she wanted. I placed my lips on her dewy mound and began with delicate kisses, gradually progressing to licks and finally parting her lips and tongue-fucking her. She cried out in ecstasy as my tongue pushed in and out of her hole. I could still taste Robbie's come in her as I sucked up all that her hot cunt had to offer, at the same time fingering her and driving her wild.

Her body writhed and her thighs were closing around my face and I could see it was becoming unbearable for her. 'Mmm ... we do everything together – coming should be no different!' she exclaimed.

I glanced at her, and she summoned me to give her my cunt, but I was enjoying eating out my first pussy far too much to stop, so, I swung my naked body round and over her, resting my horny little cunt on her face. She wasted no time and began eating away. I loved the feeling of her tongue slipping around between my pussy lips. I could feel her nose pressing against my ass as I squirmed, trying to position myself for another orgasm. Getting back down to eat her out caused quite a stir among the two practical strangers and they began to moan louder at the sight of two young friends enjoying a sixty-nine.

I held her chubby little lips open and licked her clit hard and fast. Within moments she began to quiver and yelp, her mouth still hidden between my thighs. Her cunt filled with her juices as she came hard and I drank up every bit. I continued to ride her face, pushing my clit hard against her mouth. Despite being in a state of afterglow from the orgasm I had just given her, my little friend continued to work hard, not even stopping for a second. She took my clit between her lips and sucked almost to the point of sweet pain and that was all I could take; my cunt exploded as I rode her face, crying out loud in pleasure.

She lapped up every bit of my cum as I had hers, until I collapsed on top of her and just lay there, revelling in the feeling and, for a moment, even forgetting about the men. When we snapped out of our sexy trance-like state, we began to giggle uncontrollably – who'd have ever thought that we would have sex with two strangers, let alone each other! When we were finally able to pull ourselves together, we thanked the guys for the hot time and left, not accepting their offer of a ride home.

It was dark as we walked the familiar route back to her mom's place, giddy from our afternoon adventure. We had shared so many great times during our friendship already, but this was by far the best. Smirking wickedly, Pam said, 'Gee, guess we've got somethin' new to do the next time we're bored!'

I patted her sweet little ass in agreement as we entered her mom's house for the night.

– V. F. Toronto, Canada

Stella

I'm something of a confidante where I live. If you stuck a pin in the map to find the centre, you'd find me. Hotel Stella. My home and my business, we're right on the crossroads. Everyone has to pass by, or come in, at some point in the day. Or night.

Some say I'm like the woman in *Chocolat*, who just appeared one day and opened a shop. She tickled everyone's fancy, didn't she? They all circled round at first, typical backwater types, all suspicious, then they came flocking. Because she was like a magnet. She made everything right, just by showing the screwed-up locals how to tuck into something sweet.

I look a little like her, too. Dark hair, dark eyes, too much hair, all from my Italian mother. Not what you'd normally find around here, but even in a sleepy English village by the sea people expect gourmet hospitality, so I give them what they want.

In the film she was too girlie, too Hollywood slim. People like their *chocolatiers* to look as if they love the stuff, for goodness' sake. Live on it. To look like they lick the spatula in secret, catching every oozing glossy drop, just as they'd lick a good hard cock. Shocked, are you? But anything to do with food, especially sweet food, is sexy. Why do you think they ran those Flake adverts for so long? Everyone remembers the blank-faced bimbo giving head to that candy stick.

You open your mouth, there's your tongue, you put chocolate or cake or strawberries in, you lick, salivate, taste, swallow – and you know how popular girls are who swallow.

And I bet that character wouldn't have a clue what to do with a Mars Bar other than deep-fry it. You wouldn't find her baring her breasts, opening her legs out on the cliffs, not even for Johnny Depp.

But just imagine her maybe ten years on, with a bigger bosom and better legs, and you've got me. I won't tell you exactly what age. Just that there's always a whole new generation to satisfy, because unlike her I haven't buggered off at the end of the fairy tale. I'm not going anywhere. People have to eat, don't they? I do a wicked cream tea and my chef will rustle up any pasta or steak or dessert you desire. People have to drink. My bar is famed for its log fire in the winter, big white umbrellas on the seaward terrace in the summer.

They have to sleep, don't they? I've got rooms. In the holiday season I'm packed to the rafters. They get the exposed beams, the four-posters, the chintz. Everything you'd want from a hotel off the beaten track.

It's humming in high season, and in the last few years it's been youngsters flocking here. To the area, not just to me. Word of mouth? I'm sure of it. Boys, mostly. They come for the surf, and then the word spreads. They come to get stoned. They come to get away from their parents.

Oh, and they come to get laid.

I've never been maternal, not got kids of my own, but I love them young. I love just watching them. Especially when they're sprouting, you know. Cocks of the walk, or so they think. And what cocks! Permanently hard at that age. Permanently ready. And permanently grateful.

God, the mothers round here would kill me if they knew. After all, they're my friends. The things they've confided over the years! I know things about some of the relationships around here would make your hair curl – or your legs cross.

But when these boys are grown it's not mummy's business any more. They're not kids any more, coming by after school for a Coke and one of my sticky doughnuts.

And the mothers of all those surfers, miles away in London or wherever, will see my picture-book website and all the thatched cottages and sparkling waves and they'll assume that nobody could possibly be led astray at Hotel Stella.

When I first came here I thought the same thing. I didn't have time for fun. I worked to make this a perfect home from home, cosy on the outside, clockwork precision behind the scenes. Just like me, in fact.

Finally, last summer, I got there. I handed over the cooking. Employed a manager, even a housekeeper. Could cook or pull pints or choose pillows or arrange flowers, take holidays, make nice with the guests. Do nothing, or do whatever I wanted.

And so came the day when I caught young Scottish Stuart sniffing my knickers.

It was one of those astonishing hot afternoons that are normal in Amalfi, where my family comes from, but wipe this country out.

Everyone had disappeared. The only things moving were the insects in the grass. The sea was fuzzy, the horizon wobbling with heat.

The housekeeper was in town and while the place was deserted I was prowling. I like to do that. I like to come out of my flat if I'm bored and survey my little domain. Do some cleaning, water the flowers, rearrange the furniture.

I thought everyone had gone to their rooms, or their campsites, or down to the beach, after I closed the bar. But someone was still hanging around in my front courtyard. A tall boy I'd seen earlier. He was arguing with his girlfriend. To me she looked like jailbait. Cute enough, pink crop top with Playboy logo, frayed denim pussy pelmet, blonde hair piled messily up on her head, spindly brown legs. But a round, child's face made ugly by a frown, and sulky big lips. Arms crossed, puffing on a fag, pissed off.

I leant on the reception desk, undid a couple of buttons on my old silk blouse. Sweat was collecting in my armpits and I swiped at them with my damp duster. All that did was make me dusty, still too hot, and smelling of laundry and furniture polish.

'Oh, sorry. Didn't know anyone was there. Some water?'

The boy was staggering in. He was momentarily dazzled by the darkness inside. I was dazzled by the silhouette framed by the open doors. Broad shoulders, torso tapering to a bony waist. And such a deep voice.

He started blundering about in my lobby. He nearly knocked over the huge vase of lilies I'd just placed there.

'Not going home for siesta?' I asked.

I waited for him to focus on me. I looked like a peasant. Bare feet, skirt hoiked up my thighs ready for mopping, hair twisted into a scarlet shawl.

'She wanted to talk.'

'Fight, you mean.' I swayed towards him, aware that my shirt was falling open. Aware of the sweat shining on my skin. 'I don't allow that here, young man.'

'Stuart. That's my name.' He was breathing hard and staring straight at my breasts. Men love breasts, don't they? Obvious, I know, but true. Analyse it all you like, but that's what they want. Big breasts, like mine. Did you read that stupid survey asking enlightened young businessmen what they looked for in a woman? There was the predictable stuff about success, sense of humour, equality – but at the end they all added: 'And great tits.'

Who needs surveys when you've got a young stud right here just pumped full of testosterone? That day I was wearing a dark-pink lace bra, the balconette style that offers your breasts like puddings on a plate. I've always taken care over my underwear, even when I'm slumming it. My aunts, who lived in Rome, taught me that. So he was getting the full works. My Scottish boy was ogling some mighty fine lingerie.

He wore just a loose pair of board shorts, bright blue with splashy flowers, slung low round his hips. Suddenly he took hold of the waistband and yanked them up. But not quick enough to hide the outline of his prick, which was trying to stand straight up in his pants.

'So. May I have some water?'

I came closer, thinking he'd dodge away. But he didn't. I swiped a hand across his forehead. His striped blond hair was wet, as if he'd been swimming. I whistled.

'It's too hot for fighting, Stuart. This time of day is no good for walking or talking. You should be lying very still somewhere.'

His face was so smooth, golden spikes of stubble pushing through his chin and cheeks. He licked his lips, which were dry. 'Where, exactly? She's gone storming off, the fucking –'

He closed his eyes. I smiled, knowing how devastating this all was for him. He was so beautiful and tragic, like one of those Greek heroes cursed by an evil goddess.

'I'll get that drink.'

I led him towards one of the armchairs by the dead fireplace, pushed him down into it. He sprawled backwards, eyes shut again. I went into the bar, splashed water into a tumbler. I thought he'd fallen asleep when I came back, because he didn't move.

I sat on the arm of the chair, bent low to study him. His eyelashes were long and curved, but unlike his piggy-faced girlfriend his bones were finely chiselled. This was the summer he became a man.

I held the glass and listened to his breathing for a moment. As for me, I was puffing, as if I'd been running. I pressed the tumbler between my breasts and gasped as the coldness brought my skin up in goose bumps. I rubbed the glass over one breast, under my shirt, and it was so good. I couldn't help shuddering. My nipples tightened, shrank into stark points. I pulled my shirt right open, moved the glass slowly over first one nipple, then the other, poking up under my bra. I pinned my tongue between my teeth to be silent. One shirt button popped off, and rolled across the tiled floor.

As I leant across him to see where it had gone Stuart's eyes opened. His nose and mouth were level with my nipples. I held still. He swallowed, his Adam's apple jumping in his throat. I could feel his breath on my skin. He could easily shove me away, do a runner if he wanted. He glanced up, beautiful blue eyes smouldering. Quarter boy just then, three-quarters man.

Oh, God, now what? What do I do? There was one thing I wanted him to do, more than anything. In the hot silence, the hot breathing silence, I couldn't remember when I'd last wanted something so badly.

But shit! How professional was this? I was practically falling across his knee. He was a customer, sitting in the lobby of my hotel asking for a drink of water. Anyone could walk in and see me thrusting my breasts in his face, urging him to look, undress me, take, suck –

That silly girl could flounce back in. The housekeeper back from shopping. Chef. With his cold box full of meat from the market and his crates from the local vineyard.

All this was racing through my head, but I didn't, couldn't move. Very slowly Stuart lifted his hand, pushed my blouse to one side, and exposed my left breast, bulging in wisps of lace. He wasn't blinking; it was as if he was in a trance. Then he touched. My heart was juddering, making my breast shake. Surely he could see it too? My lips parted, such ferocious desire stinging me, but still I kept silent.

He moved his hand over the lace, and over my skin, squeezing a little. He had to spread his fingers to get proper hold. He must have been waiting for me to slap him. But I didn't want to slap him. I wanted to scoop my breasts out for him, push them naked into his beautiful face, smother him with them, feel his firm young mouth nibbling and searching and closing round my burning nipples.

But I didn't do any of that. Can you believe that? Not quite. Not then.

I laid my hand over his to show him I liked it, this was fine, he could do it some more if he liked. He liked. He pressed harder. Then I licked my finger, ran it down the crack of my cleavage. Held it there, near his hand, to show him while he squeezed. Then I dragged my finger over to the breast he wasn't touching, stroked the soft swell, then let it trail down into the lacy cup of my bra. I circled my nipple for a moment, then I pushed the bra down to expose my breast and to show him how my finger, wet from my mouth, was teasing my nipple.

He followed the movement as if I was a hypnotist. So now his finger was inside my bra, too. He circled that nipple, then hooked his thumb over the bra to push it down. Now they were both out. I looked down at them. Both breasts, all bare. So proud. Jutting like a much younger woman's. Not drooping. Nipples stiff as nuts to show him my excitement.

I stopped. He stopped. All we could hear was the ticking of the clock in the lobby, and outside the insects in the grass.

I rubbed the cold glass across both breasts again. I pushed myself nearer, so close, nearly touching his mouth. I rubbed the glass across the nipples, making them sing, stand out. He stared. I wanted him to suck them.

But instead, dear God, I pulled my blouse closed and moved my body gently away.

'I'll have that water now,' he croaked, after a pause. He took the glass. His hand, the one that had been touching my breast, was shaking.

I was hot with shame. I got up, but not too fast. Just went to pick up the duster I'd left on the reception desk. Behind me I could hear the water glugging down his throat.

'Do you want to talk about it?' I asked, my voice all high. I knew what that meant. I was all turned on with nowhere to go. 'I mean, about your fight?'

He wiped his mouth, held the empty glass out for me to take. Surely he wanted to get away now? 'She won't leave me alone. They're like limpets, girls, after you've fucked them.'

We both listened to the rude word reverberating in the air. It was the perfect word.

'This was meant to be a boys-only holiday. Then she pitches up yesterday as a surprise and so I have to turf my mates out of my room and now she won't leave me alone and she thinks I don't want to sleep with her again because I fancy her friend.'

I was hardly listening. I was just looking at his mouth. 'And do you?'

'What? Want to sleep with her again?'

The air felt even hotter than before. He was sitting up straighter in the chair, staring at me. I could barely stand, I wanted him so much.

'No. Fancy her friend.'

'Maybe. But mostly I just want the pair of them to piss off back to London.'

'You don't want to sleep with her? She's very pretty.'

He shrugged. Typical teenager. So I walked quickly behind the desk and turned my back to unlock the door to my private staircase.

'She's a pain in the arse. Women should be motherly, and sexy, like you.'

I started to blush like a schoolgirl. I didn't look over at him. I just laughed, much too loudly, nonchalantly checked the switchboard for messages, and opened the door to my private quarters.

'I could put you across my knee for saying things like that, *bambino*.'

'I'd much rather take you across mine.'

He was walking away now. These boy-men have a way of pulling the rug out from under you. One minute all helpless babies, the next coming on to you like a practised Lothario. The way he said it, his voice so low and rough and rude, was all the more thrilling for being so unexpected.

'Glad I was some help, Stuart.' God, I sounded prim. But what else could I do? Run across, drag him up to my lair, show him how sexy, motherly women like to do it? Oh, yes, please.

But he was going back out into the blazing heat. He stretched his arms lazily above his head. He wanted to get back to his mates. And I needed to get the hell upstairs to take a very cold shower.

People always remark on how small my flat is, just a couple of airy rooms looking out over the sea, but I don't need much space. I have the run of the hotel, after all.

'And the run of the tastier male guests, I bet,' Stuart remarked later, 'with your appetite for a stiff one.'

But I'm getting ahead of myself.

I ripped my skirt and knickers off as soon as I got inside, and kicked the door shut. My hotel is immaculate, but you'd think a slut lived in my quarters. And you'd be right.

Anyway, I couldn't get that boy out of my mind. I was creaming for him. My breasts were aching to be sucked, nipples hardening just thinking about it. I flung myself into the bathroom, reached into the shower to turn it on. It was hotter up here than anywhere else in the hotel.

I stared at myself in the mirror. Peasant? I looked like a gypsy. My hair had fallen round my face. Thank God I never went anywhere without my lipstick. It matched my scarlet scarf. I started humming a theme from *Carmen*, twiddled my fingers under the cold jets of water.

Air conditioning. I wanted a nice cool flat to wander back into. So I came out of the bathroom, swooping and flicking my red scarf around my naked haunches as I danced like a diva.

And that's when I caught him. My Scottish Stuart with his ribbed bare torso and his baggy shorts and his bony feet, standing in the middle of the room, holding my discarded knickers up to his nose and closing his eyes to sniff.

I stopped in my tracks, trying not to scream with excitement to see him there.

He rubbed his face into the gusset, and then he looked up.

'Pussy juice and pee,' he said, mouth splitting into a grin. 'Horny combination, Madam Stella.'

'Christ, you're the horny combination around here.' I needed to get hold of him, immediately. My knees started to knock as I tottered towards him, swishing the scarf about to cover myself. 'How did you get in?'

'Followed you. Door unlocked.' He sat down on my old sagging sofa and tugged the scarf, and me, towards him. 'I wanted to see what it was like.'

'See what what was like?'

'Your place.' His hands were on my buttocks and he pulled me again. 'You.'

Somewhere along the line the tables had turned. Suddenly he was in charge. What had I done to him downstairs?

'I was going to take a shower, Stuart. I'm sweating like a pig.'

He stopped me moving. 'No. Don't shower. You smell great.'

I was standing, he was sitting. I looked down at him, cupped my hands round his head. His skull was finely shaped, narrow, the bleached hair all messed up into random points.

'You want pussy juice and pee?'

He shrugged. 'I want you dirty.' He nuzzled his face closer. 'I want to see what you taste like.'

'Hey! Who said I was dirty?'

I held him away from me in mock horror.

'OK. Sweaty, then. But it's so horny. She – Patsy – she's always washing.'

A woman of my age, and there I was, at the mention of the sulky moppet, hearing her name, there I was steaming with jealousy. I yanked him hard against me, burying the bone of his nose roughly into my muff. He didn't resist. I could smell myself now, the sharp scent of arousal. His nose pushed into the soft give of my pussy lips, and I parted my legs a little. His head tilted, then I saw his long red tongue snaking out, felt the tip of it touch me. I held my breath. I didn't want to scare him off, I suppose. Pretending I hadn't felt it. How could I not feel it? It was like he was striking a match on my clit.

But I'd done too good a job of pretending, because he hesitated, and I panicked.

'I thought so. You don't like – you know what you want.' I wrenched myself away from him, turning my back to wrap the red scarf round as much of me as I could cover. 'You shouldn't be here, Stuart. Go after her. Patsy. Let me get on with my work.'

He grabbed me again. He was surprisingly strong. I like that. I like them young, but I don't like wimps. He spun me round. He may have been strong, but he hadn't reckoned how heavy I was as I tumbled about, all clumsy on top of him.

I landed on him, skin on skin, the scarlet scarf flying off me like discarded foliage, and now I could feel all the warmth of his gorgeous young body spread out under me but mostly the battering of his heart and the urgent hardening of his cock inside his shorts.

I tried to land on my hands and catch my own weight, let it and him sink into the sagging sofa rather than knock my elbows or knuckles into his face and ruin the moment, but then it was my breasts that fell forwards out of my blouse, bouncing against his face. I languished for a moment, then raised myself up to look at him.

He was mine. All mine. My prize on a hot, lazy day. A feast of young manhood laid out on my sofa, comfortable as you like, not going anywhere, any doubts knocked out of the ring by the force of his lust. I was rubbing myself against him without knowing it, hungry to get him inside me. Everything about him was irresistible, his eyes, his full lips, the little bubbles of saliva at the corners like a kid impatient to tell you something, the pulse pummelling in his tanned neck.

And that big young cock barging up in his shorts. Any minute now, at a time I was going to choose, I was going to have a damn good look at it. I was going to touch it, hold it. I wouldn't be able to help myself sliding on to it –

It makes me horny even now, can you tell? Remembering the sight of him, the smell, the heat burning off him. The sheer bloody newness of him. I wasn't his first, but I was going to make sure he'd never forget me.

'Oh my God, those tits, good enough to eat. Oh God, I want to fuck you.'

I held myself out of his reach. 'Have you seen breasts like this before, Stuart? Do you get turned on, seeing breasts in magazines?'

He nodded.

'How about real ones, nice big ones?' I cupped my breasts, massaged them together, licking my lips like a porn star. 'Has a woman like me invited you, begged you, to touch?'

He shook his head, watching me fondle myself.

'Different, aren't they?' I whispered. I was chancing it, but I knew he was hooked. His Patsy and her

189

friends would have cute white baps. Not even a handful each. More like the Californian babes he wanked over. Flat nipples folding into shell pink cones when she ran into the sea or let Stuart touch them.

'Dark, aren't they?' I said softly, leaning nearer, dangling them over him, juicy like fruit. My nipples are the colour of cappuccino. You can't ignore them, if you know what I mean, especially if they're attached to a horny Italian mama. He couldn't take his eyes off them. They were inches from his mouth and lips and tongue and teeth. He was a boy, a very young man. I wanted to cradle him. I wanted him to suck me. The tension was so electric you could hear it.

My nipples went hard. Nothing I could do. I arched my back to thrust them towards him, and they stretched into long teats. The more excited I get, the darker they are. How blatant they were, how demanding. How impossible it was to pretend they were designed for anything other than a man's lips, anything other than pure, selfish pleasure.

His Adam's apple jumped again. His hands came up from my hips, where they'd tried to steady me in falling, slid up my ribcage until they reached the outward curve of my breasts. I breathed in tiny gasps as his hands slid closer. I could hardly breathe. The room was so hot. His body was straining up under me. My nipples were chocolate-brown now, each one the size of the tip of his little finger.

'Let me,' he groaned. I rubbed one across his mouth. I felt as if I'd been punched in the stomach. His face flooded with red heat. Did he flush like that when his little floozie opened her Bo-Peep blouse for him? Did he get rushes of excitement when she gave him a flash? Or a full-on erection like the one banging out of his shorts right now?

I let my nipples hover just above his mouth, torturing us both. I ran my hand over the front of his shorts, felt the rigid outline. I reached inside to cup his warm balls.

Outside, the village was roasting gently in the heat and so were we.

'OK. Now, where were we?'

I picked up one of his hands, placed it on one swollen breast. My nipple spiked up, poking against his palm. I went limp as his fingers closed round. I spread my knees to lower myself, my pussy opening, my breasts jumping into his face with each heart beat.

I had a boy here with the body of a god, just waiting for me to show him.

My stomach tightened as he played with both breasts, moulded them, squeezed until I could bear it no longer. I lay on him, smothering him, so that he had no choice but to nuzzle in between, press each breast against each of his hot cheeks. I took one breast, so heavy with wanting, and rubbed the taut nipple against his mouth again and again, like coaxing a lamb to suckle. Just the sight of me holding it, offering it to him, made me want to come. I jammed myself against his legs, but my pussy was twitching with frustration.

His tongue flicked out and I angled the tit right into his mouth. His lips nibbled up, tongue lapping round, then, aah, at last, he drew the burning bud in, pulling hard, and began to suck. Sparks pricked at me. I looked down at his bleached blond head, salt water dried in granules and flecked white across his cheek bones, and I closed my eyes as the sensation nearly finished me off.

He brought the other breast up and turned his head this way and that, lapping and sucking, snuffling through his nose to breathe, groaning, biting and

191

kneading harder and harder as if he owned my breasts now. It wasn't enough for one breast to be suckled, they both had to be. That's what really does it for me. Suck one, pinch the other until they're both singing with pain. So the harder I pushed into his face, the quicker he learned, the harder he bit and chewed and pinched, and the sharper my pleasure.

'Fuck me,' a woman howled, and it was me.

'Show me,' he grunted back.

I wanted him to go on and on sucking and biting my tits, but I wanted his stiff cock in my cunt, too, feel it ramming up me. But somehow I still kept it slow. I wanted him to remember every single move.

I planted my knees on either side of his thighs so I was straddling him, still crushing his head between my tits, still making him suck. I wanted him to suck and suck forever, except that soon I would come against his leg like some randy bitch and what sort of education would that be?

As my nipples burned and throbbed, I rolled his shorts down. He raised his hips so obligingly to let me undress him, I wanted to weep with victory. And then I wanted to shriek with it when his penis came thumping out from the rough tangle of blond curls, pulsating golden brown like the rest of him, its surface smooth like velvet.

God, anyone would think I'd never seen one before. It thumped all heavy and warm into my hand and its owner bit me, hard, so that I screamed out loud.

'You're a quick learner,' I breathed, pulling away, letting his head follow me, still nibbling and biting. 'So here's a little reward.'

He fell back, mouth all wet with licking, and I slithered down till I reached his dick, standing there like a beacon. The tip was already beading. If I wasn't careful he'd come like a bloody train, before I wanted him to. But I wanted to show him. So I took that boy's cock right into my mouth until the knob knocked the back of my throat.

His buttocks clenched as I sucked on him, holding his balls and biting my way down his shaft and sucking the sweet length of it. He started bucking. I wanted him to think he'd died and gone to heaven. Any minute now I was going to heaven, too. As I sucked, I rubbed my aching tits and wet pussy up and down his legs, the sofa cushion, any surface I could reach. I was like a randy mare scratching against a fence. He pulled at my hair. I was in danger of wasting this golden moment by coming all over his shins. My pussy was convulsing frantically now, leaving a slick of juice on his legs.

I gave his dick one last, long suck, pulling it and nipping it, then I let it slide out past my teeth. Next time I'd swallow. I clambered back on top of him, my toy, my boy, as he started to rise up on his elbows, seeking my tits again. I tilted myself over him.

'See how beautiful it is,' I crooned at him, showing him his cock in my fingers, wet with my licking. 'See how well it's going to fit.'

I aimed the tip of his cock towards my bush, let it rest just there, but it nudged into my wet lips and I shuddered as each inch went in. The tension was ecstasy, but I was going wild here, especially when he grabbed my breasts and started sucking on them again. I couldn't hold on to it for much longer, and I let the boy's knob slide up inside, all the way to the hilt. It was tempting to ram it, but once it was right in I forced myself away again.

'Let me fuck you!'

We'd both lost the power of language. Fuck was the only word we knew.

I moaned in answer, tossed my head back, and down I went on to him again and this time he was with me, pulling at my hips so that he was in as I ground down.

He filled me. God, there were years of wild lovemaking ahead for him and any woman lucky enough to get near him. I pressed myself over him, let him bite and fondle, saw the blood rushing in his face as we started to jerk and rock together, I was really riding him, really wanted to hurt us both, wanted him to suck me while we did it, suck me so hard it would make me scream with pain, knowing my willing pupil would do whatever the hell I told him.

I got hornier as I thought how I'd be even more brazen next time, I'd stay dressed, make him find his way in through my clothes, that's so sexy, so I'd make him sit at a table or on my balcony and I'd open my blouse a button at a time, show him my tits, take one out of my bra for him, hold his head against it, make him open his mouth and take it in because I'd seen how he wanted it, make my pupil taste and suck and do it as long as possible, all night if need be.

I was riding him now, jacking up the rhythm, rocketing up and down his cock. I needed to ease the urge to come, but of course that only made it worse and more intense and I was getting tighter and tighter, holding him like a vice and his cock was getting even harder, harder with each frantic thrust, ramming right up inside.

'Tell me I'm the best you ever had,' he suddenly shouted, grabbing my hips and lifting me off him. 'Want to hear you say it.'

'Enough talking now. Shut up and fuck me, big boy.'

His nails dug into me. 'Tell me, you bitch on heat, tell me I'm the best.'

I stared at him. He was trying so hard, succeeding, to be the hard man. His cock was enormous now, so swollen, standing away from his flat stomach and aiming like a battering ram at my wet, waiting cunt.

'You're the best, baby,' I said. And I meant it. I'd never had someone so young, so gorgeous, so well hung, so strong, so eager, so fresh, so obedient, all in one package.

Then I flicked myself so that his cock slipped up inside again. He couldn't stop me. I was trapping him inside me and going at him so that we were welded together, releasing him so that he could draw back, trapping him again as he tensed his buttocks and thrust inside, throwing his head back, pulling my tits with his teeth, thrusting faster now and faster, hearing my own crackling gasps of pleasure as I came and he saw me coming and he laughed with disbelief as he tensed and hardened to bursting point and shot it up me.

I slumped forwards on to his chest and listened to the drumming of his heart. I thought my head was empty, but I heard myself say, 'I wish that was your first time. I wish I'd been the one to break you.'

His laugh rumbled under my ear. 'Make me, you mean.'

I stretched my arms and legs and got off him. I went to sit on the chair opposite, my legs sluttishly apart. I started to do up the buttons of my blouse, just a couple of them.

'Wait till the boys hear about this.'

He sat up, pulled on his shorts, cracked his knuckles. The boys. He was just a boy, here for the summer. For God's sake, what was I thinking?

'You're going to brag? Boast to them back at camp how you had the old dear from the pub? Do you think they'll look at me different?'

He shrugged as only youngsters can. He went over to the mirror and raked his hair with his fingers.

'The old dear can take it!' he said. 'Respect! Think how the takings will go up when they hear how horny she is!'

'Do you think they'll want a piece of me, then?' I said, getting up. I picked up my knickers, flicked them over his shoulder, round in front of his nose. I saw his long eyelashes curve down as he breathed in. 'Oh, I do hope so!'

He turned his head and looked at me. 'I was only joking, Stella – don't be pissed off.'

I kissed him, licking inside his mouth and very gently putting my hand on his dick. Not quite subsided. They can do it over and over, these randy lads.

'Do I look pissed off? Quite the reverse, honey.'

I tossed the knickers over a chair and pulled a silky dress over my head.

'I'd better go, then –'

'When you do bring them back to the pub, tell them they can come up here after hours.'

He stopped at the door. Oh, this was almost the best bit, because I knew it would happen. I knew there was going to be so much more of this. Such a baby, he couldn't tell if I was serious or not.

'If they want to have a laugh, I'll show them how. You know I can do that, Stuart, don't you?'

I licked my finger, just as I did downstairs, held my dress open, and rubbed my nipple. He bit his lips.

'I bet I can put it into words better than you can. Wouldn't they like to hear how you touched me, touched me right there in reception, how you followed me up here, how you sucked my tits just like I wanted it?'

'Sounds pretty horny, doesn't it?' He swallowed hard.

I nodded, working my fingers, pinching my nipples as desire tore at me again. 'But how about instead of telling them, you and I just show them? They can come up here, they're always welcome.'

'All of them?'

I started to stroke both breasts now, spreading my legs over the arm of the sofa. 'Sure. How I was on top, they can all come and watch how we did it, and then they can all take turns. I could have two latched on at a time, one on each tit –'

My pussy clenched furiously at that thought. It's doing it now as I'm telling you.

'– like puppies they can suck, and then you can fuck me, or they can do it, your mates, one by one, all together, from behind, underneath. Baby, I don't give a shit how they do it, so long as they can go on all night.'

He didn't need telling twice. He was right there, this time throwing me down on the sofa, scrabbling to get his cock out, pinning my arms over my head, biting at my breasts. He was the big man now.

Did Stuart brag? Did anyone guess? All I can say is we had an unforgettable summer. Everyone else is still talking to me. And they're still flocking for food and drink and Stella's legendary hospitality.

There goes the little brass bell. The season's hotting up. So I have to go down to reception. Come with me, if you like. Let's see who's checking in today.

– Stella, South Hampshire, UK

Slap Happy

This is really quite kinky, and first I want to make a few things clear. I had an idyllic childhood entirely free of both physical and mental abuse, and my only regret is that it did not last for ever. My father was the rector of a parish that shall remain nameless but is in Leicestershire, and both he and my mother took a progressive stance on bringing up children. None of us were ever punished, and if we did anything wrong it was simply explained to us that such behaviour was not acceptable. By and large it worked. I say that because I hate it when people assume that because of the way I am sexually it means I had an abusive childhood. My childhood was perhaps more perfect than anybody has a right to ask.

It was Miss Melton who corrupted me. When I say corrupted you have to understand what I mean. The reality is that I was her willing partner, although perhaps rather naïve, but I like to think of her as having corrupted me. It turns me on.

She used to spank me.

I was nineteen when it started, which means more years ago than I care to remember. I was setting out on the path my parents had chosen for me, as an accomplished young lady who would eventually find a suitable husband, perhaps even another man of the cloth. It never occurred to me to question this, nor is there any reason I should have done. Life was pleasant if rather austere by today's standards, and having spent some time as a hospital visitor for men convalescing after being wounded in the war I knew that I was very lucky indeed.

Part of becoming accomplished was learning to draw and paint. Art had been an important part of my curriculum during school and I wanted to continue my studies. Miss Melton had recently moved into the village from London and was offering tuition in painting, drawing, music and I think other things as well. Looking back, she was the most obvious butch I have ever come across, but at the time I was completely unaware of this, as were my parents.

At first everything was completely innocent. She was a good teacher, if a trifle severe at times and impatient with incompetence or what she saw as stupidity. I was technically quite good, and she was full of praise for me save that she felt I lacked freedom of expression. This was a great thing for her, and she would often go off whatever topic we were supposed to be studying to expound her beliefs. They were an odd mixture of the Bohemian and the frankly fascist, but as she was so much older than me, and I had always been taught to respect my elders, and so obviously intelligent and well educated, I simply accepted what she told me.

In fact I was fascinated. The world she had belonged to, London in the 20s and 30s, seemed impossibly glamorous to me, and the freedom of expression about which she spoke so eloquently had soon become my dearest goal. Which is how I ended up naked but for a scrap of gossamer in the long attic room she used as a studio, posing for a series of nude studies in the delicate, somewhat impressionist style she favoured.

200

Looking back, she might have, and probably did, set the whole thing up for my seduction, or if not that, at least the seduction of some unwitting young girl. The house she had bought was further down the same lane on which the church and rectory stood, and quite isolated. She had had the attic converted into a long, open room with big windows to the north, set at an angle. Nobody could look in, and nobody could disturb her by accident, while if somebody did knock, her work and the distance from attic to front door provided the perfect excuse for taking her time to answer.

She had no real difficulty in talking me out of my clothes, but she was quite skilled at it, making it seem quite casual and yet managing to imply that for me to object would not only be bad manners but suggest that I lacked artistic temperament and even soul. Nor did I have any inhibition about going nude, at least not in front of another woman, after spending years sharing a room with two sisters. I also had the most fearful crush on her. So off came my clothes.

I can't remember how long it was before she made her next move, but I do remember that I had become so used to being naked in her presence that I would frequently stay that way for the entire afternoon, often without even the light gossamer drape she frequently liked me to pose with. She never even touched me, save to make the occasional adjustment to my position, until the day she decided she wanted some colour in my cheeks.

Now, her motive seems utterly transparent, but I swear it never even occurred to me that she might have anything other than artistic considerations in mind. Even today I don't know if she did my face first because she enjoyed it or to take the attention away from my bottom. Either way she did it, telling me she wanted a pose as if I was recovering from exertion, draped face-down on a couch with one hand hanging down to the floor. I still have the painting, and it is quite obviously of a young girl in a sulk after a nude spanking, but back then no such idea entered my head.

She even told me what she was going to do, and apologised because it would sting. I assured her that I didn't mind and stood very bravely while she slapped me three or four times across the face, leaving my cheeks a rosy pink. Then she did my bottom, bending to see as she slapped both my cheeks all over, and quite hard, pausing occasionally to admire my rear view and to ask my opinion as I looked back over my shoulder to watch my little pink cheeks in a mirror.

I didn't even realise I'd been spanked, but that was what she'd done to me, no question, and I couldn't help but react. How odd it felt, to have a warm bottom as I lay on that couch and she first sketched, then painted. Occasionally she would break off to slap me gently around the face or plant a few more firm swats on my bare bottom cheeks. My only bad emotion was embarrassment at what was happening to me, because every time she smacked my cheeks I found myself wanting to stick my bottom up, which seemed the oddest thing to want to do. I was aching for a touch between my thighs and very wet. I was horrified by the thought of her knowing, but I did at least realise that it meant I was in love with her, which made me happy.

She took her time, no doubt thoroughly enjoying my compliance and her power over me, perhaps not wanting to lose her excuse to spank me, or perhaps just waiting until I was ripe for her touch. If so, she waited a lot longer than she need have done, because by the time she was done I just couldn't resist. She came to the couch, sat down and placed a hand on my warm bottom, rubbing me as she asked in the most soothing of voices how I felt.

Heavens knows what I answered, probably just a sob, but I remember her reply, how she told me she knew what I needed even as her hand slipped between my thighs. I let her do it. Not that I understood it as wrong, not from another woman, and I was in no state to resist. It seemed as if she knew my deepest secrets and was kindly helping to assuage my feelings. When she told me to open my legs a little I did it, allowing her to see exactly what she was doing as she manipulated me from behind.

She must have done it many, many times before, to judge by the skill with which she manipulated me, and it felt so good I'm sure you'll excuse me if my description is a bit graphic. Her hand cupped my vulva, with two finger pressed between my lips to do amazing things to me, while her palm was over my vagina and her thumb up between my cheeks, rubbing my anus. She could probably see that I was a virgin, although I could hardly have been anything else, and I remember thinking how kind she was not to spoil me, goodness knows why. I also assumed that the reason she was playing with my anus was that she couldn't enter me.

How naïve I was. That was her special thing, to have me so open to her, so relaxed and so aroused that I'd let her see my anus, and rub it. Later, when there was no longer any pretence between us, she used to like to wipe my bottom for me after going to the toilet, because she wanted to feel that I was utterly dependent on her and that I had no secrets whatsoever, that nothing was too intimate.

She made me come, for the first time in my life, holding me by my sex and stroking my bottom with me nude and exposed in front of her while she was fully dressed. I had a vague understanding that to touch between my legs was pleasurable, but not that it was wrong, because that sort of thing was simply never spoken about. That may seem odd these days, but my mother never even explained to me about menstruation, a task that was left to a nurse.

Never had I imagined the ecstasy of which my body was capable, feelings so wonderful, and so full of joy as well as pleasure. I felt it was an expression of my love for Miss Melton, and it would never have occurred to me to wonder if something so nice could be wrong.

She left it at that, explaining to me that it was something private between us and that I shouldn't tell anybody. You may say that was wrong of her, but remember that I was a grown woman, if young, and, more importantly, I felt it was right. I was singing as I walked back down the lane, hardly the reaction you would expect of a girl who's been abused, and for the rest of the week all I could think about was what had happened that glorious afternoon.

I was going to her once a week at the time, but we would frequently meet in the village, and of course at church on Sundays. She behaved exactly as she had always done, but it was an effort for me not to be over-eager, and had the idea of her seducing me not been quite so unthinkable I'm sure people would have been suspicious. It was after church that Sunday when she suggested I might like to spend the afternoon painting with her down by the river, at once so friendly and so formal that even I wasn't sure if she had an ulterior motive.

She did. We walked well beyond where we might normally have stopped, on the pretext that there was a particular view she wanted to capture. There was:

me, first naked in the river and then sunning myself on the grass as I dried off, both scenes she captured for what she called our private collection, as well as a few more innocent studies. I was terrified we'd be caught, despite enjoying myself immensely, but I would have let her touch me if she'd wanted to. She held back, doubtless considering it too risky outdoors, but as we walked back past her house she suggested a cup of tea, and there, in her kitchen, it was explained gently to me that I should return the favour of last week. I agreed, she took me upstairs to her bedroom, and for the first time I was put down on my knees to lick another woman's sex.

Again, you might think I would have been resentful, but I was in love and wanted only to please her. It made me excited too, and I ended up cuddled into her arms as she masturbated me for the second time. She often did me that way, providing a feeling of such blissful abandon it still makes me feel weak to think about it, just to be held, so lovingly, and kissed and stroked while she manipulated my sex, sometimes with a finger in my anus, sometimes with my rear cheeks rosy with spanking, sometimes both.

She loved to spank me, and she loved to play with my anus. As the weeks passed she grew bolder in response to my acceptance of her desires. I think it was on the third or fourth occasion that she first put me down across her knee, simply telling me she wanted me with blushing cheeks that afternoon and that I should bend over her lap. It never even occurred to me to resist or to object. I was still dressed, and experienced for the first time the pleasure of having my clothes disarranged for a smacking. I vividly remember the sensation of having my dress lifted and my knickers turned down to leave me with my bottom bare and available. It was bliss.

That is how a girl ought to be spanked, held gently across a woman's knee, her bottom bare and her head hung down, completely available and completely accepting. She used to spend ages over me like that, never seeming to tire of smacking my cheeks, until I was rosy and gasping, when her hand would go between my thighs to bring me to ecstasy. That first time, and many after, I undressed after my spanking and spent the entire afternoon nude, not only while I was acting as her model, but while she taught me and even for ordinary activities, which in its way was as pleasurable as anything else. Later, I would be put on my knees.

It was never punishment for me, always erotic and an affirmation of how our relationship worked, with her very firmly in charge. She never once undressed, and so as not to lose her dignity she would remove her knickers before I went down on my knees to her, and then put her skirt over my head. I never even saw her bare breasts, while I myself would often be crawling playfully at her feet, stark naked, or even standing with my bottom stuck out to be wiped, or my cheeks held open to have my anus inspected.

Our relationship lasted almost a year, during which time I became deeply addicted to being nude and being spanked. We never argued, because I never disobeyed, nor did I want to, while she was always considerate of my needs if for one reason or another it was not a good time. I loved her with an intensity I have never experienced since, at least, not in the sense of sexual love.

I like to think that had I been forced to declare my love for her I would have done so, and accepted the consequences. It never came to that. She accepted a place teaching art at a girls' school in Sussex and moved south. I promised to follow, although it was hardly a realistic suggestion, but she gently but firmly declined. To this day I wonder if she wanted to spare me the troubles of life as an avowed lesbian, or if in reality I was simply one of a long string of seduced girls.

With Miss Melton gone from the village my life felt empty, but there were several people keen to fill it: three young men, all keen to win my affection. I suppose they must have been around all the time, but while I was with her they barely seemed to register, and I know now that I was considered aloof, even frigid. If only they had known.

My father's living was comfortable enough, I suppose, but with seven children he was understandably keen to see some of us married off, my mother even more so. Those men whose attentions were considered suitable were encouraged, in a very proper way, and that autumn I was married to the Hon. Philip Lancelles.

I never loved Philip, nor any man, but I did do my duty by him, as I had been brought up to. I believed in duty, you see, and still do, for all that the idea seems to have fallen by the wayside these days. He was kind too, and it would be uncharitable to claim that my life was in any way unpleasant, or even that I disliked having sex with him. He was rather clumsy about it, and I don't think it ever occurred to him that I might enjoy anything other than the feel of his penis in my body. Still it was pleasurable enough, but as he drove into me, supported on his elbows as gentlemen should be, I would be thinking of lazy summer days spent naked in Miss Melton's attic studio and the smack of her hand on my bare bottom. That is also what I would come over, once he was asleep, with my teeth pressed hard on my lips to stop myself crying out her name and my fingers busy between my thighs, just as hers had been so often.

Our marriage lasted twenty-three years, almost to the day, and might have lasted longer. I was still prepared to be his wife, despite a string of affairs, if only to keep up our position in society, but when he finally left to live with another woman there seemed little point in maintaining the pretence. We finally divorced, leaving me comfortably off, and with my children grown up I was living alone for the first time in my life.

I moved back to Leicestershire to be near my now elderly parents, and for four years lived a quiet and respectable life, busying myself with whatever came to hand. Then Caroline came to me.

The first day I met her, queuing at the village shop, I recognised something of myself in her, so much so that it made me ache for my early years, which now seemed impossibly distant in time.

She was the daughter of a wealthy couple who had recently moved to the village. Both her parents worked in the City of London, with high salaries and long hours, so that she was left largely to her own devices. I found myself drawn to her, both as a kindred spirit and physically, because just watching her face, which was always full of expression, or the way her sturdy young bottom moved in the tight blue jeans she liked to wear, made me yearn to touch her, all of her.

I told myself very firmly that my feelings were inappropriate and she could not possibly be interested in me anyway, and yet she was the same age I had been when I started my affair with Miss Melton. She enjoyed my company, coming over to my house ever more frequently. How I yearned to touch her, or at the very least to see her naked; better still, to spank her pretty bottom the way Miss Melton had spanked me so long before, then to put her gently to her knees and teach her how to lick a woman's sex.

Why I had changed from wishing to be spanked to wishing to do the spanking I do not know. Perhaps there is something natural in it, that a young woman should take and an older woman give. I do not know, only that I ached to take Caroline across my knee and warm her bottom for her, perhaps as Miss Melton had once ached for me.

As the weeks passed and her visits grew ever more frequent and longer I considered every possible angle, from the possibility that she needed me as badly as I needed her to the thought that I must be going mad to even imagine such a thing. Then came the fateful moment, on the first proper summer's day of the year. I was still washing up after breakfast when Caroline arrived, as beautiful as ever in a light summer dress and sunglasses. She was carrying a bag, and asked if she might sunbathe in my garden as her own was overlooked and there was apparently a boy next door who would peep at her.

With a flush of guilt for my own reaction to her body, no doubt little different from his, I said she could and continued washing up. Despite feeling a little uneasy, as I always did in her presence, it never occurred to me for a moment that she would be doing anything other than lying on a towel in her bathing costume, so you may imagine my feelings when I went out into the garden to find her stark naked.

The picture she presented is fixed in my mind as if it were a photograph held in my hand. She had spread out a tartan rug, and lay on it face down. She had been reading a book, but had turned to look at me as I came out, her large brown eyes peeping out over the top of her sunglasses, her mouth just a trifle open, her dark golden hair framing her face. With one elbow propping her up, her rather full breasts were prominent, while her back made an elegant curve from beneath the tangle of her hair to the rise of her firm, cheeky bottom. She had one leg cocked up, with her flip-flop dangling from between her toes.

I recognised the pose, and I knew she did. What could I do?

I made a joke of it, allowing myself a way out if she reacted badly, putting on a voice of mock severity as I told her that in my day any girl who did what she was doing would have been spanked. Her answer was a giggle, and with that it was as if the world outside no longer matter. I went to kneel down beside her, where I gave her a single, light swat across her bottom. Just to feel the warmth of her skin and see the way her cheeks bounced to my touch set my heart hammering – and as for what she said . . .

She asked if I was really going to spank her. There was a little doubt in her voice, or perhaps it was more like curiosity, and surprise, and excitement. I told her I was, still playing at giving her discipline as I began to smack her bottom, very gently, a cheek at a time. She didn't mind, lying still and silent, the only sound the pat of my hand on her skin. I kept thinking she'd tell me to stop, that I'd gone far enough, but she didn't, even as her skin began to go pink, and when she did speak it was to tell me that it felt rather nice, and to do it a bit harder.

I could never have been so bold, not to say that, and certainly not to start sticking my bottom up the way she began to after a little while. Her cheeks were now nicely flushed and although nothing was said we both clearly knew I was no longer merely playing with her but spanking her for our mutual pleasure. She had begun to moan softly and with her bottom raised and her legs a little apart I could see and smell her excitement.

I thought of how Miss Melton had so often brought me to orgasm. There was a last moment of doubt, and then I slipped my hand between her legs. She let me masturbate her, just as Miss Melton had done to me, with a spanked bottom and a kindly hand between the thighs. I even used my thumb to tickle her anus, which she accepted with a breathless, open pleasure.

When Caroline had come I took her by the hand and led her up to my bedroom. Not a word was spoken, our understanding now complete, until we were laughing together on my bed, in each other's arms, as she told me how nice the spanking had felt. I told her it should really be done across the knee and she let me, giggling and pretending to pout as I smacked her bare bottom up to a rosy glow before letting her come between my thighs on the bed and lick me to ecstasy with her hot red bottom pushed up to let me see.

I learnt afterwards that, like me, she had never been spanked before, and that it had come as a complete but delightful surprise. That was where the resemblance ended, for she was no innocent and had had several lovers, both male and female, although her favourite fantasy had always been to be the lover of an older, assertive woman. I was that woman. Apparently she had not simply guessed that I was a lesbian at heart, but it was commonly assumed.

She might not have been spanked before, but she took to it like a duck to water. Her need had been to take a playful, irresponsible role in contrast to my calm and mature one, and she found the idea that she might be punished for her misdemeanours delightful. In that she differed from me, because my spankings had never been anything but physical pleasure and a reinforcement of my position in the relationship. Caroline always liked to think of it as a punishment, if only an imaginary one.

Compared with how I'd been at her age, she was delightfully uninhibited, not merely accepting my ministrations but often instigating her own punishments and also sex, while she took a delightful and unashamed pleasure in her body. That first week she came to me every day, most of which we spent in bed or in the garden. Like me, she loved to go nude, and to be nude while I was dressed. I found I couldn't quite live up to Miss Melton's standards and, while it felt good to be dressed while Caroline was naked or had her bottom bare, I had no compunction about being naked in bed with her, or even spanking her while we were both in the nude.

That week was bliss, and the ones after it, as we explored each other's bodies and each other's minds and grew ever more intimate. I well recall the first time she kissed my anus, in the garden after a particularly hard spanking. She had been teasing me all morning, as she always did when she wanted to play, being deliberately cheeky and challenging me to catch her and punish her. She was in a plaid skirt, very short, and when I failed to rise to the bait she began to taunt me, first flashing the seat of her knickers and then her bare bottom.

I finally managed to catch her by pretending I was looking elsewhere and grabbing her by the wrist when she came too close. She was all giggles and mock protests as I led her to the cast-iron bench outside my French windows, where I sat down and took her across my knee. Only then did she go quiet, enjoying her exposure as I lifted her skirt and took down her knickers, leaving her delightful bottom bare for a punishment spanking.

She loved to be told she was a naughty girl while she was spanked, and generally chided for her misbehaviour, which I did as I punished her. Soon she was lifting her bottom, now a lovely glowing pink, then asking for more, which she got. I spanked her really hard, always prepared to stop and very much aware of the note of her cries and gasps but greatly enjoying the pain of her reaction.

I had already decided that she would make me come first, to pay her back for all the teasing. Once her bottom was a rosy pink ball and she was shivering with pleasure I stopped and told her to stand up. She obeyed, pouting a little because she had expected to be masturbated, and went straight to her knees, kneeling on the lawn with her eyes looking up at me and her mouth a little open in anticipation of having to lick.

Had she not been quite so eager I would have taken my pleasure of her as I usually did, but she always brought out the cruel streak in me, and I wanted to make her feelings as strong as possible. So I turned around, pushed down my slacks and the knickers beneath and told her to kiss my bottom. What I expected was a kiss on each cheek. What I got was a moment of hesitation, then her hands around my thighs, her face pressed firmly between my cheeks and her puckered lips pressed tight to my anus in a long, deliberate kiss.

She was immediately giggling with embarrassment for what she had done, but it had felt wonderful, both physically and to have such a beautiful girl do something so intimate and so servile. I told her to do it again, and this time there was no hesitation. Now sure I didn't mind, her lips stayed pressed to my anus and after a moment I felt her tongue poke out, uncertain at first, then eager as she began to lick deep.

I had never imagined anything could have felt so nice and so wonderfully assertive at the same time, to have Caroline lick my bottom and to push her tongue as deep in up my anus as it would go, not just willingly, but gladly. So gladly, in fact, that she had begun to masturbate, her fingers busy down her half-lowered knickers as she licked my anus, and reaching orgasm in just moments. I told her she'd be spanked again for coming first, or tried to, because no sooner had she finished her own orgasm than she was bending me forward to allow herself to get her mouth to my sex from behind. She licked me like that, with her nose wriggling against my anus, to bring me to an orgasm in which every facet of my sexual desires came together: a girl, newly spanked, playing with my bottom hole.

Curiously, although I did not realise it at the time, Caroline bending me forward to allow herself to bring me to orgasm was the first gesture of a different and unsuspected part of her sexuality. I should have guessed, I suppose, from my own life experience, but I did not.

After that day there was no act too intimate for us. We spent our days together, too enrapt with each other even to pay proper attention to the possibility of scandal, with Caroline often naked from the moment she dropped her clothes in my hall until when she picked them up again before leaving. She didn't seem to care, which allowed me plenty of ways to find excuses for punishing her, such as applying a rolled-up newspaper to her bare bottom fifty times for walking into the living room nude and risking being seen from the road.

We never were caught, although more by luck than anything else, and no doubt some of the gossips in the village were at least suspicious, but my habit of punishing Caroline for taking risks was my undoing in a different way. Many a time I had spanked her for going near windows from which there was a risk of being seen, but I thought nothing of it when I myself opened the bedroom curtains while in just my underwear.

Caroline was lying on the bed, nude, her bottom red from a spanking session with my hairbrush and her face set in a blissful smile from the orgasm I had given her. She was facing me, one hand resting on her chin, and she said it so calmly, pointing out that I had just committed what for her would have been a spankable offence.

At first I tried to resist, feigning indignation and then trying to make a joke of it, but she persisted, pointing out that it was only fair, which I could hardly deny. Finally I agreed, with my heart pounding and a sick feeling in my stomach. She bounced up and into a sitting position, her voice full of laughter but also authority as she ordered me to go across her knee. And over I went, to have my knickers pulled down and my bare bottom spanked, just as Miss Melton had done so many times; and just like Miss Melton, once Caroline was done with me and I was glowing behind and too aroused to resist, she slipped a hand down between my thighs and masturbated me to orgasm.

I did try to exert my authority again, but it was hopeless. Allowing myself to be spanked by her had destroyed something of my mystique in her eyes, although none of her feelings for me. For myself, I had always enjoyed the sense of being put in my place when Miss Melton used to spank me, and of putting Caroline in hers when it was the other way around, but the feelings that came from being spanked by a woman more than twenty years my junior were stronger by far.

We continued our relationship as before, at first with both of us giving and taking, but the balance of power shifted until it was always me who got her bottom smacked, always me who went nude about the house, and me who would go down on my knees with a bare red bottom and lick her to ecstasy. I even returned that gloriously servile favour she had given to me, with her laughing and taunting me as she stood with her jeans and knickers down in my kitchen, her bottom cheeks held wide to expose the tight knot of her anus, which I kissed.

From the moment my lips puckered up against Caroline's anal ring I was completely her slave. I would have done anything she asked, and frequently did, including numerous spankings, being made to touch my toes while a garden cane was applied across my bottom, being sent into the wood to pick a birch with which I was then beaten, and having her sit on my face with my tongue well up her bottom hole as she masturbated.

Sadly nothing ever seems to last for me, and when Caroline's parents moved away our relationship began to fade and eventually died. That might seem rather a sad end to my confession, except that my relationship gave me new confidence, which in turn has led to several encounters since, although nothing permanent. And, whatever may or may not happen, I will always have those memories, first of Miss Melton and having my bottom spanked as a young girl, then of Caroline and spanking her in turn, and lastly of Caroline taking me in hand to teach me the joy of being punished across another woman's knee.

– *Margaret, Leicestershire, UK*

The Summer Ball

The company holds a dance twice a year: once at Christmas and once in the summer. Employee holidays usually mean the Christmas party gets the larger turnout but, for those hungry for promotion, the summer ball is a valuable opportunity to rub shoulders with senior management. That was the only reason I was there.

'Why do we have to come to these damned things?' Tina complained.

'It's an opportunity for social climbing and advancing up the career ladder,' I explained tiredly. I had explained the same thing a dozen times that evening. I know it's not seen as a particularly good way of getting on within a company – sycophancy is never seen as being admirable – but there were always a couple of unexpected promotions each year that could be traced directly back to the summer ball. This year, mainly thanks to Tina's expensive tastes, I was in need of such a promotion so that we could keep the figurative wolf from the door. 'We just need to have a couple of drinks, act friendly to a couple of important people, and then we can go home.'

Her eyes sparkled with an unspoken challenge. If I hadn't found the expression so exciting I would have been infuriated by her obvious lack of respect. Tina is a habitual flirt and I could see from the shine in her eyes that she intended to take me literally when I had said that we needed to be friendly toward a couple of people. I knew I had to say something to tell her to rethink the lurid escapade she was plotting. But there was no chance for me to say a word.

'Harold?'

Thomas Carlton – my current manager's manager – interrupted our conversation before it could continue. He beamed at me, then Tina, and asked how we were enjoying the ball.

Tina didn't allow me the chance to respond. 'Harold isn't asking me to dance,' she complained. 'And I'm getting restless waiting for someone else to make an invitation.'

Thomas shook his head and tut-tutted in my direction. He was always a smartly dressed individual but he seemed to have made an extra effort for the summer ball this year. His tuxedo looked new and resplendent and his round pink face was freshly scrubbed and meticulously shaved. Even with the greying hair at his temples, I had to concede that the man who was twenty years older than me managed to look more impressive than I could ever hope to. When he turned his charm on Tina I was reminded he had a reputation for being something of a lech. There was no way to warn Tina of this before he said to her, 'Perhaps I could escort you to the dance floor?'

Tina slipped from her chair and offered him her hand. Her smile was wide and eager with anticipation. And I was left to watch my wife and my boss step eagerly toward the dance floor.

It's embarrassing to admit it but my dick was suddenly very hard.

The music came from a light jazz band, playing easy-listening sounds that didn't intrude on anyone's conversation. A handful of other couples were already stumbling around the dance floor but Thomas and Tina found a space by squeezing close together. His hand immediately went to her backside. She held him at the waist and shoulder.

I couldn't swallow. My gaze never left them. She was behaving so intimately with Thomas that I didn't think anyone would be able to mistake her outrageous behaviour. Tina had dressed to impress that evening, wearing a skimpy red dress that revealed her shapely legs and far too much cleavage. Each time Thomas glanced down at her I knew his gaze was going straight to the plump mounds of her breasts. Tina's smile, probably unnoticed by Thomas, actively encouraged his interest. When Thomas leant close to her ear, either whispering something or blatantly kissing her, I watched Tina blush, glance in my direction, and then giggle like a schoolgirl. I don't know what he said to her but I knew it had to be something risqué.

I did think of going to the bar, getting myself a drink, or trying to establish other social contacts within the company. That was the real purpose of the summer ball and I knew I ought to be trying to make friends and influence people. And yet, on this occasion, I couldn't tear my gaze from the sight of my wife dancing with Thomas.

She touched his dick.

I gasped, not sure I'd really seen it, but convinced it couldn't have been anything else. She had her left side facing me. Her left hand was on his waist and her right was on his shoulder. I saw the right hand move away from him, disappear from view as it shifted lower, and then go between their bodies. And then, as they separated slightly, I saw my wife's hand stroke the shape of Thomas's erection.

I held my breath. I pressed a hand against the bulge in my trousers and quickly called for a passing waiter. Ordering a bottle of lager I tried to look casual as I watched my wife flirting and intimately touching Thomas Carlton.

He leant close again. Once more I didn't know if he was whispering or kissing her ear. Either would have been exciting enough to make me feel sick. The situation was driving me to the brink of desperation. When the waiter finally brought my bottle of beer I snatched it from him and continued to glower at the dance floor. My erection ached as I watched my wife dance with my boss. Each time he pressed his mouth close to her ear his hand touched the side of her breast. More shocking was the observation that Tina made no attempt to pull away from him.

She smiled and nodded for him, her cheeks now crimson but her eyes shining eagerly. Easing herself from his embrace she stepped off the dance floor and headed to the toilets. Tina didn't bother sparing a glance in my direction.

Thomas sauntered slowly over to my table and grinned. 'You'll have to forgive me, Harold,' he began. 'But I've forgotten the name of your lovely wife. Can you remind me what she's called before I embarrass myself?'

His arrogance was exasperating. He had danced with her, ogled her cleavage and touched her breasts, *yet he didn't even know her name*. I considered lying, saying she was called Agatha, Gertrude or Sweaty Betty, but that wasn't the way for anyone to get promotion at the summer ball. 'Her name is Tina.'

'She's a charming dancer,' he said with a laugh. 'I hope you don't mind my keeping her on the dance floor a little longer this evening?'

'Not at all,' I said, not sure whether I minded or

not. 'It's good of you take the time to dance with her.'

He laughed and glanced toward the toilets as Tina reappeared. 'It's hardly good of me,' he said moving away from the table to greet her. He had his back to me and was walking back towards my wife as he added, 'I'm happy to dance with any woman who assures me that she swallows.'

The arousal hit me so hard it was like a punch to the stomach. Even if I'd wanted to follow Thomas, and demand that he repeat what he had said and then apologise, I wouldn't have been able to move from my chair. I could only sit and watch as he took Tina's hand and led her back to the centre of the floor.

They made their dance look overtly sexual. I don't know if anyone else was watching and thinking the same thing but I thought it was way over the top. His hands kept slipping to her buttocks and breasts. He stroked her through the fabric of her dress and touched her bare skin above the plunging neckline and beneath the short hem. His caresses were outrageously intimate and, although Tina repeatedly moved his hands away at first, she let them linger a little longer each time they found their way back. After ten minutes of fighting his advances she simply allowed Thomas to touch bare skin as they danced happily together.

When she pressed her face close to his neck, whispering something and then glancing toward the toilets she had just visited, I sensed she had visited that room to do more than just answer a call of nature.

Another shock of hateful excitement slapped me across the face.

My suspicions were confirmed when Thomas backed away from her and extended a hand.

I watched my wife place her curled fist inside his hand and realised she was giving him something. I couldn't imagine what it was and the present would have remained a discreetly exchanged mystery if Thomas had possessed an ability to keep things subtle. Because he almost dropped the gift, and only managed to catch it as it fluttered toward the floor, I was able to see that Tina had given him a pair of silk panties.

They were the ones she had worn for the summer ball.

I groaned. My excitement was so powerful I could have climaxed in my seat. Not only was my wife no longer wearing her panties, she was dancing with another man and handing him her underwear.

Thomas pushed the present into his pocket, briefly looking flustered, with his gaze scanning the room for the nearest exit. I saw him flash a smug grin in my direction, and then I was being ignored again as he tugged Tina away from the dance floor. The pair headed toward the back doors.

I snatched my bottle of beer and followed. I had just watched my wife flirting with Thomas. The man had boasted that Tina promised she would swallow. And I had seen her hand him the panties she had been wearing when she arrived at the summer ball. It wasn't my intention to stop them doing whatever they planned but I had to see what was happening.

Outside, in the dusky glow of late twilight, I wondered where they could have gone. The car park was busy but I heard the sound of a giggle and a car door closing. I guessed they had gone to Thomas's Porsche.

I walked discreetly to his car, trying not to look conspicuous, but desperate to see what they were doing. When I found the bright red vehicle, I dropped to my haunches and approached as quietly as I could manage.

The memory of what I saw inside the car has stayed with me ever since. Thomas had clearly shifted the driver's seat so it was close to being horizontal. He was laid on his back and my wife knelt over him, facing the windscreen. Her dress was hitched up, over her hips, so he had full access to her buttocks, anus and pussy. His tongue was pushed deep into the sopping confines of her sex.

My erection throbbed with the need for release.

I was so aroused the sensation brought with it a physical pain.

Thomas wasn't looking at me. His attention was fixed on my wife's pussy as it pressed over his mouth. I could have stood for hours and watched his tongue slip between the pink folds of her bare flesh and he would never have registered that I was there.

But I wanted to see what Tina was doing for him.

I slipped stealthily to the front of the vehicle and glanced through the windscreen. Tina was inside, grinning at me as she devoured Thomas's long, pink cock. There aren't words to describe how that image has remained with me. Or the effect it inspires. On one hand I'm appalled that my wife could do something so shameless with any other man. On the other hand, I'm so excited I could climax from the mere memory. My beautiful wife's mouth – ripe and freshly painted with lipstick – was wrapped around the obscene girth of Thomas's erection. Her eyes shone with devilish excitement as she moved her head up and down. When she saw me watching she wrapped a fist around his erection, held him steady, and then drew her tongue from the base of his cock to the tip.

I could have exploded as I watched. A part of me wanted to masturbate ferociously at the sight. But I knew that doing something so daring would be more than I could ever manage. All I could do was watch. Tina moved her lips back around Thomas's erection. She sucked until her cheeks dimpled.

And then she winked at me.

That single intimate wink will stay with me forever.

With one hand she gestured for me to go away. I was pained to obey but knew there was no other choice. Tina didn't want me watching and, if I continued to linger in the car park near a Porsche, someone was bound to notice and it would draw unnecessary attention. I grudgingly backed away, struggling to tear my eyes from the sight of Tina's head as it bobbed up and down over Thomas's erection.

I went back to our table and sat alone for half an hour until she finally returned. Her hair was no longer as elegant as it had been when we entered the summer ball but other than that she only looked like a woman who had been doing a little too much dancing. Feigning nonchalance, and simply summoning a waiter to get a fresh drink for Tina, I asked, 'Are you enjoying the summer ball this year?'

She shrugged with such a cool innocence I had difficulty believing this was the same woman who had just sucked another man's cock. 'It's been better than most years,' she admitted. 'I've done like you asked and spent my time being nice to people. I hope it's helped improve the prospects for your career.'

I couldn't think of a thing to say. Tina had made no attempts to hide her behaviour from me but, if I thanked her, it would be tantamount to condoning what she had done. 'So you won't complain about coming to the summer ball in future?' I managed eventually.

Tina didn't respond with words. She simply kissed me. And, when I tasted the flavour of Thomas's come, still slick on her lips, I knew it was all the answer I needed. She wouldn't complain about coming to the next summer ball – and I wouldn't mind taking her.

– Harold Scott, Portsmouth, UK

Sharona

Three years ago I had sex with a woman for the first time. I consider myself gay now, wouldn't touch a man even if he paid me . . . well, maybe if a man paid me a huge amount of money I might agree to give him a handjob. I mean, money is money and I'm not stupid. But I sleep with women exclusively now. That's how I get off, from being with another woman. Both of us naked, touching and fucking each other.

Women's bodies are just so different from men's. Smooth, hairless, all those curves and bumps instead of flat chests and hard bones that stick into you when you're fucking. Now it has to be tits and pussy for me to have a hope of getting off. But three years ago, I wasn't like that. Three years ago, I was strictly men only. You know, if it didn't come with a cock attached, then it wasn't a real fuck.

Is my language too crude? My girlfriend – I call her Pepper, because that's how her pussy tastes, hot and spicy, really sharp on the tongue – she says I swear too much. That I'm like a man.

I prefer to think of it as being honest, not wasting time on the niceties. I'm a Londoner, born in the East End, and people swear all the time there. So it's how I was brought up, calling it cock, pussy, tits, and it's never 'making love', it's fucking. Pepper hates it, she expects me to be all dainty with the way I speak, but I can't help it. So when I tell you how I got to be a lesbian three years ago, how I swopped from men to women in one day and never looked back, I hope you'll forgive the dirty words. Because I don't know how to talk about sex without using them.

One year, I was working for an old lady who had a big house out near Hainault Forest – the posh part, one of those old detached houses with big gardens. She needed someone to run errands and help around the house, and my gran had been one of her best friends back in the 50s, so it wasn't hard to land the job. I lived in one of the spare rooms and had weekends off. I was only just out of school then, so it was great to have a place of my own. Well, a room of my own. And my window looked out over this big garden of hers, all lawns and tall trees, with an old greenhouse and a shed half hidden by a weeping willow.

So the old lady had this gardener. A woman called Harriet, about ten years older than me, who used to come in and do the gardening most weekends. I hardly ever saw her, though, because I was always out partying or seeing my mates at the weekends. Then one Sunday in August when I was broke from the night before and the weather was hot and sunny, I decided to stay home and just hang in the gardens all afternoon. And Harriet was there, weeding one of the flowerbeds right near where I was lying on the lawn.

Harriet was quite well-built, one of these big-boned women with a full arse and big tits, but a neat little waist. Her skin was honey-coloured from the sun and she had thick dark waist-length hair that she always kept curled up under this old green oilskin hat, and she had these big eyes, clever and watchful. And because she was in her late twenties and didn't have any kids, her belly was flat as a table and all the gardening had really pumped up her muscles, especially in her upper arms and thighs. She used to wear these tiny high-legged shorts and halter-tops or T-shirts without a bra, and I could see all the muscles rippling in her arms and chest, and bunching in her thighs whenever she squatted down to do the weeding. I don't mean she was some muscley bodybuilder or looked like a man or anything like that – Harriet was one of the most feminine women I ever met – but you just wouldn't argue with her, because you knew she'd be able to punch you right out.

That Sunday in August, I was feeling a bit horny. I often do at the weekends, like most people, I think. Just lying out in the sun in my bikini, thinking about sex. And there was Harriet right in front of me, bending over with her long honey-coloured legs and her arse pouring out of those tiny shorts and no bra under her T-shirt – I could see her pointy nipples peeping through the material – and I couldn't help staring and getting really turned on by this lush body.

My pussy was getting hotter and wetter, and I wanted to fuck her. But it made me feel weird and off-balance, because she was a girl and I was a girl, and in those days I only fucked men.

Still bent over the flowerbed, a trowel in her hand, Harriet turned round and stared at me. I think maybe I'd started panting or something, like a dog. And she said, straight out, something really practical, like 'You'll get sunstroke lying there all afternoon. Why not come into the shed with me, get out of this heat? I've got some iced tea in a thermos.'

I got up and went into the shed with her, and she was right, it was good to get out of the sun for a while. She showed me where to sit down – there were upturned crates for seats and a rickety old table for potting up flowers – and gave me some of her iced tea. It was delicious and cool and I soon stopped feeling dizzy. But then we were sitting so close together in the dark little shed, and her smooth thigh was pressing against mine, and I just wanted to touch her. It was like an itch, something inside me that I couldn't control, and I knew I'd go mad if I didn't tell her how I felt.

But Harriet must have guessed, because next thing I knew she had her hand on my breast, cupping it through the striped bikini top. 'You don't mind, do you?'

I was a bit shocked, but couldn't believe my luck. So I shook my head and put my hand on her thigh. Right there on her bare thigh below her shorts, bold as anything, as though I had done it hundreds of times.

Her leg was firm and muscular under my fingers, yet her skin felt so soft compared to a man's, it was like touching a piece of velvet. And I stopped feeling uncertain because Harriet seemed to know what she was doing, calmly undoing the string fastening at the front of my bikini and loosening the cups until they fell into her hand.

Unlike me, she probably *had* done this hundreds of times before. I mean, she was in her late twenties then and must have fucked loads of women before she met me. And you could tell, she was so confident in how she moved, the smooth unhurried way she touched me. Like we had all afternoon ... which we did, actually.

'Well,' she said, 'you just shout out if you don't like it and I'll stop. Or you can say you do like it and we'll keep going.'

I watched her in silence as she took off my bikini top, looked at her big dark eyes, her wide-lipped mouth, trying to imagine what it would feel like to kiss her, to lie underneath her. Then my bare breasts were cradled in her hands, and she started to laugh, stroking and squeezing them, leaving little flecks of dried mud all over the white skin there. 'Oops, perhaps I should have washed my hands first. I'm getting your tits all dirty.' My nipples were almost as stiff as hers now. But I wanted us to be closer, to sit naked, chest to chest, so I pulled at her T-shirt and got it over her head. I nuzzled into her body and our breasts jabbed at each other, mine embarrassingly small and girlish with such baby-pink nipples, and hers full and brown-circled and firm with excitement.

She pulled off her oilskin hat and all this hair spilled out, over her bare shoulders and down her back. She lifted one of her big tits towards me, motioning me to suck it. I lowered my head and put my lips round her breast, drawing it into my mouth. I'd never sucked another woman's tit before but I must have been doing something right because Harriet groaned and pressed the other tit into my mouth, wriggling and rubbing herself against me. Which made my pussy so damp I thought I must be leaking through my bikini bottoms

I wanted to get down to business but wasn't sure where to start. 'OK, so how do we . . . I mean, what am I supposed to . . .?'

'We may not have dicks but God gave us ten fingers.' She laughed at my expression. 'You know how to masturbate, don't you?'

'Yes.'

'Then you know how to fuck a woman.'

Harriet showed me how to undo her shorts, then kicked them off. She was only wearing a little thong underneath, see-through lace over her pussy and pale pink strap disappearing up the crack of her arse. She half-turned away and I ran my hands over her buttocks, firm and silky, then bent to kiss her skin there, right along the crack, loving the musky scent of it so close to her arsehole.

We messed about like that for a while, keeping it nice and slow, just playing with each other's bodies. I think Harriet must have realised how new I was to lesbianism and didn't want to scare me off. Though I hate that word now, 'lesbian'. It sounds so hard and political. Being a lesbian just means you love pussy. What's wrong with that?

I remember how weird it felt, touching another woman's pussy for the first time, sucking on her tits like a man. These days it's all I can think about, of course, naughty girls and what's under their clothes. But with Harriet it was like being a virgin all over again. All shaky and embarrassed for those first few minutes. Though it felt right to be kissing another woman too, really natural, like coming home.

It was shady and prickly with heat in that shed with the door shut. I remember the branches of the weeping willow brushing against the tiny side window, turning the light pale green. We were soon sweltering in the heat, eagerly helping each other to strip off the rest of our clothes. She wriggled out of her shorts and I stood up while she pulled down my bikini bottoms, telling me to step out of them.

I was a bit shy – I mean, who wouldn't be? – trying to cover myself with my hands, but Harriet laughed and told me to drop them, saying 'Don't be ashamed of your cunt, darling. That's the sweetest part of yourself.'

If a man had said that to me, it would have sounded like bullshit. But coming out of another woman's mouth, it seemed true. So I lay down on the rickety table, even though it was filthy with soil and old spiders' webs, and let her arrange me on my back with my legs open, knees hanging down over the edge so she could get in real close, right up to my bare pussy. It was like being at the doctor's for an examination except that Harriet was smiling, her fingers walking up my thighs for fun, tickling me because I was bit tense, making me laugh too.

She took down a box from the shelf, marked Plastic Gloves. 'My fingers are dirty, I don't want to give you an infection.' She slipped a white latex glove over one hand, pulling it tight round the wrist with that scary snap of plastic, and said she hoped I was wet enough.

Of course, I was soaking by then, so lubrication was not a problem. She helped me bring my knees up, really opening me up, and slipped one of her fingers inside. It felt good, but I wanted more. So she pushed further inside and felt around until she found what she was looking for, which was my G-spot. My legs jerked in reaction when she found it, my knees trembling. I'd read about the G-spot in magazines but hadn't really believed it existed until that day. My face was suddenly burning hot and I couldn't breathe properly. I thought I was going to die there in that shed. It was like someone tripping a wire and everything exploding, just blowing up inside.

She leant over me and we kissed while I enjoyed that first orgasm. Real French kissing, deep tonguing. The rickety old table was wobbling all over the place, and I still can't believe it didn't collapse under our weight. Then she started kissing my throat, my breasts, my belly. She kept asking if it felt good but I couldn't speak.

My knees were still drawn up and she bent her head between them, put her mouth right on my clitoris, and started to suck. I was moaning and begging her to stop, but I didn't mean it. You know how you get when the sensation is so strong you don't think you can bear another minute? But you can, of course, it just feels so good that you're delirious with pleasure. Well, that's what it was like with Harriet. So there I was, groaning and fidgeting, and the dirty old table juddering all over the place. Then she wriggled her hand up there, pushed her fingers back into my cunt, that sticky night-nurse feel of the latex glove, but kept her mouth clamped firmly over my clit. I started to come again, it was something I couldn't control, and that's when I realised just how much I loved being fucked by another woman.

I wanted to give her the same sort of pleasure too, so when my orgasm had died away I sat up and pulled Harriet towards me.

We kissed and touched each other, and I couldn't get over how beautiful her tits were, how smooth and full in my hands. Her nipples were a darker pink than mine, firm and erect, and they felt sharp and ridged under my tongue, perfectly suckable. I think I must have been making a groaning noise under my breath, because she started laughing and pulled my hand down between her legs.

'Try there.'

She was wet down there, hot, the full lips gaping slightly, and I let my fingers crawl upwards, hunting for the sweet spot, for her clitoris.

It was odd how she had exactly the same equipment as me, yet everything felt different; her cunt lips were fatter, her clitoris was more protruding than mine, and she seemed to enjoy me being quite rough with her, pinching her lips and clit until she cried out, whereas I prefer a light touch, being gently licked and sucked to orgasm, at least until I'm good and warmed-up. I've found since then that all women are different down there, but that first time it was a shock, a bit of a revelation. I'd just assumed all pussies are the same but, of course, all cocks aren't the same, are they?

I felt nervous again, in case I hurt her or did something wrong, so I just fingered and pinched her pussy for a few more minutes, exploring it silently. But there was really no way round it. She'd licked me out and I would have to return the favour by licking her out too.

So it was my turn and I went down on Harriet, spreading her thighs wider apart and trying to copy what she had done to me, licking round her soft full pussy lips first and then sucking on her clitoris. She tasted a little bitter at first, then sweet and delicious as the juices started to flow. I got two fingers inside her at the same time and sucked like crazy on that taut little nugget of flesh at the top of her pussy.

Quite soon her hips began to jerk and it was such a great feeling, knowing that I'd made another woman come just with my mouth and fingers, I was smiling for days afterwards.

Harriet was whimpering and swearing as she came, just like I'd done a few minutes before, only much less inhibited than me. She knocked a few plant pots flying and she even hit me, she was flailing about so much. There was damp soil everywhere and one of the rickety table legs collapsed under our weight so that we ended up in a sweating, tangled heap on the floor of the shed. It didn't matter though, the sex was fantastic.

'You bitch!' she kept groaning, but she didn't mean it, it was just a sort of release for her orgasm, the pleasure she was feeling.

Even though I was completely inexperienced that first time, I don't remember Harriet complaining or being impatient. Perhaps my clumsiness was a turn-on. I know it is for me now, when I get into bed with a girl who's never done it before with a woman. It can be quite exciting to fuck if they're eager and up for it but not sure what's expected. I must be a quick learner, because I really know what I'm doing when I take a woman to bed these days. And I love fucking a 'virgin' – that's what Harriet called women that have only ever done it with men – and showing her how good it feels to have another woman's tongue in her pussy.

– *Sharona W., Chigwell, Essex, UK*

nexus

The leading publisher of fetish and adult fiction

TELL US WHAT YOU THINK!

Readers' ideas and opinions matter to us so please take a few minutes to fill in the questionnaire below.

1. Sex: Are you male ☐ female ☐ a couple ☐?

2. Age: Under 21 ☐ 21–30 ☐ 31–40 ☐ 41–50 ☐ 51–60 ☐ over 60 ☐

3. Where do you buy your Nexus books from?

☐ A chain book shop. If so, which one(s)?

_____

☐ An independent book shop. If so, which one(s)?

_____

☐ A used book shop/charity shop
☐ Online book store. If so, which one(s)?

_____

4. How did you find out about Nexus books?

☐ Browsing in a book shop
☐ A review in a magazine
☐ Online
☐ Recommendation
☐ Other _____

5. In terms of settings, which do you prefer? (Tick as many as you like.)

☐ Down to earth and as realistic as possible
☐ Historical settings. If so, which period do you prefer?

_____

☐ Fantasy settings – barbarian worlds
☐ Completely escapist/surreal fantasy
☐ Institutional or secret academy

- ☐ Futuristic/sci fi
- ☐ Escapist but still believable
- ☐ Any settings you dislike?

_____

- ☐ Where would you like to see an adult novel set?

_____

6. In terms of storylines, would you prefer:

- ☐ Simple stories that concentrate on adult interests?
- ☐ More plot and character-driven stories with less explicit adult activity?
- ☐ We value your ideas, so give us your opinion of this book:

_____

_____

_____

7. In terms of your adult interests, what do you like to read about? (Tick as many as you like.)

- ☐ Traditional corporal punishment (CP)
- ☐ Modern corporal punishment
- ☐ Spanking
- ☐ Restraint/bondage
- ☐ Rope bondage
- ☐ Latex/rubber
- ☐ Leather
- ☐ Female domination and male submission
- ☐ Female domination and female submission
- ☐ Male domination and female submission
- ☐ Willing captivity
- ☐ Uniforms
- ☐ Lingerie/underwear/hosiery/footwear (boots and high heels)
- ☐ Sex rituals
- ☐ Vanilla sex
- ☐ Swinging
- ☐ Cross-dressing/TV
- ☐ Enforced feminisation

☐ Others – tell us what you don't see enough of in adult fiction:

_____

_____

_____

8. Would you prefer books with a more specialised approach to your interests, i.e. a novel specifically about uniforms? If so, which subject(s) would you like to read a Nexus novel about?

_____

_____

_____

9. Would you like to read true stories in Nexus books? For instance, the true story of a submissive woman, or a male slave? Tell us which true revelations you would most like to read about:

_____

_____

_____

10. What do you like best about Nexus books?

_____

_____

11. What do you like least about Nexus books?

_____

_____

12. Which are your favourite titles?

_____

_____

13. Who are your favourite authors?

_____

_____

14. **Which covers do you prefer? Those featuring:**
    (Tick as many as you like.)

☐ Fetish outfits
☐ More nudity
☐ Two models
☐ Unusual models or settings
☐ Classic erotic photography
☐ More contemporary images and poses
☐ A blank/non-erotic cover
☐ What would your ideal cover look like?

_____

15. **Describe your ideal Nexus novel in the space provided:**

_____
_____
_____
_____

16. **Which celebrity would feature in one of your Nexus-style fantasies?**
    We'll post the best suggestions on our website – anonymously!

_____

THANKS FOR YOUR TIME

Now simply write the title of this book in the space below and cut out the
questionnaire pages. Post to: Nexus, Marketing Dept., Thames Wharf Studios,
Rainville Rd, London W6 9HA

Book title: _____

NEXUS NEW BOOKS

To be published in March 2007

BEASTLY BEHAVIOUR
Aishling Morgan

Genevieve Stukely is working as an erotic dancer in the American west when she learns that her uncle is dead and that she is to inherit the family estate on the borders of Dartmoor. Only when she returns to the mother country does she discover that Sir Robert Stukely did not die simply of old age, but was found with an expression of utmost terror frozen on his features. Nearby were the footprints of a gigantic hound.

Now Mistress of Stukely Manor and known to have a colourful past, Genevieve quickly finds herself the centre of attention for half the rakes and ne'er-do-wells in Devon.

Beastly Behaviour follows the Truscott saga into its fifth generation with a tale of bizarre lust and Gothic horror drawn from several historical and literary sources to make it one of the most elaborate erotic novels ever published, to say nothing of being irredeemably filthy.

£6.99   ISBN 978 0 352 34095 5

CITY MAID
Amelia Evangeline

City Maid recounts the erotic adventures of an innocent young woman in Victorian London. When Eleanor enters service in the Hampton household she has no idea that beneath the façade of respectability the house is a secret world of lust and depravity. Her mistress, Lady Hamilton, soon teaches Eleanor her position in the sternest and most shocking manner. Immediately, Eleanor realises to her horror that once you've felt the thrill of submission, life will never be the same again.

£6.99   ISBN 978 0 352 34096 2

RUBBER GIRL
William Doughty

The Nexus Enthusiast series brings us a definitive work of fiction about the hugely popular world of rubber fetishism. In *Rubber Girl*, Jill has an overwhelming fetish for rubber – the sight of it, the scent of it, the feeling of its texture around her skin, its aerodynamic and aesthetic qualities as a sensual fabric and second skin for her voluptuous body, as well as its flexible properties for restraint and bondage. And her neighbour Matt is drawn into her shiny latex orbit when she combines her love of rubber with his weakness for female domination. Kinky Sue, who has a crush on Jill, is the next to join in the perverse and rubbery games in an isolated country house in Dorset. Together, they reach the very heights of rubber fetishism.

£6.99   ISBN 978 0 352 34087 0

If you would like more information about Nexus titles, please visit our website at www.nexus-books.co.uk, or send a large stamped addressed envelope to:
Nexus, Thames Wharf Studios,
Rainville Road, London W6 9HA

NEXUS BOOKLIST

Information is correct at time of printing. To avoid disappointment, check availability before ordering. Go to www.nexus-books.co.uk.

All books are priced at £6.99 unless another price is given.

NEXUS

☐ ABANDONED ALICE Adriana Arden ISBN 978 0 352 33969 0

☐ ALICE IN CHAINS Adriana Arden ISBN 978 0 352 33908 9

☐ AQUA DOMINATION William Doughty ISBN 978 0 352 34020 7

☐ THE ART OF CORRECTION Tara Black ISBN 978 0 352 33895 2

☐ THE ART OF SURRENDER Madeline Bastinado ISBN 978 0 352 34013 9

☐ BELINDA BARES UP Yolanda Celbridge ISBN 978 0 352 33926 3

☐ BENCH-MARKS Tara Black ISBN 978 0 352 33797 9

☐ BIDDING TO SIN Rosita Varón ISBN 978 0 352 34063 4

☐ BINDING PROMISES G.C. Scott ISBN 978 0 352 34014 6

☐ THE BOOK OF PUNISHMENT Cat Scarlett ISBN 978 0 352 33975 1

☐ BRUSH STROKES Penny Birch ISBN 978 0 352 34072 6

☐ CALLED TO THE WILD Angel Blake ISBN 978 0 352 34067 2

☐ CAPTIVES OF CHEYNER CLOSE Adriana Arden ISBN 978 0 352 34028 3

☐ CARNAL POSSESSION Yvonne Strickland ISBN 978 0 352 34062 7

☐ COLLEGE GIRLS Cat Scarlett ISBN 978 0 352 33942 3

☐ COMPANY OF SLAVES Christina Shelly ISBN 978 0 352 33887 7

☐ CONCEIT AND CONSEQUENCE Aishling Morgan ISBN 978 0 352 33965 2

☐ CORRECTIVE THERAPY Jacqueline Masterson ISBN 978 0 352 33917 1

☐ CORRUPTION Virginia Crowley ISBN 978 0 352 34073 3

☐ PENNY PIECES	Penny Birch	ISBN 978 0 352 33631 6 £5.99
☐ PETTING GIRLS	Penny Birch	ISBN 978 0 352 33957 7
☐ PET TRAINING IN THE PRIVATE HOUSE	Esme Ombreux	ISBN 978 0 352 33655 2 £5.99
☐ THE PLAYER	Cat Scarlett	ISBN 978 0 352 33894 5
☐ THE PRIESTESS	Jacqueline Bellevois	ISBN 978 0 352 33905 8
☐ PRIZE OF PAIN	Wendy Swanscombe	ISBN 978 0 352 33890 7
☐ PUNISHED IN PINK	Yolanda Celbridge	ISBN 978 0 352 34003 0
☐ THE PUNISHMENT CAMP	Jacqueline Masterson	ISBN 978 0 352 33940 9
☐ THE PUNISHMENT CLUB	Jacqueline Masterson	ISBN 978 0 352 33862 4
☐ THE ROAD TO DEPRAVITY	Ray Gordon	ISBN 978 0 352 34092 4
☐ SCARLET VICE	Aishling Morgan	ISBN 978 0 352 33988 1
☐ SCHOOLED FOR SERVICE	Lady Alice McCloud	ISBN 978 0 352 33918 8
☐ SCHOOL FOR STINGERS	Yolanda Celbridge	ISBN 978 0 352 33994 2
☐ SEXUAL HEELING	Wendy Swanscombe	ISBN 978 0 352 33921 8
☐ SILKEN EMBRACE	Christina Shelly	ISBN 978 0 352 34081 8
☐ SILKEN SERVITUDE	Christina Shelly	ISBN 978 0 352 34004 7
☐ SIN'S APPRENTICE	Aishling Morgan	ISBN 978 0 352 33909 6
☐ SLAVE GENESIS	Jennifer Jane Pope	ISBN 978 0 352 33503 6 £5.99
☐ SLAVE OF THE SPARTANS	Yolanda Celbridge	ISBN 978 0 352 34078 8
☐ SLIPPERY WHEN WET	Penny Birch	ISBN 978 0 352 34091 7
☐ THE SMARTING OF SELINA	Yolanda Celbridge	ISBN 978 0 352 33872 3
☐ STRIP GIRL	Aishling Morgan	ISBN 978 0 352 34077 1
☐ STRIPING KAYLA	Yolanda Marshall	ISBN 978 0 352 33881 5
☐ STRIPPED BARE	Angel Blake	ISBN 978 0 352 33971 3
☐ TASTING CANDY	Ray Gordon	ISBN 978 0 352 33925 6
☐ TEMPTING THE GODDESS	Aishling Morgan	ISBN 978 0 352 33972 0
☐ THAI HONEY	Kit McCann	ISBN 978 0 352 34068 9
☐ TICKLE TORTURE	Penny Birch	ISBN 978 0 352 33904 1
☐ TOKYO BOUND	Sachi	ISBN 978 0 352 34019 1

------ ✂ ----------------------------

Please send me the books I have ticked above.

Name   ....

Address   ....

            ....

            ....

            .... Post code ....

Send to: **Virgin Books Cash Sales, Thames Wharf Studios, Rainville Road, London W6 9HA**

US customers: for prices and details of how to order books for delivery by mail, call 888-330-8477.

Please enclose a cheque or postal order, made payable to **Nexus Books Ltd**, to the value of the books you have ordered plus postage and packing costs as follows:
    UK and BFPO – £1.00 for the first book, 50p for each subsequent book.
    Overseas (including Republic of Ireland) – £2.00 for the first book, £1.00 for each subsequent book.

If you would prefer to pay by VISA, ACCESS/MASTERCARD, AMEX, DINERS CLUB or SWITCH, please write your card number and expiry date here:

....

Please allow up to 28 days for delivery.

Signature ....

Our privacy policy

We will not disclose information you supply us to any other parties. We will not disclose any information which identifies you personally to any person without your express consent.

From time to time we may send out information about Nexus books and special offers. Please tick here if you do *not* wish to receive Nexus information.   ☐

------ ✂ ----------------------------